PeL IS PuZZLed

MARK HEBDEN

HOUSE OF STRATUS

This edition published in 2001 by House of Stratus, an imprint of
Stratus Books Ltd., 21 Beeching Park, Kelly Bray,
Cornwall, PL17 8QS, UK.

www.houseofstratus.com

Typeset, printed and bound by House of Stratus.

A catalogue record for this book is available from the British Library
and the Library of Congress.

ISBN 1-84232-894-8

Though Burgundians will probably decide they have recognised it – and certainly many of its street names are the same – in fact the city in these pages is intended to be fictitious.

one

There was no wind and the interior of the church was as still as a tomb. As in many old churches, the light inside had a quality of dusty violet about it and its smell was that of incense mingled with dust and damp. As the sacristan made his way down the side aisle, his mind was full of happy anticipation.

His feet made little noise on the stone floor. He was an old man and little had happened in his life to change the pattern of his days. St Sauvigny-le-Comtesse was not a very big place. Little more than a village situated in a hollow of the hills to the south of Pouilly-en-Auxois, in summer the steep sides of the valley made it a sun trap so that it was said that the finest dahlias in Burgundy grew there. In winter, however, with a tributary of the River Amançon running alongside its main street, it was a place of fogs and frost, because the sun, in its lower arc, managed to reach down into it only for short periods at a time.

Because of the resulting damp and the fact that – since it was far too big for the little town – there was always a chronic lack of funds, the church the old man ministered was slowly falling into decay. It wasn't something that troubled the sacristan a great deal. The church had been falling into decay for generations and as long as he remembered there had been workmen pottering about the place, replastering, shoring up or rebuilding. He'd lived with it most of his life.

As he reached the Chapel of the Sacred Heart, his footsteps slowed. Glancing inside, he almost smiled. As he always did. Because in the Chapel were the Daunay Panels and, of all the ecclesiastical gems he knew, the Daunay Panels were his favourites.

As he shuffled to a stop, however, his expression changed. To his surprise, instead of five panels, which was what he had expected to see, there were only four.

Four, he thought, his mind working slowly.

Four?

FOUR!!!!!

For a while he stood still, staring at the place where the third and centre panel should have hung, wondering what had happened to it, half-imagining he was having some sort of mental black-out. Then, gathering his thoughts, he convinced himself there must be a proper explanation for the mystery because he had hung the five panels in the Chapel himself. They were not only his pride and joy, they were also his responsibility.

The town had little history because in 1870, when the Prussians had overrun France, it had not been touched, and in 1914 it had been safe behind the lines. In 1940, when the Germans had occupied the area once more, there was nothing in the district of much use to them and because St Sauvigny was close to the German border and among the last places to be liberated, even the Resistance had never managed to be very forceful. Finally, the agents of Reichsmarschall Goering, searching through the occupied countries for all that was beautiful to grace the rooms of his exquisite Karinhalle, had quite failed, because they weren't scholars of ecclesiastical art, to notice the famous panels which were the little town's only real claim to fame.

Normally they hung from the stone arches near the choir but for almost 200 years in the summer months from the first day of spring they had always been kept in the small Chapel of the Sacred Heart. Such was their colour they seemed to cover the crumbling stone walls and, although the windows were far too small, filled the place with light. After the Feast of All Saints on November 1, they were transferred back to the stone arches near the choir where they were fastened to the pillars until the following spring.

The pattern had not changed since the 18th Century and as usual on April 21 that year, the sacristan had made the usual transfer.

Since Mass was being celebrated, the bewildered sacristan did nothing for a while but, as the people streamed from the church, he intercepted the priest on his way back to the Presbytery.

'Father,' he asked. 'Have you removed the third Cardinal Daunay panel?'

The priest looked surprised at the question. 'Of course not,' he said.

'Perhaps for cleaning? Or restoration?'

'No.'

'Then, Father, it's disappeared.'

'It can't have,' the priest said.

'Father, I've just been to look. It's not there.'

'Can it have fallen?'

'Father, I have eyes.' The sacristan was growing angry. 'One on either side of my nose. They see well. Even without spectacles.'

The priest touched his shoulder. It was almost a pat of reassurance.

'Let us look together,' he said gently. 'When I arrived this morning I saw them – all five. Each hanging in its usual place.'

'Then, Father,' the sacristan said sharply, 'you were either suffering from a hallucination, as I have just thought I was, or it has disappeared since.'

The priest smiled indulgently but, reaching the Gothic chapel, he stopped, his jaw sagging. 'It's gone!' he said.

'Father –' the sacristan's voice betrayed a measure of self-satisfaction – 'that's what I've been trying to tell you.'

Within twenty minutes the ancient church was resounding to the clomp of the boots of policemen and within twenty-four hours the problem had landed on the desk of Inspector Evariste Clovis Désiré Pel.

two

The alarm arrived first on the desk of Sergeant Daniel Darcy, Pel's second in command. Darcy was a good-looking, strong young man with dark hair, a firm jaw, good white teeth he enjoyed using to smile at girls and a supreme self-confidence which, while it occasionally led him astray, always served to bolster up that of his chief.

Not that his chief needed much bolstering up where his work was concerned. Though he considered himself overworked and underpaid, on the point of dropping dead from stomach ulcers caused by too much worry, from cancer caused by too much smoking forced on him by too much work, or from just plain fever caused by anxiety over cancer brought on by too much smoking as a result of too much work, he was still one of the best in the business. His record was formidable and he had a shrewd brain that saw through the tangles of lies with which he was usually faced, to the core of a case, picking out the important details with a sure skill. His private life, however, was a mess. And it was in this sphere that Daniel Darcy was invaluable.

First of all, who could expect to feel successful with a name like Evariste Clovis Désiré Pel? It had sat on Pel's shoulders throughout his life like a vulture waiting for him to wither and die. As a boy, he had found the girls he shyly approached fell about laughing at it; in his youth, ardent with love, one had actually fallen out of bed when presented with it. Now, in his approaching middle age, even seeing it on his police identity card or his driving licence made him feel ill. He blamed on it entirely his bachelor existence and the fact that he was bullied by his housekeeper. Had he been plain Jean Pel or Pierre Pel or even Jean-Pierre Pel, he felt, he would have been happily married by this time to someone who looked like Brigitte Bardot past her film star days, of course, and comfortable now, because possession of a wife as beautiful as she'd been in her prime would have terrified Pel – with four or five beautiful children, a large brand new Citroën instead of a clapped-out Peugeot, a flat in the city and a house in the country – not a château, just a small manor – and a directorship or two: Siemens. Creusot. Centre-Est Aéronautique. Something like that. Nothing pretentious. Just important and well-paid.

As it was, when Darcy put his head round the door, Pel had just arrived from home in a bad temper and was coughing like a dying man over what he chose to call his first cigarette of the day – though he'd had one after his first cup of coffee and another in his car on the way to the Hôtel de Police. He was in no mood to be worried. He'd had a bad night – Pel liked to think he always had bad nights because they made him feel martyred and that, he considered, was good for the soul. At breakfast he'd had the mother and father of a row with his housekeeper, Madame Routy, who had switched on the television during breakfast. Television at breakfast was one step too far. But Madame Routy was an addict and, watching far into the night, ruined Pel's reading, spoiled his sleep and generally added to the difficulties of what he already considered a difficult life. Being an overworked underpaid police inspector who couldn't stop smoking *made* it a difficult life. However, he considered himself a reasonable man and believed – just! – that a widow working as a housekeeper had a right to a little entertainment to enliven her off-duty hours. Entertainment at breakfast, however – a time sacred to Pel for the purpose of hating everybody who sang or tried to be cheerful – was just too much.

'But it's a special programme,' she explained. 'It's the Tour de France. It's about to start!'

'At this time of the day?' Pel snapped.

'They have to talk about it a bit!'

'Not to me, they don't.'

Despite the fact that the Tour de France was the longest, most gruelling cycle race in the world, Pel had little time for it, for the masochists who took part in it, for the fifteen million spectators who were prepared to stand half a day to see it flash by, or for the hundred and sixty million who were prepared to glue themselves to television or radio to learn who was winning. As she turned the set to almost full volume he stormed out of the house and had the humiliation as he climbed into his car of seeing her through the window make herself comfortable with a fresh cup of coffee and turn the sound up to *full* volume.

It was a defeat and he knew it. The time had long passed when he should have discharged Madame Routy. Despite the fact that he paid all the bills, she was always more in charge of the house than he was and, quite wrongly, he considered he would never be able to get anybody else to look after a crotchety bachelor such as he considered himself to be. Rather than take the risk of having to do his own cooking and cleaning, therefore, he endured Madame Routy. Sergeant Darcy kept asking him why he didn't get married or at least get a new housekeeper – 'I bet I could find one,' he said. 'And no Madame Routy either.' But Darcy had a way with women. If Darcy had had a housekeeper, she would have looked like Sophia Loren, been a cordon bleu cook, and would have detested television. Pel considered he wasn't that lucky and preferred to work his bitterness out on his staff and the officials of the Church of Notre Dame at St Sauvigny.

'Why couldn't they keep the damned thing under lock and key?' he asked,

Darcy shrugged. 'It's part of the church,' he said. 'It's supposed to be on display. It's been on display there for two hundred years now. I don't suppose it occurred to them to lock it up.'

'Who's looking after the enquiry?'

'I thought Nosjean.'

'Nosjean's too clever for that,' Pel said. 'We might need him here. Send Misset. It'll keep him from worrying me to have the night off. It'll probably also stop him straying off the straight and narrow with women.

Misset's wife seemed to add to his growing family every year and Misset's eyes had started wandering over the girls again.

Darcy grinned at Pel's sour expression. 'They have women in St Sauvigny,' he pointed out. 'With befores, behinds and all the other attributes. Just like the ones here.'

'There can't be so much choice, though,' Pel grunted. 'It's too small. Besides, it's out in the country. Misset's a town bird. He likes them smart.' He paused, frowning. 'Who did it?' he asked. 'I suppose it's part of the same gang that's been getting into the châteaux.

'Looks like it, Patron,' Darcy said. 'Though there's no proof yet. There was no break-in, so we can't compare methods. It looks to me as though someone just walked in between 7.15 and 9.15 am, when the theft was discovered, and simply helped himself. He quietly unfastened the cords that attached it to the wall, put it under his arm and walked out again. The St Sauvigny boys say there are no clues and no fingerprints.'

'Nobody seen?'

'A tall guy in overalls and a beret is supposed to have been seen. But nobody's sure because there's work going on to stop the place falling down.'

Pel frowned. 'Is it valuable?' he asked.

Darcy laughed. 'You could mention any figure you care to mention, Chief. It's unique and quite irreplaceable. It has the signature of Cardinal Daunay on it and the date. It's the only one of the five that has. Whoever did it knew his stuff. He picked the most valuable of the whole lot. It's considered to be part of the national patrimony.'

'So it can't be sold?'

'Not in France, Chief. I wouldn't say the same for elsewhere. There seem to be people in other countries who're willing to take stolen treasures from Europe and keep them in underground vaults so they never see daylight.'

'Can't see much sense in that,' Pel said.

'Acquisitiveness,' Darcy pointed out. 'A bit like squirrels with nuts. Or like climbers with mountains. It's there so they have to have it.'

'Isn't the Historic Monuments Department of the Ministry of Cultural Affairs supposed to be responsible?'

'In theory, Patron. Both for its safe keeping and for its preservation, but, with ecclesiastical objects, the Church, not the Ministry, looks after its own treasures.'

'Didn't the Bishop of Paris send out a Diocesan letter after all those robberies in 1962 that churches were to make sure their treasures were kept safe?'

Darcy shrugged. 'Yes, he did, Chief. Unfortunately, everybody – especially in small places like St Sauvigny – considered that it meant everybody else but them. They just can't believe that they'll be robbed and, in fact, it's been discovered more than once that they aren't even aware of the value of the things they own.'

'They must have known the value of *these* things!' Pel snorted.

'Yes, Patron, they did. But it's been the tradition to display them in the Chapel of the Sacred Heart for two hundred years. There'd probably be an outcry if they locked them in the safe.'

'There'll be an outcry now that one's been stolen. Have the press got it yet?'

'Not yet, Chief.'

'They will. How many does this make?'

'Six, Chief. There was the statue from the Cathedral at Bourges, and four château break-ins. Everything they took was priceless. In every case there were plenty of other *objets d'art* available which looked more valuable, but in every case nothing was touched but the most valuable in the place.'

'Somebody who knows something about it, eh?'

'That's the way it looks, Chief.'

'I'll see if we can't find somebody to help us who knows something about it. Somebody who can tell us what to look for.' Pel looked up. 'Unless, of course, *you're* an expert.'

Darcy smiled. 'Not me, Patron. Girls, yes. Antiques, no.'

'I'll have a word with the Chief. He ought to be able to find someone.'

In fact, it wasn't the Chief but Judge Polverari who put Pel on the right track. Polverari, who was an old friend of Pel's, had married a wealthy woman and collected glass.

'There's a sergeant at Auxerre,' he said, 'who knows something about this sort of thing.'

'A sergeant?' Pel's eyebrows rose. 'A *police* sergeant?'

'Yes. I met him once at a sale.'

'Buying things?' Pel said. 'On a sergeant's income?'

Polverari smiled. 'No. Just looking. Advising. He's actually a bit of an expert.'

'How did he come to be that?'

'Well, his family's an old one.'

'So's mine. Goes back to Adam.'

Polverari smiled. 'But *he* grew up with *objets d'art* around him. I gather they're all gone now, but he seems to know a little about it. Name of De Troquereau. We'll get the Chief to have him sent down here to help us.'

Satisfied with his morning's work, Pel headed back to his office. There was a drizzling rain falling on the city, dulling the famous enamelled roofs and making the spires dim in a misty outline. Nobody seemed to be wanting him and as he reached his office he made a point of not ringing to find out if anyone had been enquiring. It gave him ten minutes on his own to read the newspaper.

It was full of a new scandal that had broken in Paris. A brothel had been raided for contravening the laws, and an Under-Secretary to the Minister of Defence called Philippe le Bozec had been found there. Since he was supposed to be a young politician of great morality and integrity the newspapers were having a ball, especially since also a member of the Russian Embassy was known to have been in the habit of visiting the place, too. It gave Pel a lot of pleasure. He didn't like politicians, regarding them merely as a necessary evil, and to find one in trouble always delighted him. He was surprised, nevertheless, to find the police had managed to find a good enough reason to lay on a raid. Most brothel owners knew the law inside out, certainly sufficiently well to know how to avoid getting into trouble, and he could only suppose that the presence of the Russian from time to time had set them wondering if it were being used as a posting house for secrets.

The newspapers were enjoying themselves enormously, and Le Bozec's resignation was being demanded – as much from the point of view of morality as security. Considering the standard of most newspapers, it seemed to Pel a little ironic, because alongside the picture of Le Bozec was a picture of a half-clad girl being led away by a policeman, and it wasn't there to indicate Le Bozec's low moral tone so much as to titillate the great sporting public with a glimpse of what he'd been up to, which was much more exciting.

They were also busy slating the Russians again. Embassy officials, guests in France, were expected to behave with decorum, they claimed, and anyway, there were far too many of them. *'La Grande Fraude,'* the headline screamed above a long screed demanding the heads of a few Russian attachés.

11

'A swindle is being practised in France,' Pel read. 'A great deception. It is to be hoped that the Russian ambassador is a generalissimo of the first order because he has a veritable army of military men at his command. There are too many Russian officials in France and too many of them are military experts...'

Pel was enjoying himself. He liked a good political scandal, because he was convinced that only by getting rid of every ambitious politician in the world – and quite a few unambitious ones as well – was there any hope for the future. Most politicians, he felt, seemed to behave like Judge Brisard, with whom he'd been conducting a running fight for two or three years now. When his job demanded a *juge d'instruction* it was always Pel's first object to get Judge Polverari if possible, because he was round and fat and cheerful, while Judge Brisard was tall, earnest, humourless, hypocritical, and behaved as if a steam roller had run over his personality.

Happy in his dislike of Brisard, he shook the paper and made himself as comfortable as his chair would permit. Standard issue for the offices of inspectors, it was hardly '*confort anglais.*'

Bombs, he noticed, his eyes casting over the columns beneath the funereal black of the headlines. A rash of letter bombs in Paris. Believed, it was claimed, to be sent by a breakaway group which wanted to free Brittany from the rest of France. The whole country, like the whole world, seemed to be full of breakaway groups. Everywhere would-be politicians with dreams of power were trying to split up large units into the dangerous smaller units the statesmen after two world wars had tried to get rid of. He wondered if he couldn't form a breakaway unit himself, its sole purpose to leave Madame Routy behind.

The Tour de France was also off to a good start, he noticed, and the favourite was a Belgian by the name of Camille van der Essen, a Dutch rider in the style of Merckx and Zoetemelk. As a distinctly non-sporting type, the information left Pel as cold as if the newspaper had announced 'Today happened.' All that Pel knew about the Tour de France was that it cluttered up the roads, filled the television and the newspapers, and seemed to be the only talking point for a matter of three weeks. With the Russians poised to swallow the democratic world, the Chinese multiplying so fast they could march past – so Pel had been told – a million abreast for ever without ever coming to a stop, and terrorists from one end of the world to the other throwing bombs that maimed innocent men, women and children, the result of a race involving a hundred-odd cyclists – like the result of a football match – seemed of small moment. To Pel the Tour de France merely meant twenty-one days of cycling, and that, of course, meant twenty-one days of it on television, of which Madame Routy would doubtless watch every single kilometre.

Folding the paper, he looked at his desk. There was a long screed from the Chief about a series of frauds being investigated by the electricity authorities. His assistance was not being asked because most of the offences were in the north and out of their area, but what had been discovered was set out for everybody in the Hôtel de Police to see, to take note of, and be alert for. People had been tampering with meters and there seemed to have been an epidemic so that the electricity authorities were wondering if someone had devised a scheme to make the fraud nationwide. Probably the Russians, Pel decided cheerfully, as a means, like drugs, of undermining the national character ready for the big take over.

Meanwhile – Pel sighed and put the paper aside – the art robberies. In 1962 there had been a rash of robberies from châteaux which had so irritated the French police that a special squad had been set up in Paris, and the gang had been arrested. With the precautions that had been taken since, however, it had been assumed that such art robberies – chiefly from *châteaux classés*, châteaux to which the public were admitted and therefore subsidised – would stop, because the owners had begun to forbid photographs inside as a means of preventing would-be robbers identifying the objects they were after. Guide books had also been reprinted so that they were deliberately vague about which *objets d'art* were the valuable ones, and guides had been instructed to avoid pointing out in their spiels those things which might attract the attention of thieves.

Forcing visitors to leave their cameras at the door had had the result, in addition, of course, to the side-effect of forcing them to buy photographs and slides – a useful extra source of income – of making it more difficult to obtain pictures of individual items of value. This had been expected to put a restraint on art thieves but, despite all this, an entirely new rash of robberies had started – four so far in Pel's area alone – and the police were growing worried. The case at St Sauvigny was the latest and, though it could, of course, have no connection with the châteaux robberies and be merely the work of one individual who had simply taken a fancy to the missing panel, on the other hand, it could well be the work of the gang who had been subjecting the châteaux to their ministrations. If it were, Pel decided, then they were well organised and well advised.

Could there have been an artist involved, he wondered. A man clever with a pencil, his sketch pad hidden inside his guide book, could well put down all the details of an *object d'art,* together with its exact location, so that the experts could come along later and knock it off.

As he considered the possibility, there was a tap at the door, and he looked up, expecting one of his team with a query. Instead it was Inspector Pomereu, of Traffic.

Pomereu was a thin, sallow man with a sharp alert expression. He had a reputation for missing nothing and it seemed that he was making a point of living up to it.

'We've had an accident,' he said. 'On the hill down from Destres. A Renault 6 ran over the edge and landed upside down. It's burned out. We'd like you to look into it.'

'Is it anything to do with me?' Pel asked.

Pomereu gestured. 'It might be. The driver was found dead nearby. He'd been badly burned, but it wasn't that which killed him. It was multiple injuries. Doc Minet has the report. And he must have been going down that hill as if the hounds of hell were after him, because his car leapt the barrier and landed a good five metres out into the field below.'

'That's a dangerous hill to drive fast on,' Pel agreed. 'Full of curves.' Pel knew it well. It terrified him every time he was obliged to drive his ancient Peugeot down it, because he was convinced his brakes would give and he'd end up in the bar at the bottom. Going the other way, he was afraid the engine would give and he'd have to park and walk back to the bar to telephone for help. That bar had become an obsession with Pel.

Pomereu was agreeing. 'Yes, it is dangerous,' he said. 'And there are skid marks to show that he must have been swerving pretty wildly as he was going down it.'

'Drunk?'

'Not according to Doc Minet. There was alcohol in his stomach but not enough to make him do something as mad as that. Two or three small brandies.'

'Two or three small brandies produce a state of berserker in some people. Me, for instance.'

'Not in this chap,' Pomereu said. 'He was normally a reasonably sober chap, I gather, but he liked a drink occasionally when he was pressed.'

'And *was* he pressed?'

Pomereu permitted himself the luxury of a smile. 'That's where you come in,' he said.

'It's still Traffic's problem, surely?'

'Not quite,' Pomereu said. 'You see, there were other skid marks on the road, too, which don't match the ones from the

Peugeot. We've checked them carefully and had the Lab on to them. We've decided they were made at roughly the same time.'

'And – ?'

'And if they were, then it raises another question: Was he being chased?'

'And if he was, why?'

'Exactly.' Pomereu seemed pleased that Pel had arrived at the point so quickly.

three

The road north from the city climbed slowly upwards through the outer suburbs, through the area where the big houses gave way to small houses, then to an admixture of garages and occasional small factories. Eventually, it began to climb to a flat plain, bare and treeless, where a small aerodrome lay by the side of the road, the small Cessnas, Rallyes and Centre Ests standing in lines of brightly-coloured aluminium. It then began to climb again, through a long double avenue of ancient trees, until finally and suddenly it began to descend in steep dangerous curves to the valley of the Epreys. More than one car had gone off the road here, some into the deep ditch alongside under the high bank that rose to the plain, others over the edge on the other side into the sloping fields that bent their way down to the river. Because people seemed determined to kill themselves, the authorities had put up a heavy steel guard fence but there were still a few who were clever enough to charge it at full speed and leap their cars over it to drop into the fields and roll down, over and over through the thick grass, leaving behind them an assortment of fenders, headlamps, wheels and bodies.

Pel stared at the bent rail and rubbed his nose. On the road, above Pomereu's car, a police patrol car was parked with its light flashing, its crew staring down at the wrecked vehicle which still lay on its side below them, its paint blackened, its roof crushed, its fenders bent, its wheels out of true. It lay like a dead animal in the grass, one wheel-less axle like an amputated stump sticking up in the air. Doors hung open and the grass around was scorched in a brown circle where the flames had licked. There were still a few small wisps of smoke and the air was acrid with the smell of burnt rubber. Several metres higher up the slope was a deep scar in the turf.

'That's where he landed,' Pomereu said. 'We reckon it's almost five metres out from the road. That's quite a jump, considering he had to get over the guard rail. He must have been going at quite a speed.'

They climbed back to the highway. Pomereu's men had placed tapes and warning signs to keep passing cars clear, and they walked slowly up the road studying the black scorched rubber marks. Towards the top of the hill they stopped. Pel lit a cigarette, coughed heavily once or twice, got properly into his stride so that he sounded like a consumptive, then drew a deep breath, feeling much better.

He held the packet out to Pomeren, who shook his head. 'I don't smoke,' he said.

'I wish I didn't,' Pel said.

'You've only to give your mind to it.'

Pel gave Pomereu a bitter look. He'd been giving his mind to it for years, ever since someone had first publicised the fact that it caused cancer. He still hadn't managed to reject the habit and was convinced that at any moment he would be carted off to hospital, his lungs charred, ready to gasp out his last.

Pomereu was gesturing down the hill and they started to walk slowly back again to where they'd left the cars. 'You'll notice,' Pomereu observed, 'that in every case where a corner appears, there are marks, as though he went into it at full speed. You'll notice also, however, that there are second sets of marks doing the same, as though a second and larger car was also descending at full speed.'

'Perhaps they were having a race,' Pel said.

'People are stupid enough.' Pomereu was a humourless, pedantic individual who had a great contempt for his fellow men. 'But I doubt it. Not here.'

'Who was he?'

'Type called Cormon. Claude-Achille Cormon. Bachelor, aged forty-one. Lived with his sister, Eugénie Clarétie, of Evanay-sur-Rille. She's a widow and he had rooms in her house.'

'Queer?' Pel asked. 'Was he a queer?'

'Why?'

'Bachelor aged forty-one.'

'Some bachelors aged forty-one are perfectly normal.'

'I know that,' Pel said, sourly aware that he, too, was a bachelor approaching forty-one. 'But most bachelors aged forty-one don't end up dead in a burned-out car which gives every indication of having been chased at high speed.'

Pomereu considered. 'No,' he said. 'Not queer. A bit of a loner, though. Quiet type. Not given to drinking. Though, as I've said, when pressed, he'd have a brandy or two.'

'What do you mean by "pressed." '

'Work. That sort of thing.'

'No women friends?'

'None his sister knows about off-hand.'

'Enemies?'

'Sister knows of none. She thinks he gambled too much. Mind, she's a bit stiff. Pillar-of-the-church type. Doesn't hold with drinking and gambling. She says this is why he was often short of money.'

'Was he short of money?'

'She says so. Other times, though, he seemed to have good wins because he seemed to have a lot.'

'Know where he gambled?'

'No.'

'We'd better find out. Where did he work?'

'For a type called Louis-Napoléon Pissarro. Runs a small manufactory in the city. At least –' Pomereu paused '– he

19

worked for him up to six months ago, then he said he wanted to leave because he'd got a better job at double the wages. Pissarro couldn't better that, so he left. His sister doesn't know where the new job was but she thinks it was somewhere in Montbard.'

'Didn't he ever tell her?'

'No. It seems they didn't get on all that well. She was a good churchgoer. He never went. But she was his sister and she felt it her duty to look after him.'

'We'd better go and see her,' Pel said. 'What about the tyre marks. The second set. Do they tell you anything?'

'Nothing.'

'Not even the size of the car?'

'Nothing, except that it was bigger.'

Pel nodded. 'I'll go and see Doc Minet on the way back,' he said. 'And find out what he has to offer.'

Doctor Minet had quite a lot to offer, including the remains of Claude-Achille Cormon. Considering he had a delicate stomach, Pel never enjoyed seeing the dead – especially since most of the dead *he* was concerned with were *violently* dead. Sometimes, however, there was no choice and the problem was one that always had to be faced.

Cormon's face, hands and the front of his body had suffered most. The hair had been burned away and the face was unrecognisable, an ugly mass of charred flesh clinging to the bone of the skull. The burned and blackened fingers were curved, the shrivelled tendons drawing them into hooks like claws.

'The clothing of the upper torso was almost completely burned away,' Minet said, 'though bits of it still clung to the legs.'

'Go on,' Pel encouraged, lighting a cigarette to kill the smell.

'Extensive burns, broken ribs, broken legs, fractured skull, broken collar bone, broken pelvis.' Doc Minet shrugged. 'I'm not going to put them in medical terms because I don't suppose you want me to. But that's what he had in lay terms. But it wasn't that he died of.'

'It wasn't? The burns?'

Doc Minet was a small round plump man who drew little pleasure from the corpses he saw on the slabs in his laboratory. On the other hand, they didn't depress him much either, because he was a cheerful smiling man who enjoyed tormenting Pel and his colleagues by making them wait for what he'd discovered.

He shook his head. 'No,' he said.

Pel scowled. 'Well, come on, then,' he said. 'What *did* he die of?'

Doc Minet made him wait just a little longer. 'Have you ever done any hunting?' he asked.

'A bit,' Pel said. 'Not much. I see enough that's dead without contributing to the numbers.'

Doc Minet smiled. 'Ever shot anything big?'

'Such as?'

'Deer.'

'You've shot deer?' Pel looked at Minet with admiration. 'Who're your wealthy friends?'

Minet smiled. 'Not here,' he said. 'Algeria. Before it was given independence. I was born there. I lived there as a young man. There were a few buck in the south. Occasionally we used to go shooting. We always carried a knife so we could polish them off if we only wounded them.'

Pel studied Minet with interest. He'd always had the impression that they'd have been given the *coup de grâce* with – another shot in the head. When he said so, Minet shook his head.

'Waste of a bullet. Expensive things, bullets, in those days. A good big pocket knife was just as good.' He lifted his hand and touched the back of his head where the neck joined the skull. 'Just up here there's a soft spot under the skull. It's even more marked in a four-legged animal. We used to slip the knife in there. It was instantaneous.'

Wondering where it was leading, Pel frowned. Doc Minet smiled.

'The hunter's thrust, it was called,' he said. 'They probably call it other things in other places, but where I lived that was its name.'

'And?'

'Someone gave Cormon a hunter's thrust.'

'What!'

Pel's eyes widened and Doc Minet went on cheerfully, pleased at the effect he'd produced. 'There was blood on the body, of course,' he said. 'There were a lot of cuts and injuries. Broken limbs. Compound fractures. But there were no cuts on the head and I wondered where the blood there had come from. There wasn't much, so it seemed to indicate that it came from the fatal wound, because when the heart stops pumping the blood stops flowing. I found an incision a centimetre and a half wide and eleven centimetres deep. It went upwards under the skull into the brain.'

'In other words, he wasn't dead when the car stopped rolling?'

Minet smiled. 'In fact,' he said, 'I think he actually pulled himself out of the flames. There were grass stains on his knees and bloodstains on the grass. He dragged himself clear, but someone followed him and killed him.'

'With a knife?'

'Perhaps they intended to do it some other way originally. Perhaps as they followed him down the hill they decided they could polish him off by driving him off the road. But, after he crashed they found him quite clearly alive and, in my opinion, despite the injuries he'd received, capable of recovery, so they killed him.'

Pel sat down, his hands toying with a packet of Gauloises. He took out one of the cigarettes, stuck it beween his lips and offered the packet to Minet.

'I don't,' Minet said.

Pel's head jerked up. 'You used to,' he accused.

'I'm trying not to.'

'How do you do it?'

'With a lot of agony. So far I'm holding. I can't guarantee it, however, so don't tempt me. There's only one way to stop and that's have none about the house.'

'If I had none about the house,' Pel admitted gloomily, 'I'd probably smoke the tufts off the carpet.' He stared at his cigarette, small, dark and intense-looking. 'This Cormon,' he went on. 'If what you say is right, it was sheer cold-blooded murder.'

Doc Minet shrugged. 'That's what it looks like,' he agreed.

'Why? Most murders are much less premeditated than that. But here they seem to have been chasing him, tried to kill him by making him crash his car and, when they failed, did it with a knife. Why not with a gun?'

'Perhaps they didn't have a gun.'

'Then they'd need to know *this* method of killing, this hunter's thrust of yours.'

Doc Minet smiled. 'That would seem to be the case,' he agreed.

Pel was frowning when he returned to his office. He was smoking and scowling at his blotter when Darcy put his head round the door. Pel waved him to a chair and pushed his packet of cigarettes across.

'No thanks, Patron,' Darcy said.

'Don't say *you've* given up too?' Pel felt betrayed. Darcy was a good honest cigarette smoker who remained undeterred by the dire warnings about cancer, asthma and all the other associated diseases.

Darcy grinned. 'No, Patron. I've just finished one.'

Pel pushed forward a sheet of paper. 'Claude-Achille Cormon,' he said. 'Lived with his sister, Madame Eugénie

Clarétie, of Evanay-sur-Rille. Aged forty-one. Bachelor. Now dead.'

'Pomereu's stiff?' Darcy asked.

'Yes. Find out about him, Darcy. He was murdered.'

Darcy's eyebrows rose. 'Was he now? How?'

'What Doc Minet calls a hunter's thrust. A knife under the skull.'

'I thought he was killed in a car crash.'

'He ought to have been. But he wasn't. He was still alive and, what's more, he was still conscious and trying to drag himself away. Somebody found him there and murdered him while he was helpless. I want to know why. That sort of murder's usually prompted by something big that we ought to know about. Something as big as drugs.'

Darcy glanced at him. They had both been severely shaken not long before to find a growing drug ring in the city that had prompted murder.

'Try the bookmakers,' Pel suggested. 'He seems to have been a bit of a gambler. Sometimes he lost heavily but at other times he did well and had money in his pocket.'

'Think there was doping going on?'

'If there was, why kill him *here*? We have no major stables in the area. He also doesn't ever seem to have wandered far from home and doesn't seem to have frequented the tracks. I want to know about him, Darcy.'

'Right, Patron.'

'How's Misset doing with that art theft at St Sauvigny?'

'He doesn't know whether he's coming or going, Patron. If it had two legs, a bust and a behind and wore lipstick, he'd find it at once. He doesn't even know where to start.'

'What about the expert who's supposed to know all about this sort of thing. Has he arrived yet?'

'End of the week, Patron. He's involved in a fraud case.'

'Send Misset in.'

Misset was growing fat, Pel noticed, as the sergeant appeared. He'd never been the brightest member of Pel's team and it would have pleased Pel to get rid of him, because Misset was also inclined to be lazy, over-familiar with women witnesses, and forever asking for time off to look after his growing family. But, since Sergeant Krauss had been shot dead not long before, they'd been shorthanded. Everybody in police work seemed to be shorthanded, Pel felt. Every civil service department in the world seemed to be overstaffed except the police, and with recruits not coming up to standard lately, recruiting was temporarily in abeyance and they were having to wait.

'The art theft,' he said. 'Making any headway?'

Misset shrugged. 'Patron, I don't know anything about art. I wouldn't know a Louis XV commode from a piece of pudding.'

'I gather it's not a Louis XV commode we're looking for,' Pel growled. 'Nor a lost piece of pudding.'

Misset gestured. 'No, patron, but that's what this dame seemed to spend all her time talking about.'

'Which dame?'

'This Madame de Saint-Bruie. Runs an antique shop in the Rue de Lyon at Chagnay. I saw the priest-in-charge at St Sauvigny but I couldn't make head or tail of what he said, so I went to this Saint-Bruie dame. She was just as bad.'

'Why didn't you spend an afternoon reading it up?' Pel asked.

'Reading it up, Patron?' Misset's face was blank.

'We have an excellent library in this city,' Pel pointed out coldly. 'We also have a university which in the past has never hesitated to give us the benefit of its knowledge and experience. Two or three hours in the library there might have made all the difference. Even an hour or two at home with a book.'

'Patron, at home I don't have time to read books.'

'The trouble with you, Misset,' Pel snapped, 'is that you never have time for anything. Your family life prevents you being a policeman. Normally it's the other way round: Being a policeman normally prevents a man having a family life.'

'Well, seeing his kids is a father's right, Patron.'

Pel glared. He'd used up his ration of good humour for the day. 'This world's full of people demanding rights,' he snapped. 'But nobody ever seems to accept the responsibilities that go with them. Send Nosjean in.'

Sergeant Jean-Luc Nosjean was slim and dark and still very young. Though Pel would have died rather than admit it, he considered him, with Darcy, to be one of the bright members of his team. In fact, both Pel and the Chief considered Darcy and Nosjean to be head and shoulders above all the other sergeants in the Hôtel de Police. After a harsh introduction when he had bleated constantly about the hours he worked, Nosjean had settled down well and these days, like Darcy, he was never overcome by the prospect of putting in overtime. He didn't always go by the book, but he had ideas. If he had a failing, it was that he tended to fall too heavily for any pretty girl who happened to cross his path. There was one on whom the sergeants' room had been betting for a long time, Odile Chenandier, whose father Nosjean had helped send to prison, but of late the sergeants' room had been wondering if they'd picked the wrong horse, because Nosjean's attentions seemed to be straying in the direction of a librarian by the name of Louise Rodier, who was not only intelligent but also managed to look like Charlotte Rampling.

'How's your love life, Nosjean?' Pel asked as Nosjean halted in front of his desk.

Nosjean looked startled. 'Patron?'

'Misset's seems to be getting in the way of his work.'

Nosjean grinned. 'Mine bothers me from time to time, Patron,' he admitted. 'But it's never got in the way of work.'

Pel came dangerously close to beaming at Nosjean. 'I'm delighted to hear it,' he said. 'How busy are you at the moment?'

'I'm in court tomorrow, Patron. That break-in at Vence. I've also got a few enquiries to make about the assault at the Relais St Aubyn, and there's that stabbing in the Rue Royale.'

'You're busy then?'

Nosjean grinned. 'I don't call that busy, Patron.'

This time Pel actually did beam at him. Nosjean was perhaps his favourite sergeant because he was as clever as Darcy and never answered back or pulled Pel's leg. According to Pel, the only person who was entitled to answer back or pull legs was Evariste Clovis Désiré Pel.

'Good,' he said. 'Then I want you to work with Misset. Inevitably, that will mean you doing all the thinking, so make sure Misset does all the leg work.'

Nosjean smiled.

'Do you know anything about ecclesiastical art treasures?' Pel asked.

'Not a thing, Chief.'

'Then what would be your first move?'

'To go to the library and read it up, Patron.'

Pel eyed him. It was more than likely he would also enjoy half an hour's chat with Charlotte Rampling, but at least he could be relied on to do the reading too, and, what was more, he'd absorb what he'd read. Misset would merely enjoy the chat with Charlotte Rampling.

'Do that,' he said. 'Then get down to St Sauvigny. See the canon in charge. It seems to be way above Misset's head. I understand we have help coming at the end of the week in the shape of a police officer – no less – from Auxerre who's supposed to be an expert. He'll doubtless be as fat and lazy as Misset, so make sure you pick his brains well.'

While Nosjean headed gleefully for the library, wondering what he could tell Odile Chenandier if he could get round Charlotte Rampling and found it necessary to put off their date for the following evening, and Darcy settled down at the telephone to ring round every bookmaker in the district for what they knew about Claude-Achille Cormon, Pel headed for the Bar du Destin, which was a dark little place he favoured because no one knew him there but the landlord.

As he sipped a coup de blanc, he wondered about his own love life. Unhappily, it didn't seem to be making much headway.

For some time now Pel had been bored with his private existence. Mostly it seemed to be organised for Madame Routy's convenience. She had been wished on him some time before when his last housekeeper, also a widow, had announced that she was marrying again. Pel's younger sister, who lived at Chatillon, had found him Madame Routy and now Pel was stuck with her. He couldn't shift her and was aware that gradually she was taking him over.

He sipped his wine again, enjoying the flavour. What would they do, he wondered, without wine to push the blood through all those little veins and things? Pel was convinced that *his* veins never worked properly, which was why he always felt the cold so much in winter.

He brooded for a while, staring at his glass. There *was* an alternative to Madame Routy, of course, and Madame Routy was well aware of it so that of late her sullenness had multiplied. In fact, Pel was convinced she had a supercharger fitted to the volume control of the television. Most nights when he returned home it sounded like a re-run of the storming of the Bastille. Unfortunately, Madame Routy's alternative, who went by the name of Geneviève Faivre-Perret – also a widow who ran Nanette's, the beauty salon in the Rue de la Liberté – and Pel were having the greatest difficulty in getting together. The last time Pel had tried, with a dinner all arranged at the most expensive hotel in the district, he had found himself stuck in Innsbruck with a dead drug-pusher and a dead Sergeant Krauss, and things hadn't been quite the same since.

He was aware that with a little effort on his part he could probably bring things back to normal. Red roses would have worked wonders – long stalks, of course, and an uneven number. No Frenchman in his senses would have sent ten or twelve, because an odd number was always more intriguing – but somehow he couldn't bring himself to make the move.

Was he all that keen, he wondered. Or was he afraid of giving up his cherished independence? The one thing he certainly wasn't afraid of giving up was Madame Routy and, unless he accepted another housekeeper – always assuming he could pluck up the courage to get rid of Madame Routy, of course – the answer seemed to be marriage. And Madame Faivre-Perret, as he'd discovered by a little private detective work out of office hours, owned a splendid little villa near Talant that made Pel's house in the Rue Martin-de-Noinville look like a dog kennel. She also possessed a flat above her hairdressing establishment and a cottage near Trouville. Clearly she had more money than Evariste Clovis Désiré Pel and it put him off a little.

Nevertheless, there were times when Pel longed for an efficiently-run home that wasn't dominated by the television, where the food was eatable and there wasn't a lumpish Madame Routy sprawled in the best chair. There was another aspect to it, too, of course, which he hesitated to admit to himself. It had occurred to him more than once that the answer to that one was to take a mistress. Other people did. The things some people did with their spare time, in fact, it was amazing they survived the night. Unfortunately, there was an element of prudishness in Pel that precluded such a step. He'd been strictly brought up by parents who believed neither in divorce nor in promiscuity, and it had rubbed off. It was a pleasant idea to toy with, he decided, but somehow, not one he felt he could follow up, though sometimes his loins ached with the thought of a woman and he was terrified by the feeling that he was growing old.

When he returned to the office, Darcy was just putting on his jacket to go home. He was carrying on a heavy affair with a girl whom he'd met during their last case. She worked at the University and, blessed with a sense of humour and a great gift for fun, made a pleasant change from her predecessor, Joséphine-Héloïse Aymé, who was a Norman and had in her enough of the berserker Scandinavian blood that had peopled the province hundreds of years before to enjoy throwing things at Darcy. Since Darcy was the intermediary between Pel and the rest of the Hôtel de Police, he often had things thrown at him metaphorically and it made a pleasant change not to.

He looked at Pel with amused eyes. Daniel Darcy had a great gift for enjoying life. He was a hard-working policeman, modern as a rocket to the moon, and he took his pleasures as he found them, worrying not at all that he was sometimes on duty eighteen hours in a day. Pel always looked as though he worked twenty-five hours a day and, Darcy considered, had no idea how to run his life.

All the same, he was a good policeman who had more than once saved an over-enthusiastic Darcy from putting his foot in it and Darcy regarded him with considerable respect if only for that. At that moment, however, Darcy decided, the poor old bastard looked as if, like Atlas, he was carrying the weight of the world on his shoulders.

'Our friend Cormon,' Darcy said. 'I've telephoned round. The bookies know him. He was a regular loser.'

'No wins?'

'Not here. He picked losers so often he was a bit of a joke.'

'Where *did* he pick his winners then?' Pel asked.

'Perhaps the periods when he was in the money *weren't* the result of winners,' Darcy suggested. 'If he was up to something fishy, for instance, he'd hardly tell his sister, would he? The obvious thing to tell *her* was that he'd won the money on a horse.'

Pel nodded slowly, his mind whirring. 'I think we ought to see this sister of his,' he said. 'Also this Louis-Napoléon Pissarro, who used to employ him. After all, who's more likely to know about him than his employer?'

four

Nosjean and Sergeant de Troquereau from Auxerre got together at once.

De Troquereau was a small man, lean and slim like Nosjean and roughly the same age. He was precise-looking, with delicate, almost effeminate features, a small straight nose, large pale eyes and a neat head covered with crisp, curling hair immaculately cut. He looked about sixteen.

Nevertheless, he knew his job, and armed with the knowledge he had culled from two days' reading, Nosjean sat down with him to find out how art thieves worked.

'It's nothing new,' De Troquereau said. 'And it's growing. With inflation, it's bound to. Art's a better investment than property and has lower insurance rates than jewellery. In the Seventies, in fact, the art thefts in Italy reached such proportions the government had to call up 3000 police reservists to serve as guards at churches and museums. There were even a few suspicions that priests were involved and got a share of the loot. The same thing happened with Mayan relics in Latin America, where odd generals and engineers were caught up in it.'

'What about this country?'

De Troquereau smiled. 'Security's nothing to write home about. A visitor to the Louvre a year or two back found he'd been locked in at closing time and couldn't get out. He finally found the guards about a kilometre away down the hall, frying eggs on a hot plate. They'd no idea he was there.'

Nosjean frowned. 'It begins to look as if the underworld's become aware of the majesty of art,' he said. 'They're not only attracted by the prices but also by the glory of light, form and colour. They're probably debating inferior brushwork and tonal qualities these days.'

De Troquereau's smile widened. 'They're probably even getting fanatic enough to start stealing from each other. Do you think the people who pulled this job are the same ones who've been working the châteaux?'

'We don't know. But there certainly seems to be a connection because in every case they made no attempt to clutter themselves up with what was available but went straight for the best. At the Château Boncey-Morin they removed one picture – one only – but it was a Vigée-Lebrun and was small and easily removed. At Boureleau, near Saulieu, they took four chairs. All Boulard, whatever that is.'

'Boulard was a craftsman employed by Louis XIV,' De Troquereau said, speaking with a confidence that indicated he knew what he was talking about.

Nosjean nodded, gratefully accepting the information and storing it away. 'At Samour-Samourin it was four plates. Four only. From a case which contained twenty-four. The four were from the original set, all that remained. The other twenty were copies, good copies, of course, but more recent. I couldn't have told the difference, but *they* knew. At Lamence it was a Louis XV commode, of extraordinary value, so I'm told.'

'It would be,' De Troquereau smiled.

'At St Sauvigny it was one panel out of five. The centre panel which was not the most accessible but *was* the most valuable, because it had on it the signature of Cardinal Daunay. Whoever took it knew exactly which it was because he obviously didn't have time to examine them all.'

'Probably a graduate of the Ecole du Louvre,' De Troquereau suggested.

'What's that?'

'A more exclusive version of Arts-Déco – the School of Arts Décoratifs.'

'Is that where *you* learned all about it?' Nosjean asked.

De Troquereau smiled. 'My family had a lot of books and I had suspected nephritis as a child. It meant being in bed for weeks. I read them all.'

'Art books?'

'My family went in for art.'

'Teaching it?'

'Collecting it!'

Nosjean looked puzzled. 'They must have had some money.'

'They did. In those days. Actually –' De Troquereau looked sheepish ' – I'm a baron. Did you know?'

Nosjean stared at him. He'd never worked with a baron before.

'Sergeant Baron de Troquereau Tournay-Turenne.' De Troquereau smiled. 'There are more barons in France than there are stars in the firmament, of course, and it doesn't mean a thing. I have no money. We lost everything first under the Revolution, got it back when the monarchy was restored under Louis XVIII, lost it again under Louis-Philippe, got it back under Napoléon III, and lost it again under the Third Republic. We got tired of trying.'

'That's the worst of French history,' Nosjean agreed. 'Couldn't you use your title somehow? Get a directorship? A name like yours would look well in a letter heading.'

'Most people wanting directors these days,' De Troquereau said, 'want either business experience or money. I've got neither. That's why I became a cop, and I happen to like it.'

'Well –' Nosjean sighed ' – at least you know something about it. I don't. Where do we start?'

'Round the antique shops. Have you got any here?'

'Chiefly in the country. Most of them look like junk shops.'

De Troquereau considered. 'In that case,' he said, 'it might be a good idea to visit Paris. Have a look along the Rue de Charonne and the Rue Vanoy. There's a lot of furniture restoring and faking goes along there. The Rue St Honoré's another good place, but it's not a good time of year for there. In November and December antiques fetch double the prices, so everybody brings them out then. All the same, we might spot something.'

'I think we'd need to find something here first,' Nosjean said doubtfully.

'Very well. Who's your expert?'

'There's a Madame de Saint-Bruie, I gather. Keeps a shop at Chagnay. She might help us.'

The shop at Chagnay seemed to be run entirely by a girl in her twenties who looked more like Charlotte Rampling than the librarian back in the city. Perhaps, Nosjean thought, it was becoming a fashion and *everybody* was trying to look like Charlotte Rampling.

She was sitting behind a desk piled high with art books and was busy turning the leaves of a catalogue for a sale. In front of her was a small triangular piece of varnished wood bearing her name – Marie-Joséphine Lehmann. Nosjean, who was nothing if not impressionable, thought it a lovely name.

She looked up at him and smiled. It seemed to bring sunlight into the dusty disordered shop.

'Can I help you?' she asked.

'I'm looking for Madame de Saint-Bruie.'

'I'm afraid she's not in at the moment. She won't be long. Can't I do anything?'

'I don't know.' Nosjean produced his badge. 'I'm from the Police Judiciaire. I'm investigating the robbery of the panel from St Sauvigny. You'll have heard of it. I'm trying to fill in a little background, so I know what I'm looking for.'

'You'd better sit down.' She pushed the books aside and indicated a chair.

'Do you know anything about it?' Nosjean asked.

She smiled. 'It pays us to know things like that.'

'You'd better fill me in, then.'

She smiled again. 'When Louis XII found himself fighting against the growing power of Venice,' she explained, 'his alliance with the Papacy caused him to call for volunteers for his army, and the people of St Sauvigny, being devout and ardently French, raised troops. In gratitude, the King instructed Cardinal Daunay of Paris to provide a gift of seven matching panels to present to the district.'

'Big?'

'Big enough. A metre and a half high by a metre wide. They arrived in St Sauvigny in 1520.' The bright smile flickered on again. 'They were painted in indigos, vermilions and golds, and they depicted the trial of Christ, the Crucifixion and the Descent from the Cross. Despite the subject, they were remarkably attractive and were bordered with Burgundian roses and flowers as symbols of faith. They were priceless examples of medieval craftsmanship.'

Nosjean was entranced. 'Go on,' he urged.

The smile came once more. 'Their survival was quite remarkable because, not long after their arrival, the town was set on fire by the Huguenots. But the priest managed to hide them and, because the town was the backwater it was – and still is – they survived the iconoclasm of the Revolution and even the arrival of the Prussians in 1871.'

As the girl finished speaking, Nosjean remained silent, his eyes on her face. Then he became aware that she was regarding him with a quizzical, amused – expression and he started to life.

'Can you describe the missing one?' he asked, more briskly than he intended.

'I can do better than that. I can show you pictures.' She produced an enormous art book and laid it with a thump on the table. *Panneaux Et Tapisseries Ecclésiastiques De La France,* it said across the jacket.

'French Church Panels and Tapestries,' she said. 'It'll all be in here.' She opened the book at the index and ran her finger down the list.

'Here.' She looked up. Nosjean was a handsome young man, clean, neatly dressed, looking a little like Napoleon at the Bridge of Lodi, and she decided he was by no means the type to make a pass at her. 'You'd better come round this side,' she suggested. 'It's rather a large book.'

Nosjean joined her, trying to rivet his attention on the coloured plates. But Marie-Joséphine Lehmann was visible out of the corner of his eye and was rather a distraction. She wasn't exactly beautiful. Not as attractive as the librarian, but there was something extra about her that appealed. Confidence. Brains. Charm. Nosjean was enchanted and was already wondering what he'd seen in the librarian, or the nurse who looked like Catherine Deneuve, who'd held his attention for a time. Even old faithful, Odile Chenandier, despite her steadfastness, seemed to fade before this vision of poised intellectuality. She even had a splendid figure and wore an elusive perfume that might well have disturbed someone much less disturbable than Nosjean.

'Of the original seven,' she was saying, 'two disappeared soon after they were presented to the Church. It's believed that the Bishop helped himself. Bishops weren't very fussy in those days. You'll notice the pictures – the trial of Christ, the Via Dolorosa, the Crucifixion, the descent from the Cross, and the Resurrection. The Crucifixion is the most valuable because it had on the back of it the signature of Cardinal Daunay, and the colours have remained extraordinarily good because they've never been subjected to a lot of sunlight.'

By this time Nosjean had come to the conclusion that he could spend the rest of his life happily investigating art frauds.

As she looked up at him, their faces were only inches apart. 'I have other books,' she offered. 'Would you like to see them?'

'No. But do you have copies of these pictures?'

'I'm afraid not. Naturally, while we have to know about these things, they never come on the market, so we have no reason to present them to possible buyers. We often take photographs ourselves, though. I do it all the time. I'm quite skilled with a camera,'

Nosjean indicated the book. 'Could you photograph these pictures?'

'Of course.'

'In colour?'

'It'll mean rigging up lighting.'

'Could I help you?' Nosjean could think of nothing pleasanter than helping her rig up lighting.

She smiled, well aware that he was smitten. 'I think I'll do it myself,' she said. 'You'll probably get in the way. If you'd like to call back in a day or two.'

'I'll do that,' Nosjean said eagerly. 'I'll telephone ahead. Who shall I ask for?'

She indicated the plaque on the desk. 'That's my name,' she said. 'My friends call me Mijo.'

Nosjean was just wondering how he could prolong the interview, when the girl lifted her head as a door clicked somewhere in the dim interior of the shop.

'That sounds like Madame,' she said. She smiled at Nosjean. 'I think you'd better see her. She might be jealous.'

Madame Sadie de Saint-Bruie was a widow, enormously tall with elaborate green spectacles to match her eyes. Her shapeless gown and the string of amber beads she wore, that reached almost to her knees, made her look vaguely as if she had stepped out of a 1920s edition of *Vogue*. Her bright, artificially red hair was as frizzy as if it had been fried in olive oil, but was arranged on her cheeks in kiss-curls, and her shoes had straps across the insteps, so that Nosjean half-expected her at any moment to break into a Charleston.

She was of indeterminate age – young enough still to be called youngish, but certainly not old enough to be called middle-aged. She led Nosjean into an office cluttered with chairs, tables, lamps, plates, statuettes; busts and portraits of Napoléon by the thousand; and paintings of the Battles of Gravelotte, Mars-la-Tour and Sedan in which pale-faced French soldiers in red képis and trousers were dying in dozens as they held off the Prussians with their last cartridges.

'Influence of Détaille,' she said loftily. 'After the war of 1870 it became a deplorable convention and led to numerous developments on the theme of *gloria victis,* so that the typical hero was not the man who beat the enemy but the one who fell protecting the retreat of his comrades. It probably led to France's defeat in 1940. *La Dernière Cartouche* became a popular fad.'

She had, she said, been reading reports on thefts from country houses since 1960, and had noticed that over a period of years what were often blatant fakes had been hauled away.

'It needs an expert, of course,' she said, 'to recognise the touch of an expert.'

Nosjean was faintly awed by the brain inside this strange angular, yet very feminine frame. 'Are *you* an expert?' he asked.

Madame de Saint-Bruie looked at him with the noble sadness of an aristocrat of the bluest blood obliged to live in something as vulgar as a republic.

'Arts-Déco,' she said. 'Oh, yes, I studied. But then, so did many more and it might turn out to be any one of them. Their names are still in my mind. Artists stick together, you see, and don't forget each other. They know exactly how they work, and just as artists can recognise each other's work, whether it's good, bad or indifferent, so art experts can recognise each other's touches, too. I, for instance, can tell you without difficulty just who makes which fakes because, believe me, some of them are as much craftsmen as the people they copy. The only difference is that they weren't born two hundred years ago in the Haute Epoque.'

'It's as easy as that?'

'To an expert. An artist can recognise his friend's work whether it's signed or not, or even if it's disguised. There are touches which always escape. It's the same with craftsmen. Of course – ' a languid hand gestured ' – you have to have a bit of a gift, too. There must be only as many as you can number on one hand who know *exactly* when a thing is "right", when it hasn't been tampered with.'

Nosjean permitted a look of admiration to cross his face. She seemed to expect it and, since she'd been helpful, he saw no reason not to oblige.

'There was a period of pure error in the châteaux robberies in the Sixties,' she went on in her strong husky voice. 'Then the crooks took away whatever was handy. But this was followed by a period when they grew more discriminating – as if they were being advised by an expert. As indeed they were. They went to jail in the end, of course, as you know, because they became too greedy – they had found it so easy, they tried it once too often – and after that, the amateurism started again, and as much that was rubbish as was good was hauled away.' She paused and stared at Nosjean through the big green spectacles. 'Now, however, the pattern's being repeated. They have someone helping them once more, someone who knows what he's doing.'

Nosjean frowned, trying to absorb everything he'd been told. 'This panel that's disappeared from St Sauvigny,' he asked. 'Where could it be sold?'

'Nowhere.' Her hands lifted and dropped to her side. 'It would be like trying to sell the *Mona Lisa* or the English Crown Jewels. No one would dare touch it.'

'Not even a wealthy American? There must be a few who do not ask where such things came from.'

She gave him a bored smile. 'They're becoming less and less, young man. Since Van Meegheren did all those fakes about the time of the end of the war, they've grown more wary about what comes from Europe. American houses must be full of Canalettos, Fra Angelicos, Titians and many others that never had their origin in the Middle Ages.'

'Are there any other sources? I mean, where do the antiques go these days?'

'Germany. The bombing of German cities destroyed most of what was old and valuable, and lorryloads go there every week from France. Whole shiploads from England – but *they* need the money more, of course. Most of what goes is rubbish, but the Germans don't argue. They're eager to build up their "background" again. Some of it's "improved", some's sold just as it is.'

She talked for a long time about hall marks and estampilles, and offered a lot of names of craftsmen – Roentgen, Riesener, Weisweiler, van Rysen Burgh, together with a few known fakers like Vrain-Lucas and Mailfert.

'There are plenty more,' she said. 'Some not as honest.'

'Honest?'

'Mailfert was selling fakes and he knew it. But he always made sure his fakes were classified in the catalogues as reproductions, even though he allowed his buyers – very often *nouveaux riches* with too much money to spend – to think that they knew better than he did. Nowadays, Paris is full of people like Mailfert. The Flea Market has workshops within metres of the stands where the fakes are sold as genuine, and there are plenty of shops behind the Eiffel Tower with small factories attached, while the Rue de Charonne and the Rue Vanoy have scores of cabinet makers – half of them making fake furniture, half restoring genuine antiques. You're looking for someone who knows exactly what they're after.'

She gave Nosjean the benefit of her dazzling superior smile once more. 'And people like that,' she ended, 'are so clever they'll have thought of everything – even how to evade the police.'

'So the chances of finding them are slim?' Nosjean said.

She smiled. 'Very.'

It was most encouraging.

five

Claude-Achille Cormon's sister, Madame Clarétie, though totally devoid of sex appeal, was physically a similar type to Madame de Saint-Bruie, even to the frizzy hair.

She was tall and thin with a frigid, expressionless face, and her living room showed her attachment to the Church, with crucifixes and pictures of Christ. A Bible was noticeably prominent, and religious pamphlets were stuck into the frame of the mirror hanging over the dresser alongside the table.

Her home was one of a row of stone-built cottages in a small cul-de-sac in the village of Evanay-sur-Rille. Next door was an épicerie and further along what looked like a disused stable, on which were posters advertising the Tour de France and a few enthusiastic comments in chalk from the village youth about its favourites – Van der Essen, Aurelian Filou and Jo Clam.

Madame Clarétie clearly hadn't much time for her brother. When Darcy arrived she was preparing lunch and was cutting up a baguette with a long slender knife held in her fist like a sword, and she gestured angrily with it under Darcy's nose.

'I always said he'd bring disgrace on himself, the way he behaved,' she said.

Her brother, Darcy thought, had brought on himself more than merely disgrace.

'It was in the paper,' she went on. 'I read it in *La Bien Public.*'

She ought perhaps, Darcy thought, to have read it in *France Soir* and *France Dimanche*. They gave you much better value for money. The men who covered the district for the press had appeared outside Pel's office clamouring for a story and the cautious outline devoid of too many details they'd been offered had been seized on joyously. What hadn't been supplied they'd made up, and *France Soir* had gone to town with a splendid account, in gory detail, of how Cormon had met his death in his burnt-out car. There was only one thing wrong with it. Pel hadn't made known what Doc Minet had told him and all they could do was make a lot of song and dance about the dangers of the descent from Destres.

'What did your brother do for a living?' Darcy asked.

'My brother was an instrument maker.' Madame Clarétie gestured at a portrait on the sideboard round the frame of which a piece of black crêpe had been draped and fixed in place with pieces of sticking plaster. 'That's him.'

'I suppose,' Darcy said, 'that we couldn't borrow that, could we? For identification purposes. We'd copy it and let you have it back at once.'

She shrugged. 'I don't see why not.' She frowned. 'This would have killed my mother. He was often in dubious company – even as a boy. Once he disappeared for two whole years. I don't know where to. He lived with her until she died, then, since my husband had also recently been called to meet his Maker and I was in need of money, he moved in with me here.'

'It had its advantages, of course,' she went on without waiting for Darcy to ask another question. 'Without him, I could never have got into the city and he occasionally ran me in on his day off so that I could do a little shopping. This place has nothing more than a small draper, which sells only the crudest of clothing for agricultural workers and their families – and I've always been more than that.'

'How long had he worked for Louis-Napoléon Pissarro?' Darcy asked.

'About eight or ten years. But I think he was always underpaid because he never seemed to have any money. Of course – ' Madame Clarétie's face was thin with disapproval ' – he wasted most of it on gambling and last year he seemed to grow restless and said he'd decided on a change. He gave in his notice and moved to Montbard.'

'Where in Montbard?'

'I don't know. It wasn't my business so I never asked, and he never told me. As far as I can make out, it was a similar place to Pissarro's. He said his wages had doubled.'

'Did he have any special friends?'

'Not to my knowledge.'

'Women friends?'

'It might have been better if he had. A wife would have kept him on the straight and narrow. When he went to Paris I suspect he got up to all sorts of things.'

'He went to Paris?'

'Occasionally.'

'Why?'

Madame Clarétie's lips tightened. 'To enjoy himself, I suppose.'

'Not on business?'

'That's something I don't know about. It was something that was fairly recent. He became very secretive.'

'In what way?'

'He never talked about what he was up to. He received telephone calls occasionally.'

'Did you ever take them? When he wasn't here, for instance?'

'Once or twice. When I asked who it was they always said it didn't matter, they'd ring back.'

'What about acquaintances? Did he have many of those?'

'Well, he must have had some, because of the telephone calls.'

'Did you ever ask him who the telephone calls were from?'

'Sometimes. He just said they were from work.'

'Why would the people at work want to telephone him at home?'

'I don't know. He wasn't that important. He did once say it was some secret gadget he was working on. Perhaps that's why he went to Paris.' She spoke as if going to Paris was going to the moon. 'He used to be satisfied with this part of the world but I suppose his extra money went to his head.'

Something, Darcy decided, certainly went to Cormon's head.

'I shall have to search his room, Madame,' he said. 'Would that be possible?'

'Will it make a mess?'

'Not if you help me.'

She seemed far more concerned with disorder than with her brother's death but she grudgingly helped. There seemed nothing very unusual. Cormon's bank book showed a steady rise and fall that looked, Darcy thought, like the working of a yo-yo. Sometimes there was a lot in it, sometimes there was almost nothing. There was also a file of notes of electrical gadgets and a few sketchy drawings. He picked them up.

'I'd better take these, Madame,' he said. 'Do you mind?'

'Are they valuable?' she asked.

'I shouldn't think so.'

'Then you might as well. Why do you want them?'

'We'll have them checked. They might tell us what your brother was working on. It might give us a lead.' Darcy turned over one of the sheets. On the back was a half-finished pencil drawing of a church, that had been scribbled across with figures. Here and there on it were dabs of coloured paint.

'Was your brother an artist, Madame?'

'Oh, yes,' she said.

'This his work?'

'I shouldn't think so. Mostly he drew plans for radios. That sort of thing. All wires and valves. He was always tinkering with radios and working out where to put things.'

'That was the sort of drawing he did?'

'Yes. He was very good at it.'

'But nothing like this?'

She stared hard at the drawing. 'It looks vulgar,' she said.

'It's a church.'

'I don't think my brother would draw anything like that.'

Montbard wasn't very far off Darcy's route back to the city. It was a little town on a hill, old-fashioned with narrow-gutted buildings and a hump-backed bridge. There was scarcely any water in the river but there was still enough for two intent men to be trying to fish. All Darcy knew about the place was that at Montbard was born the Comte de Buffon, naturalist, keeper of the garden of Louis XVI, and husband to a wife who was said to have 'no neck any more, her chin making half the journey, her breasts the other half, as a result of which her three chins reposed on two soft pillows.'

His first visit was to the library to get a list of all the manufacturers in the place, then to the police station where he begged the use of the telephone to ring round to find out which of them knew Claude-Achille Cormon.

None of them did.

It was a wonderful way to make a living.

Meanwhile, Evariste Clovis Désiré Pel, still not on speaking terms with Madame Routy, had left without breakfast and headed for the Bar Transvaal near the Hôtel de Police where he ate a croissant and drank a cup of coffee in gloomy silence. It was admitting defeat, he knew, because even as he'd climbed into his car, he'd heard the television come on and the raucous tones of the man who was describing the antics of the hundred-odd masochists who were riding in the Tour de France.

At the office, he found Judge Brisard waiting for him.

'This business at Destres,' the Judge said. 'I'm handling it.'

Pel sighed. Why, he wondered, did God have it in for him so? While there was a perfectly good Judge Polverari, with whom he got on splendidly and whose one joy in life – because he had a rich wife and no worries over money – was to take Pel out to expensive meals and fill him full of wine and brandy, why did he have to work with Judge Brisard?

Polverari was small, fat and jolly and believed that vice was good for the soul so long as it was kept well under control. Brisard was tall, pear-shaped with a large behind and women's hips, a gloomy face and a clear dislike for Pel that was well and truly reciprocated. He was young and pompous and, while posing as a good family man – pictures of his wife and children were always on his desk – to Pel's knowledge, he had a mistress somewhere near Beaune who was the widow of a police officer. When he'd been young and new to the game, Pel had bullied him unmercifully but by this time Brisard had learned a few tricks himself and, being a judge, took advantage of the fact to get a little of his own bark. He hated Pel. Pel hated him. It was a good working arrangement.

'Polverari's mother-in-law died,' Brisard said. 'He'll be away for a few days. I'll need to know a few facts.'

Pel gave them to him and he sat back and began to make suggestions.

'Have we brought in this sister of his yet?' he asked.

'There didn't seem much need to,' Pel said.

'She might have had reason to do away with him.'

'Even if she did,' Pel pointed out, 'she hardly seems the type to go scrambling in the dark down what's virtually a vertical grass bank to where her brother was dragging himself from a blazing car with enough broken bones to make him to all intents and purposes jelly, and shove a knife blade into his brain under his skull. Even if she knew how.'

Brisard clearly hadn't thought of that. 'Nevertheless,' he said, 'like all the rest, she should be brought in. I may be able to discover something that you've missed.'

Pel's eyes glittered and the silence became menacing. Pel was determined not to be more helpful than he could manage and Brisard tried to push the affair a few steps more.

'What are your plans?' he asked.

It was Pel's job to work with Brisard, but most judges behaved like Judge Polverari and did no more than keep an eye on what was going on. Judge Brisard liked to think he knew more about police work than the police.

'I have still to see Louis-Napoléon Pissarro,' he said.

'Who's he?' Brisard decided to be amusing. 'He has a name of unsurpassing splendour. A king, an emperor and a painter of the first order.'

'He was Cormon's employer until he left to take another job,' Pel said coldly. 'He may be able to tell me something about him that we don't know already.'

Brisard quite failed to notice Pel's annoyance and went on, blithely self-important. 'I understand Sergeant Nosjean's handling the art theft at St Sauvigny.'

'Yes.'

'I'd better see him, too. Everybody connected with these two affairs, in fact. Until Judge Polverari returns, I'm keeping an interest in his cases. I might be able to help Nosjean. I have many friends among the priesthood. It's important for a judge to set an example, and I'm regularly at church.'

Judge Brisard, Pel felt, was sometimes so concerned with God's love he was inclined to forget human love which, after all, was only a manifestation of the same thing, and his concern with his future in the hereafter seemed rather a waste of time. God wasn't that stupid, Pel felt, and would choose His own candidates for celestial bliss. And they wouldn't all be churchgoers either. There might even, he thought darkly, be a bishop or a judge or two who'd get a shock when the time came.

As Brisard vanished, he sat staring at his blotter for a while. He was not a very important-looking man. On the slight side, with dark hair he brushed close to his skull, he suffered from a tendency to be self-denigratory. Nevertheless, he'd been a policeman a long time and knew all the ins and outs of the game. In recent years the law had become more difficult as do-gooders leaned over backwards to stop policemen harming criminals – they didn't seem to worry overmuch about the criminals' victims – and more and more the police had come under the influence of the Palais de Justice. It wasn't possible to quieten Brisard by evading the rules but there were other ways.

For a moment, Pel looked like a snake about to strike. If Brisard wanted to see everybody, he decided, then, very well, he would see everybody. If he wanted work, then that was what he was going to get. Brisard would find people queuing up outside his door to be interrogated. Pel hoped it would interfere a great deal with his work, stop him getting home to meals on time, and prevent him paying the calls Pel knew he paid to the woman near Beaune.

Nevertheless, he made certain that he wasn't laying himself open to charges of obstructiveness.

'Judge Brisard expressed a wish to see everybody connected with the case,' he told the Chief.

The Chief looked startled. 'Everybody?' he said.

'Everybody.'

'What in God's name for?'

'He thinks he may be able to elicit information that it's beyond my powers to acquire.'

The Chief stared hard at Pel. He didn't like Brisard much either, but he was supposed to be a responsible official.

'You two feuding again?' he asked.

Pel was all innocence. 'No,' he said. 'But, knowing Judge Brisard, I felt I ought to follow his instructions to the letter.'

The Chief frowned. 'Well, I know he's a bit pernickety,' he agreed. 'Perhaps you'd better do as he says. Are there likely to be many?'

'It's more than likely.'

The Chief grinned. 'Very well,' he said. 'It's a protest you're registering, I suppose. Well, handle it your own way. Let him have them.'

Louis-Napoléon Pissarro was a big man with greying hair, shoulders like an ox, the ruddy face of a farmer and enough gold teeth to dim the sun. His factory, Pièces de Rechange Pissarro, was a small affair of three large sheds in the centre of the city, tucked away behind a garage and close to the Hôtel Central. When Pel arrived he was reading *L'Equipe* with a pencil in his hand and his feet up on his desk. Behind him were pictures of Louis-Napoléon Pissarro on horseback, holding a rugby ball, and sitting on the stern of a fishing boat with the name, *Annick,* painted on the transom just below his behind.

'Named after my wife,' Pissarro explained. 'She's a Breton. Daughter of old Aloïs Hyaric, of La Roche-Bernard. He sat in the House of Representatives for the Villaine district there until he died two years ago. We still have a house which belonged to her mother on the coast at Penestin that we use in the holidays.'

In the picture he was holding a fishing rod and a fish that looked big enough to have swallowed Jonah – and several brothers, too, if necessary. Alongside it were more pictures – of Pissarro skiing, swimming, rowing, sailing, even hanging over the edge of a cliff on the end of a rope, complete with ice pick, crampons and climbing clothes. Outside the window stood a heavy old British Bentley with a strapped bonnet and copper exhaust.

'Bit of a sportsman,' Pel observed dryly.

Pissarro smiled and waved to a chair. 'Always keen on sport,' he agreed. 'You name it, I've had a go at it. That's my car outside. Old, but I've had it specially tuned. Once drove at La Mans and once very nearly played for France at the Parc des Princes. At the moment I'm just reading up the chances in the grande boucle – the Tour de France. You interested in sport?'

Pel's idea of a good day's athletic endeavour was a quiet afternoon in the sun with a fishing rod – it didn't matter much about the fish – dominoes in the Bar Transvaal, or, for really fierce activity, a game of boules. He shook his head.

'You don't know what you've missed,' Pissarro said enthusiastically. 'I've got the winner this year. Maurice Maryckx. He's going to wear the yellow jersey this time.'

'I'm delighted to hear it,' Pel said. 'I thought it was going to be Van der Essen or Jo Clam.'

'They're nothing but wheel-suckers, opportunists, limpets. They let others make the pace and tag on behind.'

'Isn't that the idea?'

'It's not bike-racing. They might be good downhill but anywhere else they ride like a postman. This man Maryckx is another Coppi, another Merckx. He's the one with the kilometres in his legs.'

Pel was well aware that speculation as to the winner was the favourite pastime of Tour enthusiasts and he waited patiently for Pissarro to get it out of his system.

'There are fewer than two hundred real riders in the world,' Pissarro went on, 'and Maryckx is one. They call him "the cannibal" because he devours opposition. They'll be coming through our area this year, you know; round Aurelles and over the top to Bagneux-les-Doles. Stage Nineteen. They stop the night at Morny and there's a feeding point at Boine. That's a good place to watch, if you're interested.'

'I'm not,' Pel said discouragingly.

Pissarro was not put off. 'Feeding points are always considered good places for breakaways,' he went on. 'It's my guess Maryckx will have established a substantial lead by that time. He'll be first home and first over-all. I shall be at Boine to see him pass, then drive up to Paris for the finish,'

Pel continued to listen quietly, letting him have his head. You could often learn a lot by letting a man have his head.

'This year,' Pissarro went on, 'a group of us have got together to finance a team – Pis-Hélio-Tout. So look out for the diamond-decorated green jerseys. Bit too expensive for one firm, of course, so there are twelve of us involved. I make sprockets of course. Twenty-two- and twenty-four-toothed. Some of the riders like them. I also make above-standard crank arms – longer than normal – which the sprinters use. We make other things, too, but those give us an interest and a reason for taking part.'

The gold teeth glittered as Pissarro smiled. 'If I find the winner has anything of ours on his machine,' he said, 'I can use it for advertising. And with Maryckx I feel we even have a chance of winning on our own. He's a Belgian, and the Belgians know how to win the Tour de France. Eddie Merckx won it more times than anybody.'

'Except Jacques Anquetil,' Pel pointed out. 'And he was a Frenchman.'

'Maryckx is good, all the same.'

To Pel bicycling seemed a difficult way of getting about – after all you didn't have feet for walking or cycling, but for pushing the pedals of a motor car – but he still read the newspapers and he would have been less than human to know nothing of the Tour de France. 'He's nobody I've heard of,' he said quietly.

'No,' Pissarro said. 'He isn't. But he's the winner. Make no mistake about it. I've picked the winner three times running and this year I'm putting my money where my mouth is. We provided his machines and they've been tailored like wedding suits. Every weight-reducing dodge you can think of. Alloy wheel rims, tape instead of handlebar grips, rat-trap pedals, brake levers like slices of gruyère cheese. They cost money but we've got sufficient faith in Maryckx to back him to the hilt. Not that anybody knows who we are, of course, but they'll ask all right when they see the name on his jersey when he wins.' Pissarro stopped dead and smiled. 'But, of course, you didn't come here to discuss the Big Loop, did you?'

'No.' Pel was growing a little tired of the Tour de France and his answer was brusque.

'I expect you've come about Cormon.'

'That's right.'

Pissarro tossed down *L'Equipe,* lowered his feet to the floor, and sat back. 'What did you want to know?'

'Chiefly what he did here?'

Pissarro shrugged his huge shoulders. 'He was my fore-man,' he said. 'I don't employ many people but he looked after things for me. He was good at his job, too. He was quite a nice type. Bit silly, mind you. All that stupid gambling – '

He looked set for the day but Pel wedged a question into a chink in the diatribe. 'Why would anyone want to kill him?' he asked.

Pissarro shrugged again. 'I don't know.'

'What do you make here?'

Pissarro smiled. 'Nothing much,' he admitted. 'But it's a living. Gadgets, I suppose you'd call them. Spare parts. Spare parts for vacuum cleaners. Spare parts for typewriters. Spare parts for televisions. Spare parts for bicycles. Plastic with a bit of metal spring and a length of wire. That sort of thing. Mostly other people's gadgets. Anything that anyone wants manufacturing. We're not bad at it.'

'I believe Cormon was with you up to six months ago.'

'That's right. For about eight years. He was good at the job. In addition to being foreman, he was also my chief copyist.'

'Copyist?'

Pissarro gave a wide unembarrassed grin. 'Other people's things. Things that were brought in.'

'For sale?'

'Oh, yes.'

'You copied them?'

'Of course. It's business. Everybody's at it. They weren't patented things. Just gadgets. We sold them in the south. Sometimes in Belgium. Sometimes in England. They'll buy anything there.'

'Why did Cormon leave?'

Pissarro gestured with a hand like a leg of lamb. 'He said he'd had a chance to do better for himself. I was sorry to lose him but you can't stop a man if he wants to do that.'

'Where did he go?'

'Montbard.'

'Where in Montbard?'

'Haven't the foggiest.'

'Didn't he tell you?'

'No. I haven't the faintest idea.'

Pel sighed. They were getting along at a great rate.

six

The conference in Pel's office was gloomy. The newspapers had the whole story now and they were wanting to know why it was possible in this day and age in a country as well-ordered as the Republic of France that a man could be murdered without the criminal being arrested within twenty-four hours. For the moment, they'd even forgotten Philippe le Bozec, the Under-Secretary at the Ministry of Defence who'd been found in the same bawdy house as one of the attachés from the Russian Embassy. The previous day they'd been demanding his head. Today, they appeared to be after the head of the man responsible for the running of the police. It was a line they always followed. It didn't mean they believed in it or that anybody was panicking and that France was entering a state of anarchy and was likely to fall apart at the seams at any moment, but it nevertheless left Pel's team a little low in spirits, because nobody, it seemed, had anything to report. They had all drawn blanks. They were even all wondering whether to hand in their resignations and join the fire brigade when Misset – Misset, of all people, who couldn't have cared less if the Republic of France disappeared under a welter of criminality – set them going. He appeared at the door to indicate that there was a certain Brigadier Foulot, from St Symphorien, wishing to see Pel.

'What about?' Pel snapped. He didn't like being interrupted, even when they were only sitting round wondering where to look next.

56

'Cormon,' Misset said. 'This Foulot seems to have been one of the last people to speak to him. We were in the canteen when it came out.'

Brigadier Foulot was a young man who looked a little like Sacha Distel. He was neat, smart and briskly alert, and Pel decided he was doubtless a wow with the girls at St Symphorien.

'I was telephoned by Claude-Achille the night he died,' he announced at once.

Pel leaned forward. 'Claude-Achille?' he said. 'Cormon? Did you know him well?'

'Yes.'

'Well enough to be on first name terms?'

'Oh, yes.' Foulot gestured. 'He was my cousin.'

'It might have helped if you'd said that in the first place,' Pel said acidly. He never liked people who were taller or better-looking than he was. 'Go on. You spoke to him just before he died, I hear?'

'Yes. He telephoned me at the station.'

'You put it down in the book, of course, as all good French policemen do? So that there's a record?'

Foulot shrugged. 'No, sir. I didn't.'

'Why not?' Pel's voice had the sharp edge of an assegai. 'Everything's supposed to go in the book.'

Foulot remained quite unperturbed. 'It was personal, sir,' he pointed out. 'Perhaps if I'd known what was going to happen to him, I might have put it down, but of course I didn't know he was going to be dead soon afterwards.'

'It's three days now since he died,' Pel pointed out, determined not to be thwarted of a victim. Madame Routy's meal the previous night had been abysmal, and he *needed* a victim. 'Why didn't you report it before now? You must have been aware of what happened to him.'

'No, sir, I wasn't.'

Pel glared. 'You mean you live in St Symphorien, which is twenty kilometres from where he was killed, he was a personal friend of yours – a cousin, no less – and you're a policeman with all the available machinery of information, yet you didn't know anything had happened to him?'

'No, sir.' Foulot smiled. 'I was in Geneva. I was due for three days leave. My wife's Swiss and I took her to see her mother.'

Pel scowled. When he was in his predatory mood he didn't like being cheated of his victim.

'Go on,' he said. 'What did he telephone about?'

'I don't know, sir. He didn't tell me. He just suggested that he wanted to see me. We arranged to meet at the Bar Domino at Fauverolles, which is about halfway between Evanay and St Symphorien, where I'm stationed. My wife wasn't keen, because we were leaving early the next morning. But officially I was still on duty so I went. He didn't turn up.'

'What do you think it was all about?'

Foulot scratched his nose thoughtfully. 'Well, he'd borrowed money from me in the past. Small sums. He always paid them back quickly but I knew he gambled and was sometimes short.'

'Did he owe you anything?'

'No, sir. That's why I assumed he was after another loan. I just assumed he'd been let down by the horses again. When he didn't appear, I went home, expecting him to telephone. But he didn't. I went off duty officially at midnight and at six next morning I set off with my wife towards Pontarlier. I gather he was found about that time. By the time the news reached my station I was well south, and, of course, it didn't appear in the Swiss papers. I didn't learn what had happened until I got back last night. I thought I'd better report the matter.'

Foulot hesitated. 'I telephoned his sister immediately, of course. She said his boss – or, rather, his former boss, Pissarro, had been trying to get hold of him the night he died.'

Pel turned to Darcy. 'Did she tell *you* that? It's not in your report.'

'She said nothing about it, Patron.'

'Think she was hiding it?'

'She didn't strike me as the type to hide things, Patron.'

Pel frowned. 'Well, Pissarro never mentioned to me either that he'd been trying to get in touch with Cormon the night he died. *He* didn't strike me as the type to hide anything, either.'

Pissarro was in the garden of his home at Daix when Pel and Darcy pinned him down. It was a new house, smart and modern, its name carved on a block of slate set into the gate post – *Ker Boukan*. Despite the newness of the building, the garden had a well-established look about it and Pissarro was pruning roses with a horn-handled knife. He seemed startled as Pel sailed into him and eventually held up his hands in protest.

'Steady on, Inspector,' he said. 'I didn't realise it was *that* important.'

'A man's been murdered,' Pel snapped. 'Don't you call that important?'

'I mean I didn't know *my* small part in it was important.'

Pissarro clipped at a rose and stuck it in his buttonhole, then snapped the knife closed and slipped it in his pocket. 'Perhaps I *should* have told you I tried to get in touch with him. But I didn't. I'm sorry.'

'*Why* didn't you tell us?' Pel said.

'Well, I'd read he'd died in curious circumstances and I began to wonder if he'd failed to pay some of his gambling debts and that the heavies had moved in. I didn't want to be involved.'

'*When* did you try to get in touch with him?'

'The night he died. I was afraid of being involved in the murder.'

59

'Nobody said it was murder until two days ago when *Le Bien Public* were given the information. It was in the other newspapers today for the first time.'

'No,' Pissarro agreed. 'They didn't mention it. I'd better tell you how it happened.'

'I think you had,' Pel said.

Pissarro gestured to a folding chair in the shade. 'Actually, he didn't come to me and tell me he'd got a new job,' he said. 'I sacked him. I didn't tell you that.'

'Why not?'

Pissarro shrugged. 'Speak ill of the dead,' he said. 'I didn't think it mattered and I didn't want to do him any unnecessary injustice.'

'*Why* did you sack him?'

'He was always in debt and kept disappearing from work – to raise funds, I thought. I decided I couldn't go on like that. Sometimes I have to be away and I need someone to look after the place who's going to be around. So I told him he'd have to go. He wasn't very happy about it but we didn't part on bad terms. I slipped him a little bonus and he knew he'd been wrong and that he could get another job easily enough. As he did, of course. Quickly, and at better wages than I gave him.'

Pel's eyes glittered expectantly. 'Where? We haven't been able to find out yet.'

'In Montbard, he said.'

'None of the places we've been to.' Pel scowled. 'You haven't told us yet why you tried to get in touch with him.'

'I'm coming to it.'

'Was it by telephoning or personally?'

'Personally. I thought it was best that way.'

'Why was it best that way?'

'I wanted him to come back. He was a skilled man and skilled men are hard to get these days. The youngsters just won't be bothered. I missed him. As a foreman he wasn't a lot of use because of his disappearing acts, but he was still a

60

very good instrument maker. I thought I'd try to get him back. I went to see him. His sister told me he was out. I'd heard he found Montbard was a long way to go every day, so I thought he might be *glad* to come back here. But I didn't want to go crawling and I thought that, since he was out, I'd let him stew a little longer. Another day or so. Then I read in the paper that he was dead. So I just never did see him.'

Darcy leaned forward. 'Did you ever try to get in touch with him by telephone?'

'Not to my knowledge.'

'*Somebody* kept telephoning him. His sister took the call once and was told that the caller would ring back. Was that you?'

'I never telephoned him at all as far as I can recall.'

'Who did?'

Pissarro shrugged. 'Not me'

Darcy sat back and eyed Pissarro quietly. 'Was he afraid of something?' he asked.

Pissarro pulled a face. 'I don't know. He might have been.'

'Why might he have been?'

'I don't know. I don't even know that he *was*. I said he *might* have been. Someone appears to have murdered him, so perhaps he had something to be afraid of.'

On the way back, they stopped for a beer at a bar at the top of the hill leading down to the city. There were alterations going on at the back that covered the counter with dust. Even the beer tasted of dust.

'Well,' Pel said, hoisting his face out of his glass. 'I suppose you could say we've made a *bit* of progress. Cormon *might* have been afraid of something, and that *might* have been the reason he telephoned his cousin, Brigadier Foulot, and arranged to meet him at Fauverolles. Perhaps he was worried about something.'

'All the same, Patron,' Darcy said, 'it doesn't tell us much.'

'What do we know about Pissarro?'

'Nothing much. Seems straightforward enough. Been in business for fifteen years or so, now.'

'Wealthy?'

'Appears to be.'

'Let's have him checked. Get Misset on to it. Let Nosjean handle the art thefts. Tell Misset to see Durois of the Chamber of Commerce. Tell him we need his help. He'll know Pissarro. If he doesn't, he'll soon find out.'

'What if he asks why?'

'Tell him we're a bit concerned about something that might bring the Chamber of Commerce into disrepute. No need to go into details. It'll be enough to get him moving.'

When they reached the Hôtel de Police, Doc Minet was waiting for them. He had a sheaf of papers and a bundle of photographs in his hand.

'Report,' he said as he handed them to Pel. 'In full. It's exactly what I told you the other day, but in medical jargon so obscure no one can understand it, least of all the court that will have to try the case when it comes up. However – ' he shrugged and smiled cheerfully ' – convention says that's the way it must be done, so there you are. There's just one thing – '

Pel lowered the report and pushed his spectacles up on his forehead to look at Minet.

' – I found something very interesting you might like to hear about.'

'If it's interesting, of course I'd like to hear about it.'

Minet fished among the papers and began to read. '...the body of a fully-developed male, a hundred and seventy-five centimetres long, weight about eighty-three kilos, overweight but not obese. Organs in good condition – '

'What is all this?' Pel demanded.

Doc Minet smiled. 'Wait. Wait. You'll learn. Knife wound under base of skull. Width one and a half centimetres, length eleven centimetres.' Sort of wound a hunter delivers to an injured animal. Known in some parts of the world as the hunter's thrust. He was not dead when it was delivered but he would be immediately afterwards. Time of death: Can't be exact, but I can pinpoint it within five hours.'

'It's not enough,' Pel growled.

'Very well, let's say between 11.30 and 1.30 on the morning he was found. This man was shot.'

Pel lifted his eyes, lowered his spectacles to his nose to stare through them at the doctor.

'I thought you said he died from a knife thrust.'

'He did. He was shot some years ago. In the shoulder.'

'War wound? No –' Pel frowned ' – he wasn't old enough.'

'It was hard to find,' Minet went on. 'Because there were extensive burns and at first it was missed, because of the puckering of the flesh and the skin under the action of the flames. In fact, this area of the torso hadn't been much harmed but the puckering of the skin made it look like an extension of the burns. There was a star-edged scar, the size and shape of a half-franc piece, near the right shoulder. The bullet had lodged in the left clavicle and smashed the bone. Whoever extracted it was not a trained surgeon and the fractured clavicle was allowed to knit as it liked. It was in a pretty bad state. It was about eleven years old.'

'Which indicates?'

Minet gave a beatific smile. 'What it indicates to you, *mon brave*,' he said, 'I wouldn't like to guess. To me it indicates some gang fracas or a police bullet in – say – a hold-up. There'd be no other reason for the bullet to have been extracted with such a lack of skill or for the fractured clavicle to knit as it did. He was shot doing something dishonest and, because it was dishonest, he couldn't go to a surgeon, so the wound was attended by someone lacking in skill. Your

Claude-Achille Cormon, in my opinion, my friend, was at some time on the wrong side of the law.'

seven

It was their first break and Darcy immediately started searching through the records to find out what it was that Claude-Achille Cormon had been doing approximately eleven years before, that had resulted in him being winged by a police bullet.

There was another break soon afterwards when Montbard Police telephoned.

'That enquiry your sergeant was making about manufacturers here,' the voice in Pel's ear said. 'There's one we think he might have missed. Accessoires Montbard. It's small. Only about twenty people employed there. Owned by an Englishman called Robinson. It's not strictly a manufactory, but on the other hand perhaps it ought not to be left out. If you care to call here, we'll direct you to it.'

Suddenly they seemed to be galloping along, because within an hour Darcy had turned up Claude-Achille Cormon in the records. 'Two years for attempted safe-breaking in Lyons,' he announced. 'Eleven and a half years ago. That must be when he disappeared for a while. Old Minet's guess was a good one.'

'Go on,' Pel said. 'Where?'

'Office of Produits Merçage. He worked there. They make electronics. There was an attempt to get into the safe but something went wrong and the police stumbled on it. The thieves tried to escape and Cormon was winged. He got away but was picked up several weeks later.'

'Interesting,' Pel observed. 'After that, I suppose, he went to Pissarro's.'

'Looks like it, Patron,' Darcy said. 'But hang on, there's more. He'd worked originally for Cornus' Safes. He was an expert on locks. That's the reason he was at Produits Merçage. To open the safe. It was a Cornu.'

While Pel's enquiry was moving ahead, Nosjean's seemed to have come to a stop.

De Troquerean, having dispensed his knowledge and helped Nosjean to understand something of what he was doing, had returned to Auxerre with a distinct understanding that he was available for further consultations if necessary. Unfortunately, his chief in Auxerre naturally preferred that he should be in Auxerre and if Nosjean wished to confer it would be necessary to arrange it by telephone and drive up the motorway and meet him.

However, although Nosjean had got no nearer to discovering who had removed the panel from the church at St Sauvigny, he had at least discovered something of the methods of the men who had robbed the châteaux of their treasures. Though no one had seen them, to judge by what had disappeared, it was obvious they had arrived by car – more than likely a reasonable-sized station wagon to enable them to remove their loot – had parked it somewhere handy under the trees where it wouldn't be seen, and completed the journey on foot across the park to the château of their selection. They had entered by different windows, but their methods were always the same. They seemed to know which windows were secured with latches and, using a 30-millimetre drill had bored a hole beneath the latch and lifted it through the hole by means of a screwdriver. At Boureleau, they had actually effected their entrance on the second floor, one of them making his way up to a decorative ledge that ran round the building by means of a hooked rope secured among the more-than-convenient protuberances in the stonework.

Having bored the usual hole and opened the window, he had then descended to the ground floor and opened a side door, and whoever had been with him had made his way inside with him and removed four excellent Boulard chairs and a small portrait of the owner's ancestor by Greuze.

Madame de Saint-Bruie had been more than helpful. 'You'll never find the chairs again,' she had said cheerfully, her husky voice vibrant with self-confidence.

'But, surely, they carried the estampille and the master's personal signature?' Nosjean pointed out.

'It makes little difference. They'd have them disguised in a matter of days. They get rid of the gilt to reveal the original unvarnished wood, remove the medallions, or oval backs, recarve the arms, obliterating all the floral decoration, do the same with the back – though they would probably preserve the centrepiece in this case – then reupholster with a faded length of authentic 18th Century tapestry.'

'It makes it difficult, doesn't it?' Nosjean said with a wry smile.

She smiled back. 'It does rather. It's very convenient for thieves that the nobles of the 18th Century were a gregarious lot who liked to build their châteaux within reach of each other. In those days, of course, it was a day's coach ride when they went visiting. Nowadays, it's only a matter of an hour or so in a motor car. It makes it possible to visit the lot in one day and make your plans accordingly. It's even worse further north. The area round Versailles, Fontainebleau and Marly is literally studded with châteaux, and they're all filled with haute époque furniture by Louis XV's craftsmen.'

Faintly uncomprehending, Nosjean made enquiries round St Sauvigny and the villages surrounding the châteaux but was able to discover remarkably little. Nobody had seen anybody suspicious, but that was not considered unusual, because the owners of the châteaux spent their weeks in Paris and only their weekends – when they weren't skiing in winter or water-skiing in summer – at their country homes.

'It makes it reasonably easy,' Madame de Saint-Bruie observed loudly. 'Especially when they're so disinterested in that part of the national patrimony they possess they don't even know its value – or even, often, what it is. For the most part, young man, many of them wouldn't miss what they own and it's only when they learn the immense value of the things they've been looking at all their lives without interest that they set up a howl.'

'You don't seem to like them,' Nosjean grinned.

She gave him a cold look. 'They don't deserve to own such beauty,' she said sharply. 'Personally, I'd allow every thief in the business to take what he wants – provided, of course, that he'd bothered to study the subject or read it up in the *Journal du Garde Meuble*.'

'Which is?'

She drew herself up, strong, colourful and oozing personality. 'The Bourbons, young man, appalling though they were, spent an incredible amount of money on the royal furniture, and Louis XIV and his minister, Colbert, devoted an extraordinary amount of energy to ensure that it was all catalogued. The book came to an end only in 1792 when the Revolution arrived. And *that* iconoclastic lot simply dispersed it all, much of it to America.'

'Even in those days?'

She beamed at him. 'Even in those days. Waggonloads went to Poland, especially when some of the Revolutionary officials saw money in it for themselves and started feeding Versailles, Fontainebleau and Marly with furniture from other sources, all of which was sold as *royal* furniture. Some of it's been returned, of course, when tastes changed and Victoriana or the Style du Métro came into vogue. But it's been so dispersed now, it's not difficult for anyone with an expert knowledge and a good wood carver to sell a fake as genuine or appraise a genuine article worth stealing.'

'Could you?'

'Couldn't you?'

'No.'

'You have nothing – ' a strong languid arm gestured at the interior of the shop ' – of this sort at home?'

Nosjean's parents were far from poor but they were largely self-made and he suspected that most of what graced their salon would come under the heading she so contemptuously described as Style du Métro.

'No,' he said. 'Do you?'

'But of course,' she said. 'I have a house full of treasures. But, then, it's my job isn't it?'

Nosjean was deep in thought as he headed for his car. He had already worked out the modus operandi of whoever it was who was busily denuding the châteaux and churches of the area of their treasures. Some expert – an antique dealer, a graduate of Arts-Déco or merely someone who was just an omnivorous reader of books on antiquities – made the rounds of the châteaux, probably visiting several in a single weekend. Since it was no longer possible to take photographs inside, and since the photographs that were sold were careful, since the robberies of the Sixties, to avoid showing details, it was clear that whoever *was* doing the rounds was either using a hidden camera – which was always a possibility in these days of minute Japanese gadgets – or was an artist who could make a quick sketch of important items. Perhaps the expert was accompanied by the artist, in which case there were at least two of them on the game and two were quite enough, provided they were strong, to remove the objects that had disappeared. On the other hand, having done their job, the experts probably left the rest of it to cracksmen, who, armed with an illicit photograph or a drawing, whichever the case might be, then did the dirty work, appearing with a vehicle large enough to remove what they were after. And, as Madame de Saint-Bruie had said, a journey which in the great days of the châteaux had taken a whole day, now took no more than an hour or so and the thieves could be at the other end of France before the alarm was raised.

Nosjean was as much in need of a break as Pel and Darcy had been and eventually it came. From his enquiries he learned that nobody identifiable had been seen at any of the break-ins, no groups of two that were noticeable. In most cases the owners were not even present and the *gardien,* who knew little of the value of the treasures beyond what was in the guide book he used for his spiel as he conducted parties round in summer, had heard no one and seen no one. However, a small boy had noticed a yellow Volkswagen Passat estate car parked outside the church of St Sauvigny. He was a bright child and had noticed the car because he'd never seen a Passat estate before and had stopped to look at it.

'See the driver?' Nosjean asked.

'No. But I later saw it move off. It was driven by a man in overalls wearing a cap. He had a lot of hair. It stuck out.'

Other people had seen this man in overalls, Nosjean remembered.

'Did you see anything of note?' he asked. 'Anything inside it we could identify? A torn seat, for instance. Something like that.'

'The back seat was down and there was a blanket inside. A grey blanket.'

'A blanket that could be used to cover something?'

'Yes.'

'Anything else? Tools? Anything of that sort?'

'I didn't notice. But I saw a sort of clipboard thing with a list on it.'

'Could you read it?'

The boy smiled. He wore spectacles. 'Not at that distance,' he said.

"Could it have been a list of *objets d'art?* – paintings, statuettes, that sort of thing.'

'It might have been. On the other hand, it might have been a shopping list. Except that they don't usually carry them on clipboards.'

Nosjean thanked him, feeling that at least he'd made some headway, and promptly visited the châteaux that had been robbed and enquired if a yellow Passat estate had been seen there at any important time.

The *gardiens,* owners and car park attendants were unable to help him, but a few enquiries at bars in the villages nearby turned up the fact that a yellow Passat estate – which Nosjean realised was quite big enough with the rear seat lowered to carry away four chairs or a commode if necessary, to say nothing of a picture or a set of plates – had been noticed outside the bar in the village of Drive close to the Manoir de Boureleau around the time it was robbed.

'Number?' he asked.

But, of course, nobody had taken the number. There had been no need to, so nobody had.

'Was it local? Or from somewhere else? Like Paris?'

Once again he drew a blank, but at least someone had again noticed that the rear seat had been down. Nosjean felt he was making headway, even if it was slow headway.

eight

Montbard was at its best when Pel arrived with Darcy early in the morning. Despite the steelworks that existed there, it managed to look like every other small Burgundian town – grey, worn and enduring.

The police station was down a sidestreet near the bridge, its tricolour floating over its flat front, and the sergeant at the desk produced a large envelope which contained a street map.

'The inspector who saw you the other day,' he said, 'apologises that he can't be here. He had to go out to a shooting at Charleville. We're not sure yet whether it's accidental or not and he had to be there. The map shows the position of the factory. It's on the outskirts of the town.'

The 'factory' consisted of a large construction with a small attachment at the end which seemed to be the office. The sole occupant of the office was a girl in her late twenties who informed them that, yes, they had had a man called Claude-Achille Cormon work there.

'He's dead, though, now,' she said. 'Perhaps you've heard.'

'Yes,' Pel said gravely. 'We have. We're the Police Judiciaire. That's why we're here. We're trying to find who killed him.'

The girl, he noticed, was looking at Darcy not at him. Quite obviously she liked what she saw and her eyelashes were going like wasps' wings. Glancing from the corner of

72

his eye, he realised that Darcy, who hadn't been behind the door when cheek was handed out, was studying her with unabashed approval. In fact, they seemed to have taken to each other straight away and it made Pel feel suddenly old and lonely. Something, he decided, would have to be done about Madame Routy, preferably through the means of Madame Faivre-Perret.

'What was his job here?' he asked. 'This Cormon, I mean.'

She shrugged. 'Just an instrument maker, I think,' she said.

'Wages?'

She looked in a file and told them. It didn't seem much. Pel looked sideways at Darcy. 'I thought he was getting *twice* what he got at Pissarro's place,' he said. He looked at the girl. 'This is his total wage?'

'Yes.'

'Overtime?'

'We don't do it. We're more experimental than anything here. We're not rushed like other places.'

'Who runs the place?'

'It belongs to Doctor Robinson. He's English. Doctor Clive Robinson.'

'What's he doing in France?'

She shrugged. 'Don't ask me. Still, if I were English, I'd live in France, wouldn't you? All those fogs and things.'

'Where's Doctor Robinson now?'

'He lives at Rambillard.'

'Why there?'

'There's a lake there. He's crazy about sailing.'

'Who runs this place when he's not here then?'

She looked blank. 'It runs itself. More or less. I answer the telephone. He rings up from Rambillard and turns up here every week for a day on Wednesdays. Jean-Pierre looks after it for the rest of the time.'

'Who's Jean-Pierre?'

'Jean-Pierre Rivard. He calls himself works manager. She beamed at Darcy. 'Actually he's just a sort of foreman.'

'We'd like to speak to him,' Pel said.

She led them through the workshop. She had a wiggle that would fry a man's eyeballs at fifty paces and it was quite clear Darcy had noticed. In the workshop, there were half a dozen long benches, with drills, lathes and soldering equipment, at which men, girls and women worked. Stored at the end was sheet metal, wire, plastic sheeting, a metal guillotine, stamping machines and shelves full of screws and springs.

'What we do isn't very big or important,' she said. 'We don't even have a canteen because it would cost money to run it. There's a little bar along the street where people can get meals if they want them, but I've noticed lately that they've all started to bring their lunch in boxes and eat at their benches. Saving money, I suppose. It's an easy place to work for, and that's all right with me. It gives me plenty of time off.'

Darcy was quick to take the hint. 'We'd better have your name,' he said. 'We shall probably need to be in touch again.'

'It's Elodie Guillemin.'

She also gave her telephone number – just in case – and Darcy wrote it down on the edge of the newspaper he was carrying.

Pel watched the manoeuvrings sourly. Darcy had a deft touch when dealing with females. Pel's efforts seemed to be those of someone clodhopping around in sabots.

Jean-Pierre Rivard seemed incredibly young. Bright-eyed and breezy, he seemed to be barely out of school, but he was brisk and didn't seem to feel the need to refer to any higher authority. He obviously did his stint of work like everybody else, however, his position as manager notwithstanding, and when they found him he had his head down, shaving off a piece of plastic with a sharp-pointed knife.

'Experiment,' he pointed out. 'Specifications from the Boss.'

'What is it?' Darcy asked.

'Switch.'

'What for?'

'Something he's busy with. We're always getting things like this to work on. Prototypes. Then he develops them for what he wants.'

'Did Claude-Achille Cormon work on this sort of thing?'

'Oh, yes.'

'Secret stuff?'

'No. He did the same work as everybody else. He turned up asking for a job as an instrument-maker and, as the Boss experiments a lot with electronic gadgets requiring precision, skill and a sound knowledge of instrument-making, he got the job.'

'Was he good at it?'

'Very good.'

'Ever in trouble?'

'Not to my knowledge.'

'Did you know he'd been in prison? For attempted safe-breaking.'

Rivard laughed. 'It wouldn't have made much difference. We've got nothing here worth stealing. The safe doesn't contain money. Only gadgets that we make.'

'What sort of gadgets?'

'Well – ' Rivard indicated a bench full of what looked like small squares of plastic to which were riveted strips of metal ' – these are television switches. It's an idea of the Boss'. Nothing new. Just an improvement on the ones in general use. They're less likely to go wrong, that's all.' He gestured at another bench where a girl in overalls was watching them with interest. 'She's assembling cut-outs for electric irons. We mould the pieces here, assemble them, and sell them to Roupnel Electric. We also have a small photo-processing lab for films, because we do a little work on projector switches.

They're pretty complicated. You know: ahead, reverse, slow, stop. Even a few more on the better-class ones.

He seemed set for the day. Almost like a Paris spiv selling dirty pictures, Pel thought, and he interrupted him before he was too well launched.

'This Doctor Robinson,' he said. 'Why does he live in France?'

'He was born in France. He lived in France until the Occupation. He's as French as I am, really, in spite of his British passport.'

'Does he go to Britain?'

'From time to time. He has a firm near Dover. Making the same things. He's probably hedging his bets. If I could afford to, I would, too. If things get bad here, he can switch to there. If they go wrong there, he can switch to here. Actually, I think they're both going well.'

'Good to work for?'

'He understands France.'

'It makes a change,' Pel observed. 'Most Englishmen regard us as savages.'

'Not these days. A few who come here to see him can actually speak French. I was in London not long ago for him and I found quite a lot. At least three.'

'What about Cormon? Can you tell us any more about him? Ever seem worried?'

Rivard considered. 'Not really,' he said. 'Often seemed tired, though. But it's a long way from here to Evanay where he lived. I think he was a worrying kind, too. Besides – '

'Besides what?'

'Well, those horses of his: He never seemed to pick a winner. It must have been a bit depressing.'

Pel glanced about him. 'There are girls working here,' he pointed out. 'Did he ever go out with any of them?'

'Not that I ever heard of. He was single, though, so if he did he was entitled to if he wished.'

'I wondered if he'd ever been in any trouble with any of them?'

'What sort of trouble?'

Pel frowned. 'What sort of trouble do men usually get into with girls?' he said.

As they left, Elodie Guillemin smiled at Darcy. 'We're always here if you want us,' she said cheerfully. 'You've only to telephone.'

In the car, Pel seethed with resentment at the ease with which Darcy picked up girls.

'One of these days,' he said bitterly, 'one of your affairs is going to blow up in your face.'

Darcy shrugged. 'What if it does, Patron? I'm not married. They can't send me to prison. And I never tamper with married women. Too dangerous.'

'You're too damned skilful at it,' Pel said bitterly, his mind full of worms with his envy.

'Of course,' Darcy was even smug about it. 'But sex is an ailment you can only cure by indulgence in it. I'm a phallocrat.' He glanced out of the corner of his eye. 'How are you getting on with Judge Brisard?'

'That one needs a transplant,' Pel growled. 'A head transplant. He insists on seeing everybody we question. I've already sent him Nosjean, Foulot, Madame Clarétie and Inspector Pomereu. Doc Minet reckoned he could keep him occupied for a good hour, too.' He smiled and cocked his head. 'I reckon that young man back there – Jean-Pierre Rivard – would also enjoy a day talking to a *juge d'instruction*, don't you? He ought to keep him occupied for the best part of the morning.'

Darcy grinned. 'You don't like him much, do you, Patron?'

Pel gave a sour smile. 'If I had rabies,' he said, 'I'd probably bite him.'

Back in the city, while Darcy covered the office, Pel treated himself to lunch at the Relais St Armand where he indulged in andouillettes, the tripe sausage of the region. It could hardly be called a luxury dish but Pel had a weakness for them and the Relais St Armand sold a splendid chablis which left your mouth feeling as if it had been worked over by a rasp.

Reading the paper as he ate, he saw that the attack on Philippe le Bozec, of the Ministry of Defence, had got under way again and he was having a sticky time explaining to his constituents what he'd been doing in a brothel in Paris that was frequented by foreign attachés, when he ought to have been busy attending to their needs. He represented Muzillac, a district on the eastern fringes of Brittany, which Pel knew to be a good respectable place, solidly religious, small and narrow-minded. Despite the influx of tourists, Bretons remained stubborn, hard-headed, moral and pious, and even if they might secretly envy their representative, they would nevertheless not hesitate to pillory him for stepping from the straight and narrow. Pel knew the district well because eighteen months before a naval officer with extravagant tastes and a spendthrift wife had been involved in a secrets case. It had led into a few tortuous areas, and a bar owner had been found murdered in a burned-out boat drifting in the mouth of the Loire. It was well-known the two cases were connected but nobody had ever discovered who had killed him and the naval officer, who had gone to prison for his trouble, had never talked.

Le Bozec's scandal was enough, Pel decided, to make his Breton ancestors spin in their graves like humming tops, but, he suspected, there was a good chance that the erring Under-Secretary would get away with it. With the Tour de France now well under way, everything tended to be overlooked in the spectacle of a hundred-odd lunatics hurtling round the country, each trying to go faster than all the others. The newspapers were describing the event in the Biblical metaphors for which French reporters were famous. A boil on a rider's behind became his 'calvary' and his agony equivalent to that of the Crucifixion, which even to Pel, who was far from an ardent churchgoer, was going too far.

The Belgian, Van der Essen, seemed to be doing the leading in every stage, he noticed. Still, Pel thought, the Belgians were known to be stupid. Perhaps that's why they went in for winning bicycle races. Everybody knew the stories about them: Like the one who was carrying a car door in the desert and, when asked why, said 'Well, if it grows too hot, I can wind the window down'. Or the one who was carrying a heavy stone in the jungle so that if a lion came he could drop it and run faster.

When he reappeared in the street, the harsh midday sun had changed to the mellow gold of afternoon. The city looked at its best, the enamelled tiles of the famous rooftops glowing in the brilliant daylight which, in Burgundy, always seemed to have a special quality. Like the countryside, he thought proudly. Like the wine. Like Evariste Clovis Désiré Pel.

The pale stone front of the Palais des Ducs shone like gold, the red, white and blue of the flag flying over the entrance a splash of colour against the mass of stonework. It even managed to make Pel feel optimistic. Remembering Darcy's success with Elodie Guillemin, he decided life was shooting by at an alarming rate while he, Evariste Clovis Désiré Pel, was still dependent entirely on Madame Routy. The only good thing about Madame Routy was that she had a nephew, Didier Darras, who turned up occasionally to stay with his aunt when his mother, her sister, disappeared to look after an ailing father-in-law. But Didier Darras, it seemed, had vanished on a month-long visit with his school to stay with the parents of the boys of an English school. A Burgundian to the core, Pel couldn't imagine why anyone should wish to go to England or, for that matter, even cross the border into the neighbouring provinces of Aube, Haute Marne, Haute Saône, Jura and all the rest.

It seemed he would have to take his courage into his hands and go and see Madame Faivre-Perret. Diving into the first florist's he came to, he bought eleven long-stalked red roses. The price rocked him back on his heels and he very nearly changed his mind.

Nanette's, the hairdressing establishment Madame Faivre-Perret ran, was the best in the city, customered by all who were wealthy enough to be able to afford it and quite a few who weren't. It was a hotbed of gossip from which Pel had managed to acquire more than one titbit of information which had stood him in good stead and now he was well known and not even regarded askance when he appeared at the door.

The girl at the desk beyond the gauze curtains that decorated the front of the premises went into raptures over the flowers.

'Oh, Monsieur l'Inspecteur,' she crowed. 'English roses! How beautiful! For Madame?'

'Of course!' The reaction quite overcame the resentment Pel had felt at the price.

'She'll be thrilled! She loves English things!'

At that price, Pel felt, it needed a little rapture. He waited. The girl waited. Pel was puzzled. He was expecting to be shown upstairs to the office Madame Faivre-Perret maintained. To Pel, being shown upstairs always made him think of going to bed and conjured up all sorts of erotic visions.

Still the girl waited. In the end, she reached out for the flowers.

'She'll be so pleased,' she said. 'I'll tell her about them on the telephone.'

Pel's jaw dropped. 'On the telephone?'

'Yes. She rings every evening. It's such a pity, because she had to go to Vitteaux. She has an old aunt there who's just died and she's going to be away for a while sorting out her affairs.'

Pel almost snatched the roses back. Perhaps, he thought wildly, he could return them to the shop and get his money back. Only his good sense restrained him because he would still need the good will of Madame Faivre-Perret when she returned. Regretfully, he watched them placed on one side and returned the girl's friendly smile with a sick look. No cup of tea. No climb up the stairs. No fantasies today.

Bitterly he stalked back to the Hôtel de Police. What, he wondered, did one have to do to get a love life off the ground? No Didier Darras. No Madame Faivre-Perret. France seemed to be coming off its hinges. It wasn't even August, when it was expected that nobody would be home. In August the whole country seemed to switch places. Nobody who was anybody in Paris would be seen dead there at the weekend but wouldn't dream of being anywhere else during the week – save in August, when they disappeared to their country homes, to the sea, to the mountains, or to strange foreign countries which couldn't possibly be half as good as France.

He regarded it as most inconsiderate of Madame Faivre-Perret's aunt to die just when he was on the point of arriving with a token of his regard, so that Madame Faivre-Perret had disappeared to Vitteaux, probably for ever – Pel was a born pessimist – causing him to fork out an unconscionable number of francs for a bunch of red roses she was never going to see.

He wished she'd hurry and get her affairs in order. He needed a little feminine company. It was only since he'd met Madame Faivre-Perret that he'd realised how starved of it he'd become, because Madame Routy could hardly be called feminine company. She was never company and sometimes he even wondered if she were feminine.

He remembered that the girl at Nanette's had said that Madame Faivre-Perret liked English things. Perhaps, he thought, it would be a good idea by the time she returned to have taken to a pipe and a walking stick and one of those caps that looked like a chequered plate. For a moment, wildly, he wondered if he might even try a dog.

nine

Pel arrived early at the Hôtel de Police next day. Madame Routy had been at her most intransigent the night before and the television had been on so continuously he had become convinced she was trying for a takeover bid. The evening meal had been dreadful and to crown everything he had slept badly. Sleeping badly, he felt, indicated he was succeeding at his job but it was nevertheless a bore.

In a thoroughly bad temper, he complained bitterly to the Chief that they were still short-handed since Krauss' death and that it was time a replacement was delivered, tore Misset a strip off for no reason at all, and even snapped at Sergeant Lagé, who, as usual was working twice as hard as he need, simply because he was ardent and willing. The work, as usual, was mostly Misset's.

Feeling better, he snatched up Darcy and they headed for Rambillard. If nothing else, he thought, he might be able to work out his ill temper on Doctor Robinson. After all he wasn't a Burgundian – not even a Frenchman – and was therefore probably so stupid it wouldn't matter. Besides, he'd heard Darcy had a date with a girl and had decided maliciously that it would teach him not to take things too much for granted.

He wasn't sure what he expected of the Englishman, but he was certainly disappointed. Sure enough, Robinson lived up to Pel's impression of a potato-faced Anglo-Saxon because he had no special features which made him easily recognisable

– merely a space with eyes and a nose, and a voice like a foghorn that he didn't attempt to restrain. On the other hand, much to Pel's annoyance, because he'd always had a good French chauvinistic belief that his was the only nation in the world which bothered to learn foreign languages, he spoke French perfectly, even with a Burgundian accent with rolled 'r's' and everything. He was clearly brainy, and, what was more, immediately offered coffee with excellent brandy and suggested they stay to lunch. The lunch was also excellent, with a splendid wine and more brandy to follow. By the time they'd finished, Pel even had a warm feeling towards the British and was prepared, if necessary, to admit that the Queen, despite the fact that she couldn't touch a French President's wife when it came to chic, at least had dignity and charm.

Only when they were feeling truly mellow would Robinson deign to talk about Cormon.

'I didn't know him very well, of course,' he admitted. 'I leave the running of the place at Montbard to young Rivard. He's a very capable young man. A little brash, perhaps, a little self-seeking, a little too ambitious – perhaps even none too honest – but he keeps the place ticking over very happily and these days that's something.'

He offered cigars and sat back. 'Cormon came to me asking for a job. Rivard said we could use somebody so I took him on. I hear he lost his wages regularly on horses.'

'He did.'

'Well, that, of course, was not my business. Sometimes he went to Paris. That again was none of my business but he'd never talk about it. I often heard the other employees pulling his leg. Perhaps he had a woman there; I don't know. And then there was this character who used to meet him outside sometimes when he finished. The others said – again in fun, of course – that he was being blackmailed.'

Considering he had a record, Pel decided, they might possibly have been right.

'Which character was this?' he asked.

'Well – ' Robinson shrugged his shoulders ' – he was only a character in so far as he didn't look local. He drove a large Citroën and he was very smartly dressed. Montbard isn't big enough for people to be dressed as he was dressed.'

'Know his name?'

'I once heard Cormon call him Rambot. It may not have been his real name. I just heard Cormon say "Look here, Rambot – ", like that. As if they were arguing. That's all. I was going to my car and I didn't take any notice.'

'Did you know this Rambot?'

'No. I saw him two or three times, that's all.'

'Do you think he could have been a representative of some other manufacturer after your secrets?'

Robinson's eyes flickered then he laughed. It sounded like a horse neighing. 'We haven't any secrets,' he said. 'Not in Montbard, anyway. I do my experimental work here. It only goes to Montbard when it's being produced in numbers and by that time it's not very secret because it's been acquired under contract.'

Curious, Pel began to enquire about Robinson himself.

'Of course I live in France,' he said. 'Of course I chose Burgundy. I was born in Beaune because my father was a wine importer and preferred to spend his time where the grapes grew. I have my works at Montbard merely because there happened to be a convenient site available.'

'But you live *here*?' Pel made it a question.

Robinson gestured down the garden to where they could see the glitter of the sun on a wide expanse of water.

'Because the Lac des Getons is here,' he said. 'And I wish to sail.' He looked at Pel. 'Do you sail, Inspector?'

Pel, to whom anything that wasn't terra firma was a dangerous element, shook his head.

'You should,' Robinson said. 'That's one of the points about the British. Nowhere is it more than two hundred-odd kilometres from the sea. Everybody knows about boats. In

France it's much more difficult, but since the authorities have permitted the use of lakes and dams for the sport it's growmg, and there are far more Frenchmen who've become sailors. That's also why I'm here.'

Pel lifted his eyebrows, and Robinson smiled.

'I make parts for electronic aids to sailors,' he said.

'Such as?'

'Switches.'

'Light switches?'

Robinson laughed. 'Oh, no. Switches in the other sense. I discovered a new means by which it's possible to reverse currents and I've used it to give an added measure of security to self-sailing devices for long-distance yachts. Loick Fougeron was one of my customers. It can be used in various ways and I have a small workshop here, where I employ only one assistant and do all my experimenting. The device – I won't go into details – can be used for lifts and for changing programmes on televisions. Do you have a television, inspector?'

Pel eyed Robinson with new eyes. Anybody who contributed to the improvement of something which made his life a misery had to be an enemy.

'You've seen what the Americans call blab-off switches?' Robinson went on. 'It's a device that was invented to switch off the sound during the commercials. Nowadays you can also change programmes. My device's used in some of these. I'm working on an improvement at this moment. I didn't go in for wine like my father. I turned out to be an engineer instead. And I work in France because France's bigger than England and it's possible to get further away from people. My gadgets sometimes have – er –' he paused ' – well, let's say they have enormous value and could be of great use to people for whom they weren't intended.'

Industrial spying?' Darcy said.

Robinson hesitated then he smiled. 'You might call it that,' he said.

'It seems to me,' Pel said as they drove back, 'that this Rambot might be the key to the whole thing.'

'What do you reckon it is, Patron?' Darcy asked. 'Think Cormon was selling secrets and got in too deep?'

'Industrial spying's never managed to reach the blood-thirsty stage of international spying,' Pel pointed out. 'They don't go in for killing.'

'Perhaps they've just started, Patron.'

Brigadier Foulot was in the city to attend court and when they arrived at the Hôtel de Police he was in the entrance. Pel drew him to one side.

'This bar at Fauverolles where you used to meet Cormon,' he said. 'Did you ever see him there with a smartly-dressed city type called Rambot.'

Foulot thought deeply for a moment then he shook his head. 'Never,' he said.

'Did he go to other bars?'

Foulot grinned. 'Of course,' he said. 'Who doesn't?'

'Which one was his favourite? Do you know?' Foulot thought once more. He seemed to go in for pauses for thought.

'Well, I've heard him talk of the bar at Voivres.'

'Which one? There are two there, to my knowledge.'

Foulot smiled. 'Actually, there are five,' he said. 'You could try them all. But the Bar du Centre's only a little single-room place with a zinc counter and no spirit licence. The Bar des Ouvriers on the outskirts is usually full of farm-workers. The Bar Harry and the Bar Bourguignon are possibles, but if you're looking for a well-dressed city type, I imagine he'd take him to the bar of the Hôtel Colbert. It's just off the centre of the town, up the hill towards Aignay and next to the garage. You can't miss it.'

The weather was still warm and pleasant and Pel decided they might as well make a day of it.

When they reached Voivres and the Hôtel Colbert, they picked a winner at once.

'Sure.' The proprietor, a tall man called Vandelet, nodded as he poured out their coups de blanc. 'I know Cormon. He comes in here occasionally.'

'He won't any more,' Darcy said. 'He's dead.'

'Accident?' Vandelet clearly hadn't associated anything he'd read in the newspapers with any of his customers.

'Murdered.'

Vandelet pulled a face. 'Wonder if that chic type had anything to do with it,' he said slowly.

This was a bonus already.

Darcy leaned forward. 'This chic type,' he asked. 'What was his name?'

Vandelet shrugged.

'Could it have been Rambot?'

'Now you mention it, I think it was.'

'Can you describe him?'

Vandelet stared at Darcy. 'Bit like you. Same height. Good-looking.' Darcy preened. 'But there was something else about him.'

'What sort of something else?' Pel asked.

'Cold. He was a cold fish. He never smiled. Come to that, neither did Cormon. *He* seemed nervous as a kitten most of the time. Worried. You know how it is. They never seemed to be here just for a drink or a day out. They seemed to be doing business together. They always used to come in about this time when there was no one in and sit over there by the window. I heard them mention Paris once or twice. Come to think of it, the guy had a car that was registered in Paris.'

'Number?' Darcy said at once.

It was a forlorn hope.

'I didn't notice,' Vandelet said. 'But I saw it drive off once when I went over to the table to remove their glasses. Through the window.'

'Make?'

'I didn't notice?'

'Colour?'

'I didn't notice that either.'

'Did you notice whether it had four wheels or five?' Darcy asked sourly.

Vandelet thought. 'No,' he said, oblivious to the sarcasm. 'I didn't.'

They obtained a description of Cormon's friend. It wasn't all that good. People seemed to go round with their eyes shut in a way which made it surprising that they didn't bump into things. Certainly, they didn't appear to use them for looking. The description was vague but at least they had some idea. Rambot, whoever he was, whatever he was, looked like Darcy.

Back at the Hôtel de Police, Darcy promptly got on to the telephone to the Quai des Orfèvres in Paris but the police there knew of no one called Rambot.

Sitting opposite Pel in his office, he began to wonder aloud. 'It begins to look to me,' he said, 'as if Cormon's money *didn't* come from wins on horses.'

'Pay-outs?' Pel asked. 'For pinching industrial secrets?'

'That's what it looks like, Patron. But, as you said, those people don't usually go as far as murder.'

Pel was silent for a while. 'You know,' he said slowly, 'that Pissarro type didn't impress me much.'

'Why not, Patron?'

Chiefly it had been Pissarro's obsession with sport. No one who was honest could be that good at sport, Pel felt; especially when Evariste Clovis Désiré Pel was beaten regularly by Didier Darras at boules, dominoes, fishing, even scrabble.

'I don't know,' he said. 'Bit too friendly. Too helpful.'

Darcy smiled. 'If we suspected everybody who was helpful and friendly, Patron, we'd have the cells at 72, Rue d'Auxonne permanently full. And that wouldn't improve our already uncertain image.'

Pel frowned. You could hardly call the police popular these days, it was true. Most people seemed to regard them as allied to a fascist dictatorship and given to breaking heads purely for pleasure; to rioting students they seemed to exist merely to have brickbats and paving stones thrown at them. At the very least they were regarded by motorists as interfering busybodies with nothing better to do than persecute people in cars, and by old ladies who found them standing on corners as lazy good-for-nothings who should have been tearing about stamping out crime. Nevertheless, occasionally there *were* people who were friendly and willing to help – especially when they'd just been robbed or beaten up – at which point the police, provided they weren't regarded as stupid idiots who couldn't see clues when they were lying round knee-deep, were transformed by a miracle into the saviours of the Republic and the hard-worked guardians of the populace.

Forcing himself from his meditations on the failings of the French public, Pel looked at Darcy. 'Those papers you found in Cormon's room? Have you had them looked at?'

'I got Dériot of Electroniques de Dijon to have a squint through them. He thought they were nothing more than the outlines for simple gadgets.'

'Recognise any of them?'

'He thought they were all unimportant. Switches. Cutouts. Nothing secret. Nothing they haven't got already.'

Lighting a cigarette, Pel drew in the smoke, sat back and allowed it to dribble out of his nostrils. It was only his tenth that day. Tenth out of his second packet, of course, but that was something he tried to overlook.

'I think we ought to know more about friend Pissarro,' he said.

'We can hardly demand a search warrant, Patron. He's done nothing wrong.'

'He didn't tell us he'd been to see Cormon. At least not until we told him we knew.'

'Doesn't make him a criminal, Patron.'

'Nevertheless – ' Pel frowned ' – I wonder what sort of people visit that place of his.'

'Not very many, I should imagine,' Darcy said, 'It's not all that big.'

'How about getting a photographer up there with a camera? Stick a placard on his chest or something. Make him look like a street photographer. There are a few about at this time of the year. The tourists enjoy it.'

'You don't get many tourists round Pissarro's works.'

'The Hôtel Central's down the street. Plenty of tourists there. It's a good enough excuse. Get him to take pictures of anybody who turns up who obviously isn't a workman.'

Darcy grinned. 'I doubt if Grenier would like the job.'

Grenier was the police photographer and he was fat, inclned to be lazy, and never in the best of tempers.

'He'd never stand there all day,' Darcy went on. 'How long do you expect it to go on?'

Pel frowned. 'A week. No one will worry with all those Americans at the Central. He might even sell a few and make a bit on the side.'

'How about Lagé.'

'Could he do it?'

Darcy smiled. Sergeant Lagé was a camera fiend who went out at weekends taking photographs all round the district, spending all his pay on cameras, lights and tripods and then wondering why he was short of money. It had started when he had tried to photograph the model aeroplanes his son built from kits. His son had long since progressed to girls but Lagé, because he was a sucker for doing other people's work, was by now secretary of the photographic society at Fontaine where he lived.

Darcy grinned. 'He'll enjoy it,' he said. 'Mind, you'll pro- bably end up with a series of studio portraits. He's a great one for light and shade.'

'I don't want portraits,' Pel growled. 'I want snaps. Good snaps. Tell him to go and talk to one of the city photographic bureaus before he starts and get to know what we want. We could do with two or three of everybody who looks as though he might be Rambot. Get him on to it straightaway.'

As Darcy emerged from Pel's office, Nosjean rose to his feet from his desk. He had been busy. Pursuing the line of thought on art thefts suggested by Sergeant de Troquereau, of Auxerre, he had decided to go to Paris and, guiltily feeling it was time he showed some interest in Odile Chenandier again, he had sadly rejected all thoughts of Mijo Lehmann and taken her with him. It was his weekend off and she had been overwhelmed at the thought of a whole day with Nosjean. The idea had boomeranged, however, because Nosjean's intention had been to enquire round the furniture and antique shops in the Rue de Charonne, the Rue Vanoy, the Flea Market, the Faubourg St Honoré, the Rue St Honoré and the Ecole Militaire, and for some reason she had got it into her head that he was thinking of buying furniture to set up a home – and with whom but her? It had been faintly embarrassing to have to admit his real interest but the day hadn't been entirely lost because there was a lot Nosjean saw that seemed to be fakes selling at genuine prices and, as he poked about, he was startled to discover how much he'd learned. With the aid of De Troquereau and Mijo Lehmann at Chagnay, he had acquired a surprising knowledge of antiques.

There were also two young men in the Rue Vanoy, near the Ecole Militaire who had interested him greatly. Just on the right side of being queers, sharp as razors, typical Parisian decorator types, knowing the price of everything and the value of nothing, he decided they were worth a second look.

By the time he had finished, both he and his girl friend were feeling faint with hunger and, since it was the end of the month and Nosjean was short of ready cash, he went to a charcuterie a few paces from the shop run by the two sharp young men and got them to make up a couple of sandwiches. In their greaseproof paper wrapping, they looked big enough to need a bulldozer to lift them but the smell was mouthwatering and the two of them sat on a bench under a tree to eat them. There were a lot of furniture shops around them and Nosjean decided the area might be worth another visit. By this time, however, aware that his interest was less in her than in his job, Odile Chenandier wasn't half so keen on furniture as she had been, so Nosjean reluctantly found the periphery road and headed south again down the motorway.

The girl's face was filled with reproach as he dropped her at the door of her apartment but he avoided her eyes and said that he had to catch Pel in his office.

He needed to talk to someone with experience. Even if the trip to Paris weren't included, his expenses sheet was already so swollen by the trips to Chagnay he was growing a little worried. He'd been told to provide meals for Sergeant de Troquereau, from Auxerre, when necessary, but despite his fragile little boy's frame, De Troquereau had the appetite of a weight-lifter and Nosjean had a growing feeling that someone would finally object to the cost.

As he put his head round the door, Pel indicated a chair and pushed a packet of cigarettes across the desk. Nosjean shook his head.

'I'm trying to give them up,' he said.

'It's become an epidemic,' Pel complained. 'Are you succeeding?'

'I'm down to five a day. With two in the evening.'

Pel eyed him bitterly. All *he'd* done was cut them down from about two million to about five hundred thousand.

'I think *you* ought to have a look at this art theft thing at St Sauvigny, Patron,' Nosjean said. 'I'm stuck.'

Pel leaned forward. 'What have you done so far?'

'I've been in touch with the Historic Monuments Department. They suggest that whoever stole this panel – in fact, everything, the châteaux thefts, the lot – was an educated type, and that he seems to have an obsessional interest in the minutiae of antiques. De Troquereau says the same and Madame de Saint-Bruie – '

'Who's she?'.

Nosjean grinned. 'You ought to talk to her, Patron. Keeps a shop at Chagnay. You'd enjoy meeting her.'

Pel pretended no interest but, without Madame Faivre-Perret in the background – even taking no notice of him – he felt it might be a good idea.

'You shall drive me down, *mon brave,*' he conceded.

'She's an expert,' Nosjean said. 'She suggests it might be an antique dealer or an aristocrat who's grown up with antiques. She suggests even that he might have received training at the Louvre School of Beaux Arts or at Arts-Déco. She suggests I look around in the South.'

'On expenses?' Pel shook his head. 'They'd never permit it, *mon brave.* You'll have to get Lyons and Marseilles in on the act. What about our friend from Auxerre? What does he say?'

De Troquereau had been even more explicit. 'He suggested we should keep our eyes on the Rue St Honoré in Paris, round the Flea Market workshops, the streets round the Ecole Militaire and the Rue de Charonne and the Rue Vanoy. All places where stolen property turns up.'

'So what did you do?'

'I went to Paris?'

'You didn't ask permission.'

'I knew I'd never get it.' Nosjean smiled. 'So I took Odile Chenandier there for a day out. Killed two birds with one stone, you might say. Not on expenses.'

Pel looked hard at Nosjean. The old innocent look he remembered Nosjean had had when he'd joined his team had gone. He was learning fast. He'd eventually be a good detective.

'And what did you find out?'

Nosjean smiled. 'I saw a lot of what I decided were fakes selling at genuine prices.'

'You're that good at it?'

'Not really, Patron. But this girl in Madame de Saint-Bruie's shop – '

'Which girl in Madame de Saint-Bruie's shop?'

'This Mijo Lehmann. She's been most helpful. I've been to see her two or three times for information. I took her out to lunch to repay her for her trouble.' Nosjean grinned. 'Again, not on expenses.'

'Is she pretty?'

Nosjean blushed and Pel decided that perhaps the old innocent look hadn't entirely gone. It pleased him.

'I've been to Chagnay a lot, Patron,' Nosjean went on. 'I've learned a great deal.'

Pel nodded approvingly. It was only what he'd expected.

'What with Madame, Mijo Lehmann and Sergeant de Troquereau, I think I can identify a few things now,' Nosjean went on. 'There are a few I saw in Paris which I reckon were stolen.'

'Worth putting the Quai des Orfèvres on to them?'

Nosjean shook his head. 'Doubt it, Patron. There's too much moving around up there. Documents, chairs, commodes, plates, chests, officers' trunks, mirrors, secrétaires. I did a bit of asking around.'

'Find anybody?'

'Two.'

'Names?'

'Jean-Jacques Poupon and Pierre Rebluchet, also known as Pierrot-le-Pourri.'

'Why?'

'Because, I gathered, he's a bad egg. So I looked him up. He's got a record. He was caught stealing as a teenager but as a first offender got a suspended sentence. It didn't work and he tried his hand at it again. This time he went down the line. That was seven years ago. Nothing since.'

'Probably only means he's grown more cunning,' Pel observed. 'What about the other one? Poupon.'

'Nothing known.'

'Any others you investigated?'

Nosjean smiled. 'One or two are well known, but not for stealing. Fiddling. Faking. Fraud. But nothing really hard. It's too difficult to prove anything, it seems.'

'These two – Poupon and Pierrot-le-Pourri: Would it be worth getting a search warrant?'

Nosjean shrugged. 'Doubt it, Patron. I bet anything they lift doesn't appear in their shop until it's well and truly disguised. They aren't collectors. They're just a couple of shysters out for what they can get. They both drive flashy cars but they're smart operators. To get anything on them we'll need to catch them red-handed.'

Pel looked at his fingers. The thought of the Rue Martin-de-Noinville and Madame Routy's cooking was enough to influence his decision.

'Tomorrow,' he decided, 'I'll go with you to Chagnay.'

ten

Pel was just about to go home when Judge Brisard rang.

'Who keeps sending all these people to my office?' he demanded.

'Which people?' Pel was all innocence.

'I've had Nosjean, Pomereu, Doctor Minet and some stupid young gasbag from Montbard who talked half the morning about electrical gadgets. Are you being deliberately difficult, Pel?'

'Of course not,' Pel at his most innocent was almost cherubic. 'I informed the chief of what you wanted and he said I was to follow instructions.'

Brisard breathed heavily down the telephone but Pel was sure of his ground. Feeling he had scored a victory, he drove home cheerfully. Anything that stopped Brisard's gallop was a job well done. Battling down the Cours Charles-de-Gaulle from the Place Wilson, Pel was almost happy and began to sing *En Revenant de la Revue* to himself. As he turned into the Rue Martin-de-Noinville, however, his spirits sagged. The house looked no bigger than a parrot's cage. On either side the houses were larger, cleaner, better-painted and with better-tended gardens. Pel's appeared to be neglected and its garden looked like a hen run.

Madame Routy – inevitably – had the television on, Equally inevitably, it was some idiot talking about the Tour de France and contained shots of hundreds of panting little men on racing bicycles, their corded legs pumping away like mad as they struggled through the mountains. There were plenty of ways, Pel decided, much easier than on a bicycle.

The sound was turned up to full so that Madame Routy could hear what was going on while she was in the kitchen. Before going upstairs to wash, Pel turned it down, but when he came downstairs again, he noticed she'd turned it up once more. It sounded like the barrage before the Battle of Verdun. It was no wonder the flowers in the vase that stood on top of the set were wilting.

The meal turned out to be a casserole – Madame Routy was a great believer in casseroles because she could toss everything into a dish with a few herbs, shove them in the oven and forget them. The meat tasted of old shoelaces, while the wine seemed to be fermented from paint stripper. Sauces were unknown. Pel sighed. In a country renowned for its food and in a province of that country that was supposed to be unsurpassed among all other provinces, he, Pel, had to have as a housekeeper the one woman who wouldn't cook. It would be nice, he thought, if thunderbolts could descend and paralyse her.

Madame Routy seemed unaware of his smouldering hatred. 'I'll clear away later,' she said. 'I'm just watching the end of my programme.'

Madame Routy would be watching the end of something when the Last Trump sounded, Pel decided. Doubtless, she'd probably stand around to watch the end of that, too. Especially if it were in colour. It was going to be a terrible night.

It was.

Just occasionally, when there was nothing on television, Madame Routy went to visit her sister, though her disappearances were few and far between because she was an addicted watcher. If she'd lived in ancient Rome, she'd have spent all her time at the Colosseum watching the lions chase the Christians round the arena.

But this was one of the rare nothing-on nights, though, of course, since there wasn't sufficient to keep Madame Routy glued to the set – and it didn't require much – it meant also that there was also nothing for Pel to watch.

Gloomily, he stared at the set through the news. The wine growers were complaining again, he saw, and farmers were blocking the roads with their tractors as a protest against government food policies. There were forest fires to the north of the Côte d'Azur – there were always forest fires to the north of the Côte d'Azur at this time of the year; one expected them, like flies – and Philippe le Bozec, of the Defence Ministry, was beginning to look as if he were going to escape the results of his misdemeanours after all, as Pel had suspected. The newspapers had dropped him and now, it seemed, his colleagues in the House of Representatives, putting on a big show of being broad-minded – in case they were ever caught themselves, Pel decided – were being magnanimous and had announced that they did not intend to condemn him for his trip to the Paris brothel, which was, after all, they felt, only a human slip. That, if nothing else, ought to quieten his more difficult constituents who if they complained, would appear by contrast narrow-minded and bigoted.

Meanwhile, there was always the Tour de France, now half-run. Van der Essen and the Belgians, riding as if bound by a suicide pact, were still in the lead, and, despite the fact that as chauvinists the French yielded to few, there was little mention of local favourites save for Aurélien Filou, who was managing to stay among the leaders. Clam was nowhere and there was no mention at all of Pissarro's man, Maryckx, or even of the team he was helping to support, Pis-Hélio-Tout.

For a while Pel gazed blankly at the screen. He was no cyclist but he enjoyed seeing other people sweat.

'Riding a racing bike,' the announcer was saying, 'requires will power.'

To Pel it also seemed to require a lack of brains. Nobody in his senses would have subjected himself to such agony as the riders in the Tour de France did. They were arriving at a night stop in front of spectators who, happily appearing from bars and cafés with their drinks in their hands, watched them swaying in the saddles, ashen with fatigue and on the point of vomiting with exhaustion. The start next morning was at the Château de Virenais where the owner was using the Tour to put the château and the Louis XVI furniture it contained on the map. People who supported the Tour weren't always devoid of self-interest.

The last riders came up the hill, *en danseuse,* standing on the pedals and pulling from side to side with their arms at the handlebars to gain thrust. They hurtled through the narrow pathway between the spectators, the publicity cars honking, the sweating police fighting to keep the crowd back. Names were scrawled on walls and a group of Clam supporters waved a flag bearing the legend "Courage, Jo-Jo! Allez, Jo-Jo!" In a last burst of speed one of the riders arrived suffering from cramps, his eyes empty, his expression dazed, and careered into the crowd. Picking himself up, he tottered away in a mincing pigeon-toed walk.

Pel watched the spectacle with a sour face, then, as the news finished, he reached for the newspaper to see what else he might watch. This, however, appeared to be the night when French Television had it worked out that its viewers, having recently been paid, would not wish to remain at home and therefore would require very little in the way of programmes. The studio seemed to have been left to the cleaners and the evening's entertainment appeared to consist of a chat show, an hour of pop music and, of course, the Tour de France. The board had been cleared, it was obvious, to provide the great sporting public with a long discussion on the chances of the various competitors over the picture of sweating, straining men with whipcord muscles dressed in coloured shirts and funny hats and carrying little food bags over their shoulders. It sounded dreadful.

Sighing, Pel climbed into his car and headed for the city. Sometimes he enjoyed the city in the evening, especially when Madame Routy was home and watching the television. Cities never slept. Pel had once worked for a while in Paris and had rented a room in Montparnasse. On one side of him were a couple who had spent the whole night quarrelling and on the other side another who spent it making noisy love, while below, out of the window and across a yard, was a workshop where they spent the night sawing steel. What with the abuse from one side, the cries of delight from the other and the high screech from the yard below, Pel hadn't got much sleep. It had put him off Paris for the rest of his life.

His own city was different. The buses and cars which normally filled the place had disappeared at this time of the evening and, apart from an occasional vehicle, the streets belonged to the strollers, while the golden stone of the Palais des Ducs had changed to violet. The narrow streets were slumbering, their tall fronts shuttered and Pel almost enjoyed himself. With a bit of a push, he felt, he might actually manage to do so.

As he reached the Rue des Forges, he stopped outside a tobacconist that was still open to sell postcards and souvenirs for tourists, and he remembered his decision to attempt to capture Madame Faivre-Perret's wandering attention by trying to smoke a pipe.

The man behind the counter was helpful and produced a selection for him. Pel chose one that was large and knobbly, because it was the sort that iron-faced Englishmen smoked in films. The tobacco he chose was in a pale blue pack because he remembered that blue was a colour that Madame Faivre-Perret liked.

'It's a bit strong,' the tobacconist suggested gently. 'Is this Monsieur's first pipe?'

By this time, Pel was faintly embarrassed and was itching to get outside. Snatching up his purchases he turned hurriedly, only to crash into a stand of walking sticks in the door-way.

'I'll have one,' he blurted out.

He got out of the shop at last, the proud possessor of a pipe and tobacco, a walking stick and a flushed face. At least, he felt bitterly, Madame Faivre-Perret ought to approve of this lot.

Because he couldn't bear to think of the French nation managing on its own without Evariste Clovis Désiré Pel on duty to look after it, he called in the Hôtel de Police. Nosjean was there, telephoning. So was Misset, reading the newspaper, and Pel guessed that he and his wife had had words and he had found it wiser to disappear for a while.

'Jo Clam's going to win,' Misset observed.

'Going to win what?' Pel demanded, giving nothing away in the way of pleasantness.

Misset looked amazed at his ignorance. 'The Big Loop, Patron,' he said. 'The Tour de France.'

When Pel returned home, Madame Routy had reappeared and, though Pel had been unable to find anything to watch, Madame Routy was clearly experiencing no such difficulty. It went on until midnight, leaving Pel a nervous wreck. By the time he left for the office the following morning, he decided he might as well give up trying to cut down his smoking. Under the circumstances, he might just as well lie back and enjoy it.

His bitterness increased when he reached his office. On the desk was a note from Nosjean.

'*Manoire de Marennes near Armur broken into,*' it stated. '*Oedon work table, Carlin guéridon table and pair of Rose vases stolen. Gone to Paris to check.*'

Yelling for Darcy to keep an eye on the office, Pel headed for his car. Crime was changing, he decided. Rape, murder and theft had been around a long time. Inflation had brought in a few new ones.

Driving down the motorway towards Marennes, he wondered if Nosjean would find anything in Paris. Nosjean was no fool and he hadn't wasted time. He'd got his suspicions of the two men in Paris and he'd left Marennes to the local police and headed straight for the capital to check on them before they could sort out alibis and hide their loot. If they'd done the job, the chances were he'd find it.

Deciding to try his pipe, he stopped in a lay-by to light it. At least, he thought, it would stop him smoking cigarettes. Ten minutes later, the floor of the car was littered with matches and, dragging at the pipe with enough effort to make his eyes stick out, he decided he'd packed it too tight. Loosening the tobacco, he tried again and this time seemed to be doing well enough to start the engine. As he drove out of the lay-by on to the road, he turned his head to see if anything was coming and the pipe crashed into the window. It almost tore his teeth from their sockets, filled his eyes with flecks of tobacco, and covered him with burning cinders.

He prevented the fire from spreading but ten minutes later, his jaws aching, he decided he might have been wiser to choose a smaller pipe, and ten minutes after that, that smoking a pipe while driving was one of the most difficult things he'd ever attempted. Aware of aching neck muscles, a sour taste in his mouth and sheer physical exhaustion from trying to draw smoke through the tightly-packed tobacco, he decided to fall back on a cigarette. Pushing the pipe in his pocket with relief, he lit up a Gauloise.

As he was about to climb back in the car, he saw the walking stick on the rear seat, and taking it out, he tossed it into the woods at the side of the road. He had not gone more than four kilometres when he found his pocket was on fire. This time the pipe went after the stick.

Picturesque and medieval, Armur, with its great round towers with their conical caps dominating the River Raçon, had always been a favourite of Pel's. The château was a bit like the one at Sémur where an ancestor of the great Bussy-Rabutin had been governor. One of the towers there had a crack in it that seemed to run down the whole wall but it had been there as long as Pel could remember. As a child he'd always expected it to fall down, but it was still standing, a tribute to the strength they put into things in the Middle Ages.

He found the police at the Manoire de Marennes bewildered by the crime. They knew nothing about Oedon or Carlin tables or Rose vases, and couldn't imagine why anyone should want to steal what had always appeared to them to be just so much old furniture and pottery.

'They say they were as valuable as a deposit in a small town bank,' the inspector in charge said. 'It's a *château classé*, of course, so obviously someone came and had a look first, because they've stolen the only valuable things in the place.'

The owner, who did some of the guide work, was equally bewildered. 'We only tried to do the house up because we felt it right not to let it fall into decay,' he said.

His wife, a small plump woman with blue hair, was in tears. 'We didn't have much that was valuable,' she said, 'but we bought a few things to make the rooms look full and it seemed to be such a success. How were we to know the things they stole had any value? They were here when we came. We bought it furnished. I don't suppose the previous owners were aware of the value either.'

'When was the last time you had people round the place?' Pel asked.

'Last weekend. A few come in the week but not many outside August.'

'Could you say whether any of them acted suspiciously?'

'Of course not. They were just ordinary people interested in an old château. It hasn't much history. The chevalier de Marennes was born here but he never did anything except get himself guillotined during the Revolution. It's about the only story we have, so we try to make the most of it. Most of the furniture was his.' She sniffed. 'So was the stuff that disappeared.'

'Could you describe any of the people who came round?'

The answer was a wail of misery. 'You don't really see them. All I remember was a small boy who wanted to climb on the beds. His mother had to take him out. And an old man with one leg who was very fat and had to be helped up the stairs. It made the tour terribly slow.'

'Nobody else?'

'No.'

'Nobody trying to take photographs?'

'No.'

'Make drawings?'

'No.'

'Nobody suspicious?'

'None that I saw.'

The theft had been discovered by the *gardien* that morning. Near the front of the house, a buttress formed a narrow chimney against the front porch and someone wearing rubber-soled shoes had pushed himself up it, using his feet and his back, until he had reached the top of the porch. There, a thirty-millimetre hole had been drilled and, following the usual pattern, a latch had been lifted with a screwdriver. The screwdriver had been left behind by mistake but the inspector shook his head.

'No fingerprints. They used gloves.'

The furniture had been carried down two flights of stone steps, out through a side door and across a narrow lawn to a belt of trees. Scrapes in the soil indicated the route, which led to the road about two hundred metres away, and a small pool of engine oil indicated that some sort of vehicle had waited on the road there.

'They carried it piece by piece across the lawn, into the wood and on to the road,' the inspector said. 'It must have taken them half the night.'

'And nobody heard?'

'Nobody.' The inspector shrugged. 'The stairs were of stone and the family slept in a small private wing at the other end of the house. They didn't have a burglar alarm, and they heard nothing. It's pretty lonely countryside round here, and nobody else seems to have seen anything either. They didn't even know anything had gone until the maid arrived and found the door unlocked.'

Because of the warm dry weather, there were no footprints and no tyre prints in the lay-by where the car had stood. There were all the usual things that normally littered lay-bys – paper, bottles and contraceptives – but nothing that could give a clue to the identity of the thieves.

Not cherishing the idea of going back to the tearful owner, Pel elected to leave that part of the enquiry to the local police and decided, though he didn't feel it would do much good, to visit Madame de Saint-Bruie, as he'd promised Nosjean.

He found her shop without difficulty. Marie-Joséphine Lehmann was at her table waiting for customers – far from beautiful, but with a splendid figure and, with her wide mouth and large almond eyes, full of charm. Pel approved silently. Nosjean's girlfriends all came in the same pattern. Neat, clean, intelligent, efficient, modest. Darcy's were different. Neat, clean, intelligent, efficient, but with a certain self-confidence – even sauciness – that stamped them as knowledgeable and aware of what went on in the world.

He introduced himself and she immediately suggested he should see Madame de Saint-Bruie.

'She's just gone to lunch,' she said. 'She went early. Perhaps you'd like to join her. She likes company. She'd be pleased to see you.

Pel could see no reason why not. In fact, with Madame Faivre-Perret still apparently consigning her aunt to the soil, he felt a little defiant. If Madame Faivre-Perret couldn't manage to be around, he decided, then it would have to be Madame de Saint-Bruie.

He found the restaurant without difficulty, explained who he was looking for and was directed to a table in the corner. There was a young attractive woman sitting by the window and he was just about to pull back the chair and introduce himself when the waiter indicated the table next door.

Madame de Saint-Bruie looked up at Pel, her green eyes flashing behind her spectacles, her wild brilliant red hair swinging. She looked gaunt, and the bangles on her wrists, the long earrings, and the long necklaces clanked like an iron foundry as she gestured.

'Sit down, Inspector,' she said. 'I've already met your so efficient young assistant. What a splendid young man he is! Quite enamoured of my assistant, Mijo. I might add she was quite taken by him, too. It's so rare one finds a policeman with manners.'

Pel blushed.

'I know what you've come about, of course. The general increase in the price of antiques due to inflation is the cause of it all. It's the desire to have something that will increase in value. It encourages frauds and thefts, though I fear some people are going to be disappointed in years to come with what they've bought.'

'You've heard of the robbery at the Manoire de Marennes?'

'I have indeed.' She beamed. 'There was nothing much there of any real value, of course. Mostly fakes. But there were a few things of which, I might add, the owners were totally unaware, and – ' she gave a loud laugh ' – now they're gone!'

Pel decided she'd been celebrating a good sale or something, because she seemed slightly drunk and was noisy
enough for Pel to be embarrassed.

'These things that have been stolen,' he said. 'Can you
describe them?'

She leaned close to him and he got a whiff of perfume. 'I
can even send you photographs. Not of the originals, you
understand, but of fakes which look exactly like them. We've
had dozens through our hands. I know them well. I'm always
on the trot, looking for them. I never go out in the car
without calling in churches or manors or châteaux to have a
look round. I note what's genuine and what isn't. In case it
comes my way. And you'd be surprised –' another loud
laugh ' – how much is claimed to be genuine that's just a lot
of rubbish. They can't fool me.'

Her voice seemed to be growing louder and he could smell
brandy on her breath. 'A thief with a bit of erudition and a
few resources,' she said, 'is well placed to make a fortune,
Inspector, believe me.' She leaned closer and Pel found
himself looking down the front of her dress. 'You're a man
of intelligence. It's easy to see that. Good-looking with it,
too, I might add. Take careful note of what I say. Are you
married?'

'No.' Pel was startled at the question.

'Such a pity. My brother was married recently. It makes
one so envious. Since my husband died, I've been so alone.
We had the whole district at the celebration. Of the marriage,
of course, not his death. We roasted a whole lamb. I know
it's against the law to roast lambs in this fashion, but we were
in love. It was a question of pure passion.'

Pel studied her gravely, wondering just what pure passion
did to you. His eyes on the front of Madame de Saint-Bruie's
dress, he felt it was something he wouldn't mind
experiencing.

'I'd never do it that way again,' she said. 'It was chaos.
Some said it was too cold. Others said the fire was throwing

off smuts. Others said the lamb was undercooked, others
that it was charred. In the end they simply disappeared. Some
played cards. Some watched television. Some even went fishing. It was a disaster. Probably that's why the marriage never
came to much.' She leaned forward. 'Marriage is so important,
don't you think?'

Pel was about to say he totally agreed with her when she
switched back to antiques and he hurriedly had to readjust
his mind to keep up with her.

'Once upon a time,' she said, 'your châteaux thieves were
nothing more than – well, thieves. Nowadays they've realised
that there's not much to be made from stealing indifferent
objects or fakes and they've gone into the business thoroughly.
They study the illustrated magazines and go to the libraries
and take out the books. Some of them contain enough
information to make their owners a fortune if they only
bothered to read them.' She was almost leaning on Pel now,
overpowering him with her perfume. Her red hair kept
brushing his face and he was in danger of having his eye
poked out by the wing of her spectacles.

'You're looking for someone who knows something of the
Haute Epoque, Inspector,' she went on loudly. 'The French
like their antiques with a high gloss so that it's sometimes
hard to see the work for the dazzle, but your expert knows
exactly what's under the gloss and isn't impressed. And that's
rare today. Most people are satisfied by Style du Métro,
Between-the-Wars Gothic, that sort of metal furniture that
looks as though it's come from a railway waiting room, and
the appalling Victoriana which has caught on with the
young. That old woman who sat on the throne of Britain in
the last century didn't know what a crime she was perpetrating.
But then, perhaps it wasn't her but that ghastly Prince Albert
she married. Everybody knows what the Germans were like.
They're bad enough now but then they were hardly down
out of the trees.'

Pel had eaten by this time but had barely noticed what he'd absorbed.

'Come and see me again, Inspector,' she advised. 'You. Not your sergeant. He's a nice boy and well suited to dear Mijo, but I like a grown man – a man of the world.' Pel preened, barely recognising himself. 'Let us arrange to dine together again. I've enjoyed this so much. Such sparkling conversation.'

Pel wondered whom she was talking about because he could barely recall saying a word.

She took his hand in hers. It was warm and her grip was encouraging. 'London, Paris and New York,' she said, 'contain not only the finest connoisseurs of art in the world, but also the most shameless swindlers in a trade where today it pays to specialise in swindling. We must talk more about them. What a pity you have to go back. I could take you and show you a house full of treasures that would take your breath away.'

He found himself outside at last, a little dazed and, he noticed, holding the bill. She had even insisted on kissing him goodbye and Pel was the sort who never made a point of kissing women. Apart from his mother, it was a habit he hadn't got into.

Glancing back into the restaurant, he decided she was crazy. But she was exhilarating, too, and Chagnay wasn't a bad place either, when you thought about it. He would have to come again. At least, unlike Madame Faivre-Perret, Madame de Saint-Bruie was outgoing, extrovert, larger than life – and available. For Pel, who thought – quite wrongly – that he was considerably smaller than life, it had been a dazzling experience. His eyes were sparkling, partly with wine and partly with the excitement of meeting Madame de Saint-Bruie.

He took a last peep at her. The restaurant seemed to have emptied by this time, but she was still there, still knocking back brandy. It must, he decided, be her birthday and she had just decided to be thirty-one again.

eleven

When Pel reached the Hôtel de Police the following morning there was another discussion going on about the Tour de France. Misset – inevitably – was leading it and seemed to have transferred his support from Jo Clam to Aurélien Filou.

'He's just lying back,' he was saying. 'Letting the others do the pacemaking. He doesn't like cobbles but he's in a perfect position now for the kill. In two years time he'll be one of the "untouchables." '

No sooner had Pel entered his office than the telephone rang. Picking it up, he almost jumped out of his skin as Madame de Saint-Bruie leapt out at him. Not physically, but certainly she was there in the room with him, with her bush of red hair and her brilliant green eyes.

'I had to ring you,' she screamed. 'To let you know I have sent on the pictures I promised. Have you found your criminals yet?'

'Not yet, Madame,' Pel said.

'No clues?'

'Not one.' Even Nosjean's Paris enquiry had come to nothing. His two suspects had perfect alibis. They had been at a night club with a couple of girls and the night club verified their story, while nobody had ever seen them driving a yellow Passat estate.

'I'm sure you'll find them,' Madame de Saint-Bruie encouraged. 'When are you coming to see me again? I have so many things to tell you.'

Pel went hot under the collar. Nobody ever seemed to want to see Pel twice. There had been a time even when he'd imagined he had BO.

'Perhaps I could get down,' he said.

'You must. Evariste, you must.'

Pel stared at the telephone as though she might poke her head out of the hole. Evariste! In the name of God, *Evariste!* After months of trying, he hadn't got past 'Inspector' with Madame Faivre-Perret. His sad heart was warmed by the interest.

'I'll do my best, Madame,' he said. 'Have no fear. I'll do my best.'

'Do that, Evariste. You are frantic to see me, I can tell. I can hear it beneath the phlegm.'

He decided again she was mad, but at least she was excitingly mad. He even wondered if he might get some advice from Darcy. In a roundabout way, of course, that Darcy wouldn't notice.

As it happened, he didn't get that far. Darcy appeared in the doorway, carrying a small sheaf of papers. He had a look of permanence about him, as if he'd been on duty all night.

'Late last night, Patron,' he explained, 'I had an idea.'

'You've been here all night?'

Darcy grinned. 'Not likely, I have better things to do with the hours between midnight and seven a.m.

Pel could imagine what. He lit a cigarette and handed one to Darcy. 'Go on,' he said.

Darcy lifted the papers he was carrying. 'I remembered these papers. Scratchings by Cormon. Nothing important, they said. Nothing that isn't new. It occurred to me, however, that if we took them to Robinson, *he* might be able to identify them. He might even recognise something of his own and that might lead to an explanation of what Cormon was up to.'

Pel moved round the desk alongside him and studied the scratchings, small sets of neat figures – mostly in centimetres and millimetres – the indicates of algebra and square roots, as if Cormon had been busy working out some problem. He turned one of them over. It was the sheet that contained the drawing on the reverse side.

He studied it for a moment, noticing that the paper, instead of being ruled like the others, was stiff drawing paper.

'Did Cormon do this?' he asked.

Darcy shrugged. 'His sister said he couldn't draw anything but plans. It's obviously a piece of scrap paper he picked up somewhere.'

Pel studied the paper again, turning it backwards and forwards, looking first at the figures and then at the drawing. 'It's a church,' he said

'Even I can see that, Patron,' Darcy said dryly.

'What's more,' Pel said, 'it looks like part of Sacré Coeur in Paris.'

Darcy took the sheet and studied it. 'That's right, Patron,' he agreed. 'The south corner. There where it's been torn off looks like the dome.

Pel studied the drawing again. 'It looks like those things they turn out in hundreds in the Place du Tertre,' he observed. 'They stand back-to-back in rows with barely room to breathe, painting the same picture over and over again for the tourists. Dogs lifting their legs against trees – because it's naughty and French. Children with big eyes and tears – real tears, sometimes, made of glass let into the wood. Sacré Coeur ad nauseam. Sunsets. Ships. Anything that's rubbish and will sell to people who don't know their backside from their elbow when it comes to art.'

Darcy was looking at a few scribbled letters in the corner. 'This bit where it's torn looks like some sort of instruction,' he said. 'Je – Ca – le – Papi – . *"Je cacherai les papiers.* I'll hide the papers." Think it's something like that?'

'It might also be a signature,' Pel said. 'Jean-Casimir le Papinot.' He looked at Darcy, suddenly alert. 'It's Nosjean's belief that some of these châteaux robberies were done by a gang who were briefed by an expert and carried drawings of the most valuable articles so they could be identified.'

'Do you think that's what Cormon was up to?'

'Let's see. Get Nosjean.'

While they waited, Lagé appeared. He had a sheaf of photographs for them to look at. He'd been unable to throw off his obsession with light and shade but his pictures were clear. They were all of smart-looking, well-dressed men, walking away from cars or just getting into them.

'Know any of 'em?' Pel asked.

'No, Patron.' Lagé ventured a complaint. 'I didn't enjoy it. I felt a fool. It made my feet ache.'

'My feet *always* ache,' Pel said unfeelingly. He gestured at the photographs. 'Try them on a few of the firms round here. Ask 'em if they recognise anyone. Try the chamber of Commerce and the Rotary Clubs and outfits of that nature. Then get back and take some more.'

Lagé gave a sad smile but he didn't argue.

Nosjean looked weary when he arrived. Pel pushed the drawing at him at once.

'Any of your suspects got a name anything like Jean-Casimir le Papi-something?' he asked.

'No, Chief. None of them.'

'Does that indicate anything to you?'

Nosjean studied the drawing. 'Nothing, Patron. It looks a bit like one end of Sacré Coeur. That's all.'

Pel and Darcy exchanged glances. 'That's what we thought,' Pel said. 'It was found among Cormon's papers. He was using the back of it to do a few calculations. We wondered if he was one of your château gang. You said you thought an artist was involved.'

'That's right!' Nosjean came alert at once and tapped the paper. 'But this doesn't seem to indicate a drawing of anything valuable.'

'No,' Pel conceded. 'But it might be worth finding out who this Je-Ca-le-Papi might be – if it *is* someone. Slip up to Paris and ask around. Try the Place du Tertre. Someone there might recognise the name.'

'If they do, Patron,' Nosjean said, 'we ought to be able to find out where he is. Madame de Saint-Bruie – '

'Whom God preserve,' Pel said fervently.

Nosjean allowed a small smile to slip across his face. 'She says artists can recognise each other's work even when it's not signed. Even when it's disguised, even when – ' Nosjean had learned a lot about art recently ' – even when it's as bad as this. We might identify who did it and that might be a lead.'

'Get up there, *mon brave*,' Pel said. 'Try the art schools. See what they say.'

It seemed a good idea to Nosjean to haul De Troquereau into the affair again. They might well have another sniff round the Rue de Charonne and the Rue Vanoy and see if they could pick anything up. His suspects, Poupon and Pierrot-le-Pourri, knew him too well by now and it might be good sense to have a new face on the job.

De Troquereau was off duty, so Nosjean arranged to pick him up at Auxerre. On the way out of the city, he called in at his own home, promised his mother he'd be careful and keep away from rough criminals, shooed his sisters away from the telephone to do a little ringing round to make sure he wasn't forgotten by Mijo Lehmann and Charlotte Rampling at the library, and to let Odile Chenandier know not to expect him that evening. Then, driving on to the motorway, he turned off at Auxerre, picked up De Troquereau, and they were in Paris in four hours, chiefly because Nosjean liked to drive like a madman. It seemed no time at all before they were circling Paris by the periphery and parking the car. Deciding that if Pel's hunch was right, it might be a good idea to sound the Ecole des Arts Décoratifs, they tried that first. They had no luck so they obtained a list of all known art schools and, separating, began to work their way round them. Meeting late in the afternoon, they decided they'd drawn a blank but at almost the last one they visited, the Ecole des Arts et Métiers in the Sixth Arrondissement, they found they had a nibble.

'No one by any name like Jean-Casimir le Papinot,' they were told by the director. 'Nothing like that and we have them all for the last thirty years – everybody who's passed through our hands. I can only suggest that it might be a boy called Maurice Jacqmin who went by the nickname of Jean Casse-le-Papillon. They often acquire nicknames and some of them actually paint under them. After all, El Greco's real name was Domenico Theotocopuli.' There was a faint smile. 'One can understand why he preferred El Greco. With a name like that on the canvas there wouldn't be much room for his masterpieces, would there?'

'What happened to this Jean Casse-le-Papillon.'

The director shrugged. 'Not much, I suspect. He was never very imaginative. An excellent copyist. Magnificent when it came to drawing things exactly, but he never knew what to do with it. You know Van Gogh's pair of old boots – ' De Troquereau did, but Nosjean certainly didn't – 'if that were the whole of art, then Jacqmin would have been a success, but even Van Gogh couldn't have lived off drawings of old boots for the rest of his life. Neither could Jacqmin. I suspect – indeed I heard – that he turned up in Montmartre drawing for tourists. Quick sketch portraits. That sort of thing. Perhaps he ended up painting Sacré Coeur. Most of them do.'

'How old would he be?'

The official considered. 'It must be eight years since he was here. Thirty-one or two, I should say. He wasn't our best pupil but he had a personality, I remember.'

'What sort?'

'Lively. He enjoyed life. I imagine he still does, whatever he made of it, which I imagine would not be much. He probably ended up with some publicity firm drawing motor car engines for advertising. He would be excellent at that. Or huts. Or chocolates. Or fountain pens. Give him a golf ball to draw and he could reproduce it perfectly. He was painstaking but entirely lacking in imagination.'

'What did he look like?'

'Big. Burly. Not an artistic type at all really. In fact, I don't think he *was* an artist. Not as we know them here.'

Outside again, they decided they still had time to reach Montmartre before dark and the artists there disappeared. As they drove up the winding road below the sugar-icing shape of Sacré Coeur and started to park the car, an officious policeman tried to stop them. Nosjean showed his badge and the policeman raised his eyebrows.

'You're out of your area a bit, my friend,' he said. 'On business?'

'You might say that.'

'I don't know of any murderers, swindlers or rapists round here. Just tourists. They're bad enough, mind you.'

The Place du Tertre was still full of painters. They were so crowded, they were almost standing on each other's heads, and there didn't seem an original idea among them. Some had dozens of identical pictures of Sacré Coeur stacked up alongside their easels. Others, as Pel had said, specialised in children with huge tearful eyes. Others in sunsets that looked like Vesuvius in eruption. It was all there – everything, Nosjean thought, that was bad in art.

The artists themselves came in all sizes and all ages, from nineteen years old in jeans and jerseys who tried to look as if they lived in a garret, and preferred earning quick money from tourists to getting down to hard work, to the seventy-year-old poseurs, dressed in flowing cravats, wide-brimmed hats and velvet trousers, whose work over the years had at

118

least acquired a veneer of polish. Nosjean had no idea where to start so they tried a middle-aged man wearing a rugby shirt, jeans and white shoes.

'Jean Casse-le-Papillon?' he said. 'What's it supposed to mean?'

'It's a name,' Nosjean explained. 'I wondered if it meant anything to you.'

'Nothing, comrade. Nothing at all.'

Trying an elderly man with a spade beard and Dundreary whiskers, they received the same answer, and they began to move among the crowded figures, wrestling with the tourists for an inch or two of pavement to walk on.

After a while, they stopped, had a beer at one of the bars that cost enough to be made of uranium, then separated and started again. After an hour of vain searching, Nosjean saw De Troquereau heading towards him, literally flinging people out of his way.

'Type over here,' he shouted. 'He recognises it.'

The 'type over here' was a man about thirty-five with long blond hair that looked none too clean and was tied with a ribbon. He wore a workman's smock, well-daubed with paint, and a wide straw hat. In his mouth was a corncob pipe. He was at work on a painting of a boat in black, white and brilliant orange that was enough to make Nosjean want to vomit. The artist saw the expression on his face.

'I have to eat,' he pointed out. 'And you'd be surprised how well they sell. They like things they can recognise. Picasso would be a dead loss here. I know this chap you're after. Jean Casse-le-Papillon. Name of Jacqmin. Maurice Jacqmin. He used to paint a butterfly with a broken wing in the corner of his pictures. I think he got the idea from Whistler.' He gestured at the drawing Nosjean held. 'That's his style. He was a specialist in Sacré Coeur. Painted it from all angles. Not here where you could see him at it, though. He had photographs and worked on them during the winter in a studio he shared in Montparnasse. Then he'd come up here and stick one on the easel and pretend to be adding the finishing touches, and sell it as an original. It always went down big that way. When he'd sold it, he'd go straight back to the studio and fish out another and start again. It was money for jam when the tourists came. Mind – ' he pulled a face ' – there wasn't much the rest of the year. You have to have good weather or they don't linger. They head for the bars.'

'This Maurice Jacqmin?' Nosjean said. 'Where is he now?'

The artist shrugged. 'I heard he'd left Paris,' he said. 'He packed up about two years ago. The dollar was doing badly and the number of tourists fell off a bit. I heard he went to Royan. Painting beach scenes, drawing quick portraits and doing a bit of mural work in cafés when things were tight. You know Royan: Bombed in mistake by the Yanks in World War Two. Now it's all painted concrete. Outside *and* in. Half the cafés in the district have murals. Enough to keep a guy busy if he's interested.'

By the end of the day they had confirmed from three other sources that Maurice Jacqmin had indeed gone to Royan. It seemed to Nosjean that he was going to have a long journey.

He drove De Troquereau, who was reluctant to leave because he'd been enjoying himself, to the station, then headed for the nearest police office and, identifying himself, requested permission to telephone Pel.

'I've found our man,' he announced. 'Name of Maurice Jacqmin. Paints as Jean Casse-le-Papillon. Uses a butterfly on his pictures. The drawing was firmly identified. He's in Royan.'

'Where?' Pel sounded shocked.

'Royan, Patron. I think I ought to follow him, don't you?'

There was silence for a moment and the sound of rustling papers, so that Nosjean decided Pel was looking at a map.

He waited happily because he was well aware that Royan was further from the Hôtel de Police where Pel operated, than it was from Paris and it would cost more to send a man over than to let Nosjean continue.

'Can't we get Royan to ask round?' Pel asked eventually.

'We can, chief. But they haven't got the drawing. *I've* got it. By the time we could get it photographed and sent on to them, he might have moved on again.'

'Very well,' Pel said grudgingly. 'Go to Royan.'

'I was only wondering, Patron. I wouldn't like my expenses queried.'

'So long as you don't detour via Cap d'Antibes and Monte Carlo.'

Nosjean put the telephone down and set off at once. He reached Royan just before midnight, worn out but feeling that he was getting somewhere. The police suggested a small hotel. He had to knock up the proprietor and it was bare and comfortless, but it was cheap enough for there to be no queries about expenses.

The next morning, he got into his car again and set out to visit the cafés on Royan's soulless front. Everywhere there were flags and loud-speakers blaring out *'En Vacance'* to whip up any flagging enthusiasm among the holidaymakers. For two hours he drew a blank then, stopping for a beer at a bar called Le Sporting, he noticed immaculate little pictures of motor cars, motor cycles and racing bicycles round the walls.

'Who painted those?' he asked.

The landlord shrugged gloomily. 'I wouldn't know. I only acquired the place this year. It needs doing up. I'm thinking of changing the name. Something a bit more intellectual. Think Le Disco would do?'

'That's more intellectual?' Nosjean asked.

'Oh, yes, a lot more.'

'What happened to the type who used to run this place?'

The landlord shrugged again. 'Retired,' he said. 'Old. Out-of-date. You can tell by the décor. Thought I might hang up a few ropes and stirrups and a dead-or-alive poster or two and call it Le Wild West.'

'This type who retired – where did he retire to?'

'St Georges-de-Didonne. Just along the coast. Name of Morlieu. Gaston Morlieu.'

It didn't take long in St Georges-de-Didonne, with the aid of a street directory, to unearth Gaston Morlieu. He was old-fashioned all right – old-fashioned enough to be plump, round-faced and smiling as if life was fun.

'Who did the paintings?' he said. 'Type called Jean-Coupe la-Pâtisserie or something.'

'Jean Casse-le-Papillon?'

'That's it. It wasn't his real name, of course. It was Jacqmin or something.' Morlieu fished out a bottle of wine which he sloshed into a couple of glasses, and they sat in his garden drinking.

'Where did he go to?' Nosjean asked.

'Well, there wasn't much doing here for an artist when the season started, was there? Nobody wants artists cluttering up the place when it's full of visitors. He did sketches of people's heads. On the beach. But they're a bit against itinerant artists and so on here. They like their beaches organised. Clubs. Clubs for the kids. Clubs for the middle-aged. Clubs for the elderly. Where you can get weight off by doing calisthenics under the eye of bronzed instructors, then put it back on again by buying a drink at their bar.' The old man grinned and patted his stomach. 'French people love calisthenics. They think it does them good. After doing nothing for eleven months of the year all it does is give them heart attacks. I never went in for it myself.'

'Where is this Casse-le-Papillon now?'

The old man shook his head. 'I heard he got a job with a publicity firm in Limoges in Haute Vienne. He wasn't look-ing forward to it but he needed money. He was on his beam ends, painting on the backs of unsold paintings. Publicité Limoges. That's who it was.'

Nosjean set off eastwards with a growing confidence. Jean Casse-le-Papillon was moving nearer home, which was an indication that he was the man they were after, and at least nobody would query Nosjean's expenses if he was heading for home ground.

At Publicité Limoges hard under the cathedral he learned that Jacqmin had moved to Vichy because he had a brother there. Finding the brother, once more with the aid of a directory, he learned the artist had moved on yet again, north-wards this time to Châlon-sur-Saône. Nosjean's heart was thumping as he headed for his car. Jacqmin was now within eighty kilometres of where Pel presided over his small department. There was no doubt now in Nosjean's mind that Jacqmin was their man.

What was more, he'd found him in record time. It was early evening and if he hurried he could make Beaune before the shops shut. He might even celebrate by pushing on to Chagnay and taking Mijo Lehman out to dinner. In his excitement, Nosjean quite forgot old faithful, Odile Chenandier.

twelve

'You have his address?' Pel asked.

'Yes, Patron,' Nosjean said. 'I spent yesterday morning finding him in Châlon. He's been working with a publicity firm called Ateliers Pierrefeu. Châlon's quite a busy place. Waterborne trade, a wine market, iron and copper foundries, engineering, shipbuilding, brewing, sugar, glass, chemicals. Plenty for a publicity firm to get its teeth into.'

'I know Burgundy,' Pel said stiffly.

'He gave up his job a few months ago. He said he was setting up on his own.'

'And has he?'

Nosjean shrugged. 'It seems he has,' he said. 'But Ateliers Pierrefeu didn't think he'd have much business.'

They were in Nosjean's car heading down the motorway, Pel gripping his seat as Nosjean indulged in his favourite sport of racing against everything else on the road. At Beaune the traffic increased as they were joined by the motorway from Paris and Nosjean's driving seemed to Pel to become even more suicidal. However, they reached Châlon, rather to his surprise, without an accident, though the pedestrians had to be pretty nippy as Nosjean slipped in and out of the old streets.

'You nearly got that one,' Pel observed dryly as an old man with a walking stick did a quick hop, skip and jump to the pavement.

'Doesn't count.' Nosjean grinned. 'You don't get any points for geriatrics.'

Stopping to consult a street map, he jabbed with a finger. 'Here we are,' he said. 'Rue Rochefort.'

They headed for the old part of the town near to the Cathedral of St Vincent with its mixture of romanesque and gothic architecture.

'What sort of work is he doing now?' Pel asked.

'Same as before. Drawing things for people who wish to advertise. They have metal blocks made from his pictures and they're incorporated in adverts. You know the sort of thing. A picture and "Peugeot Cars are Best."'

'Mine isn't,' Pel said gloomily.

Jacqmin's studio was in an old house which stood alone at the end of the street. The house looked neglected and the garden, Pel thought, was as bad as his own, with overgrown shrubs, desperately in need of pruning, moving in the breeze over shabby flowerbeds. An elderly Citroën stood in the drive, still covered with the previous winter's mud and spattered with leaves from the overhanging trees. One of the tyres was flat.

As they rang the bell, the door immediately rattled as something large and ferocious leapt at it. Through the glass, they could see the claws and fangs of a dog which to Pel looked as big as a cow. The door shuddered under its assaults and its deep baying bark was enough to strike terror into the whole neighbourhood.

Eventually, a woman appeared and dragged the dog away, screeching at it to be quiet. Obviously with some effort, she managed to lock it somewhere out of sight and opened the door. As they stepped into the hall, the dog was still barking and what appeared to be a kitchen door was shaking under its attacks.

'He's all right,' the woman said. 'He's really quite quiet. You'll be wanting Maurice, I suppose.'

She was in her late twenties, not unattractive but heavily pregnant and clearly easy-going about her appearance. Maurice Jacqmin appeared a few moments later, sharpening a pencil with a large pointed knife.

Nosjean noticed the knife at once. 'That's a large tool for a very small job,' he observed.

Jacqmin stared down through thick glasses at the knife in his hand as though he were seeing it for the first time. 'Yes,' he said, 'I suppose it is. It's a German dagger, I think. Turned up during the war. It was my father's. He was in the Resistance and had the pleasure of disarming a few of them.'

A tall young man, dwarfing both Pel and Nosjean, he had wild blond hair that stood on end, and he looked as though he hadn't shaved for a day or two. He was an enormously powerful figure but the suggestion of power was destroyed by his legs – he had knock knees and obviously bad feet. Dressed in a checked shirt and jeans, his hands were marked with indian ink. Tossing the knife on to a table, he grinned at them.

'What is it you want drawing?' he asked. 'A Citroën? I should need one to work from, of course, to be given later as a free sample. Mine's had it.'

Nosjean produced his badge. 'Police Judiciaire,' he explained briskly.

Jacqmin's face fell. 'Oh, *mon Dieu!*' he said.

'You were expecting us, perhaps?' Pel asked silkily.

Jacqmin grinned, recovering quickly. 'No,' he said. 'But you know what it's like.'

'What is it like?'

'Well, you know artists. We don't pay bills. We forget the tax for the car. The dog got out and ate somebody's baby'. Trivial things like that but important to authority.'

'This time,' Pel said, 'it's not that sort of thing. Can we go somewhere we can talk?'

Jacqmin indicated a door and they found themselves in what appeared to be his studio. A large window faced north but was almost obscured by creepers and overgrown bushes.

'I keep intending to cut those things back,' Jacqmin said cheerfully. 'But I never seem to get around to it. I expect I will one day. Perhaps I don't want to. They help keep out the north wind in winter. The draughts then are enough to suck the cat up the chimney. You'd never notice you had a fire.'

He indicated the fireplace. It seemed to be full of burned coal and wood, and the hearth all round seemed to be littered with screwed-up sheets of paper as though, dissatisfied with things he'd worked on, he'd wrenched them from his drawing board and flung them towards the flames.

There was a table alongside the window with a large drawing board propped up on a block of wood. The desk was cluttered with bottles of ink, poster white, pencils, rubbers, rulers, T-squares, a jam jar full of brushes. Alongside was a scribbling pad and resting on top of a pile of books was a bottle of yellow lemonade labelled 'Fizz!' On the drawing board was a meticulous drawing of it in black and white.

The rest of the room seemed to be occupied by piles of paper, books of reference, empty wine bottles, untidy-looking files with their contents hanging out, a swivel chair with the stuffing protruding from the seat, a woman's dress-making dummy, a three-foot-high manikin with moveable joints, round which was draped a handkerchief, a few posters, some of them outlandish and two of them distinctly erotic, piles of old drawings and paintings with dog ears and curling edges, a few dirty cups with saucers as big as bathtubs, and a basket in a corner containing a cat and several kittens. Over the fireplace was a large painting of a cockerel in reds, blacks, greens and golds. It was good but it seemed to Nosjean, who had learned a lot about art recently, to indicate the Montmartre influence, and seemed to go with the pictures of Sacré Coeur, the sunsets, the fishing boats and the large-eyed tearful children.

'Did you do that?' Pel asked.

'Yes.' Jacqmin grinned. 'It's not all that good. I'm not at my best with colours, though I've done one or two good things.' He eyed the painting, a pleased smile on his face. 'I like drawing poultry. Cockerels especially. Such splendid creatures. So arrogant. After that, ducks and cats. Cats are always graceful, whatever they're doing.' He gestured at the cat languidly washing the kittens in its basket, a picture of grace. 'Ducks never are. Flying, they're superb. On the ground, they're the clowns of the feathered world.'

Pel stared about him. 'Nice house you've got here,' he observed. 'Just the thing for what you want, I should think. Roomy. Plenty of light.'

'It's not bad,' Jacqmin agreed. 'I got it when I came here. We had my – er – Léonie's mother was living with us then. She's got her own place now.' He grinned. 'Old people are a nuisance at times, aren't they? You have to have somewhere for them to go. You could leave 'em at the side of the motorway, I suppose, but someone would be bound to object if you did.'

He seemed nervous and Pel didn't hurry. He glanced about him. 'Rented?' he asked.

'No. It's mine.'

'On a mortgage?'

'No. I bought it outright. It's the only way. With an income like mine that goes up and down, you don't let yourself in for monthly payments. I'd had a windfall.'

Pel indicated the bottle of lemonade.

'That the sort of thing you work on?'

'Yes.' Jacqmin shrugged. 'Not much of a job, really, but I do occasional portraits for the local paper. Local bigwigs. From photographs, of course. They use them to break the type. I do headings for them as well: Lettering and design. You name it, I draw it. Boxes of pills, which I'm allowed to keep, and motor cars – from photographs – which I never even get to see. I also do drawings for serials – some for magazines, which pay better – and if a manufacturer wants anything drawing for an advert he comes to me. It's a living. I've been at it ever since I finished my military service.'

'You were in the army?'

'One month. All of it at recruit-training level,' Jacqmin gestured at his feet. 'I didn't get far with these. They gave me up double-quick. Especially since I wore glasses, too. I never learned one end of a gun from the other. It suited me, of course. I'm an artist, not a soldier.'

He picked up a pile of drawings – of tubes, packages, staplers, bottles of glue, desks, typewriters, calculators, filing cabinets.

'Good job that,' he said. 'Brought in quite a bit. An office equipment firm which was bringing out a catalogue.'

Pel heard him out, then he spoke quietly. 'Did you know a man called Claude-Achille Cormon?' he asked.

Jacqmin frowned. 'Who's he? What's he do?'

'He does nothing,' Pel said. 'Not any more. He was murdered. In a particularly brutal way.'

Jacqmin looked surprised. 'You think I did it?'

'No.' Pel gestured at Nosjean who produced the half-sheet of drawing paper bearing Cormon's scratchings on one side and the part-drawing of Sacré Coeur on the other. 'On the other hand, I don't believe you when you say you don't know him. This was found among his papers. I think you drew the picture on the back.'

Jacqmin turned the paper over, his face expressionless. 'It looks like mine,' he said.

'The signature? Could that be Jean Casse-le-Papillon?'

'It could.'

'And wasn't that the way you used to sign yourself?'

'Yes. Not any more. People who want bottles of lemonade drawing don't go in for fancy signatures. In fact, they don't want signatures at all. Just bottles of lemonade.'

'Do you make a point of writing on the backs of old drawings?'

'No.'

'Morlieu said you did,' Nosjean said.

'Who's Morlieu?'

'Kept the Café Le Sporting at Royan. You did the murals.' Jacqmin beat his forehead with the heel of his hand. 'Got him,' he said. 'Fat guy.'

'That's him,'

'He said that?'

'Yes. He said you were on your beam ends and were having to paint on the backs of old paintings. Two for the price of one, he said.'

'Well –'

Pel indicated the pile of old drawings along the wall. 'Those yours?'

'Yes.'

Pel picked one up. On one side was a pencil sketch of the cathedral at Royan, all concrete spires and angular pillars. 'That your work?'

'Yes.'

Pel turned the drawing over. On the other side was the drawing of a typewriter.

Jacqmin shrugged. 'I was just going to say, *sometimes* I do.'

Pel indicated the drawing Darcy had found of Sacré Coeur. 'Did you draw that?'

'I must have.'

'Then how did it get into Cormon's papers?'

Jacqmin lit a cigarette, slowly, as if he were taking time to think.

'I knew Cormon,' he admitted.

'Ah!' Pel looked pleased. 'In what way?'

'Business. He brought me something to draw. I expect I made some notes of dates, prices, addresses – that sort of thing – and gave it to him. I do that. He must have used it for his figures.'

'How did he find you in the first place?'

'I met him at Royan last year. I was painting that bar at the time. Morlieu's Café Le Sporting. It was just at the beginning of the season and he was on holiday there. With his sister, he said. She was a tart old bird, it seemed, and he'd slipped out for a few drinks on his own to get away from her. I got the impression he was bored stiff. We got talking. He came again and we got on to what we did. He was an instrument maker, I think. Something like that. Later, after I'd moved here, he turned up on the doorstep. Said he had something for me to draw.'

'What?'

'I don't know what it was and he never told me. It was a black plastic thing about as big as a tape cassette. But it had bits of metal attached to it and a piece that slid up and down.'

'Did he bring you other work?'

'No. I never saw him again. He said it was secret and because of that he hadn't wanted to go to a studio. He'd remembered me and got my address from the old boy I worked for at the Café Le Sporting and traced me here.'

'Did he give you no idea at all what this thing was you drew?'

'None at all.'

'Have you any copies of the drawings you did?' Jacqmin looked indignant. 'It was six months ago!' he said. 'Take a look round. I can't even find things I drew yesterday.'

'Did he say who this thing, whatever it was, belonged to?'

'I assumed it belonged to him. But I knew he didn't have his own firm, so I asked about it. He said it was a gadget he was developing on his own at home. He said he hoped to make money from it.'

'Did it look home-made?'

Jacqmin thought for a moment. 'No,' he said. 'Since you mention it, it looked too good for that. The pieces of metal looked as though they'd been stamped out and the plastic was moulded, not cut. It wasn't home-made.'

Pel paused, rubbing his nose. 'Ever meet a type called Rambot?'

'Rambot?'

'We don't know his first name.'

'What's this all about?'

'Never mind what it's all about. A man's been murdered and we're trying to find out what he was mixed up in, because that way we'll find out who did it.'

Jacqmin tossed his cigarette towards the fireplace. 'Rambot? Rambot? Yes – ' he snapped his fingers ' – a type called Rambot did come here. About six months ago. He said Cormon had recommended me.'

'Could you describe him?'

Jacqmin paused then, reaching for a piece of paper and a pencil, produced a quick sketch. Once or twice he rubbed out and drew again, then he handed it to Pel.

'I imagine that's better than a description,' he said.

Pel nodded. 'Is it like him?'

'As far as I can remember. I may be wrong here and there but that's the impression I had of him.'

Pel showed it to Nosjean. It looked remarkably like Darcy.

'Any objection to us using this?'

'In what way?'

'For the newspapers? We'd like to find him.'

Jacqmin thought for a moment. 'Do I get paid for it?'

'If necessary,' Pel said grudgingly.

'Then I suppose it's all right. I'd rather you didn't mention my name, though.'

'Why not?'

Jacqmin gestured. 'Is this type a gangster? I mean, did *he* kill Cormon?'

'He might have done.'

'Well – '

Pel nodded. 'Your name will be kept out of the newspapers,' he said. 'As far as anyone will know, this was drawn by a police artist. What did this Rambot type want of you?'

'He brought some gadgets.'

'What sort of gadgets?'

'Well, I got the impression he was in the casino business and that he wasn't any too honest.'

'Why?'

'Well, there were playing cards, which he wanted drawing, arranged in a sort of fan shape. There was a roulette wheel. He also wanted a rough sketch of a gaming table with people round it. He said it was advertising. There were also a few small gadgets. One was a largish square thing, shining, with grooves on it, and a sort of hook thing at the side that moved backwards and forwards. Another was larger. It looked a bit like the fuel pump off my car but it was bigger and more complicated. He wanted them both drawn from two or three angles.'

'Did he say what they were?'

'No. But I got the impression that one of them had something to do with fiddling a roulette wheel. One of those big ones you get in casinos.'

'When did you last see him?'

'Three – four months ago.'

'No copies of what you did?'

'No. That was one of the conditions. He took all the drawings, even rough sketches.'

There was a long silence. The breeze outside kept the overgrown branches of the bushes tapping at the window.

'You ever visited the Manoire de Marennes?' Pel asked.

Jacqmin's eyes flickered. 'That the one where the robbery took place? The one in the paper?'

'Yes.'

133

'Once. Last year. It's not far from here. I took Léonie. That's my – er well, you know. The girl you saw. She'd been bitten by Hercule. That's the dog. When we first got him. We have him against intruders. She'd only just arrived and he didn't know her very well. She was pretty mad with me, so I took her out for the day. It was warm. We ate out. Sat on the banks of the river watching the fishermen. When we found ourselves near Marennes, we decided to call.'

'Ever been since?'

'No.'

'How about the Château Boncey-Morin, the Manoire Boureleau, Samour-Samourin, and Lamérice?'

'No. Not my line, really. Not very interested in old places. Only went to Marennes to please Léonie.'

'Ever been to St Sauvigny?'

'I've been through it.'

'Stop to look in the church?'

'That's not my line either, really. Léonie goes on Sunday.' Jacqmin grinned. 'To pray for my soul. She was well brought up and she still finds it hard to accept that we're – well – you know.'

'Why do you have the dog?' Pel asked.

'Why do I have the dog?' Jacqmin looked puzzled.

'Have you anything here of great value?'

'No.'

'Then why a watchdog of such ferocity?' To Nosjean Pel sounded prim and old-fashioned.

Jacqmin shrugged. 'Well – you know – '

'No,' Pel said. 'I don't.'

'Well, I don't like being interrupted. The type who owned this place before me was a friendly type. Belonged to all the clubs. Invited friends he met on holiday to call on him. When I first came here, I found there were always people staring at me through the window, looking for him. That sort of thing. I got Hercule to frighten 'em off. Also, of course, some of the things I get asked to draw are a bit private. Manufacturers are pretty secretive these days. They're all scared of industrial espionage. You'd be surprised what people get up to.'

'Yes.' Pel agreed. 'I probably would.'

As they left Châlon, Pel looked at Nosjean.

'Well?' he said. 'What do you think? Could *he* be the type to kill Cormon?'

Nosjean frowned. 'It was a large knife he was using,' he pointed out. 'A German dagger, he said. Just the sort of thing for the wound Doc Minet found. But – ' he paused ' – he honestly didn't seem the type, Patron. Big. Shambling. A bit stupid. Besides, those feet of his. And his eyesight. He didn't seem the sort to go scrambling around a steep hillside in the dark.'

'No,' Pel agreed. 'But he still *might* be. And if he wasn't involved in that, is he perhaps the type who's going round these *châteaux classes* making drawings inside his guide book?'

'That's different,' Nosjean agreed. 'I'd say he wasn't all that fussy about being honest, and it has to be something like that. They don't allow cameras any more and the guide books that are being printed these days leave out the pictures. Madame de Saint-Bruie says even the spiels the guides give have become deliberately vague about the objects the rooms contain. Instead of saying "That's a Boulard chair" they simply say "The room contains many items of exquisite art, including a Boulard chair." But they don't say which one, so if it's in a set, no one can tell which it is.'

'Unless they're experts?'

Nosjean nodded.

Pel considered a moment. 'Judging by the interior of Jacqmin's house,' he said. 'I wouldn't say *he* was an expert, would you?'

Nosjean grinned. 'The rubbish was good.'

Pel didn't laugh. 'So if he did do the drawings that led our châteaux thieves to their loot, he was accompanied by someone who knew his stuff. How about your two in Paris?'

'I think they're involved. Whether they actually carry out the robberies or get somebody else to do the break-ins is another matter. They're also probably being directed by someone a lot more knowledgeable than they are themselves, who tips them off and takes his cut with the best piece, but certainly they know their stuff, Patron. It *could* be them.'

'We could bring them in and arrange for them to have a suspended sentence – on health grounds or something. If we find they've committed some sort of crime, we can let them go, watch them, and keep bringing them back every time we get a bit of new evidence. Put them away and then re-arrest them every time they're released. The yo-yo method. Gets their nerves on edge. It works quite well.'

Nosjean wasn't so keen. He felt that sooner or later they might be able to get the lot at one go and that it was worth waiting.

'I think,' he said slowly, 'that our friend, Casse-le-Papillon, *is* involved. I'd swear he was the one who did the drawings. The sort of work he does is exactly what would be wanted. Immaculate detail. Standing in a room while a guide was talking, he could make a quick sketch of a chair or a secrétaire or a commode – even a vase or a plate. Prompted by an expert, he could have all the relevant details down in ten minutes. Perhaps more than one object. Even the details of the decoration. He could look at a plate and have its design down in no time. He's been doing it for years.'

'What about the gadget Cormon brought him? That doesn't seem to be connected with châteaux robberies.'

'Unless it was some means of opening locks. Cormon was a locksmith originally. He did time for expert locksmithing, didn't he?'

'The châteaux were broken into by a much simpler method than that,' Pel said dryly. 'A drilled hole and a screwdriver to lift the latch.'

thirteen

Nosjean requested permission to stop off in Chagnay and Pel took the car on alone.

When he reached the Hôtel de Police, Darcy was sitting at his desk reading *France Soir.* Across the front was the story, with blood-curdling pictures, of a shooting in Paris.

'British Official Shot,' the headlines announced. 'IRA Men Sought.'

'Anything else?' Pel asked.

Darcy looked up. 'Another rash of letter bombs. This time a bit closer to home. Two turned up in Lyons.'

'Anything on the home field?'

Darcy shrugged. 'Only Misset. Got a wigging in court for bungling the evidence in that break-in at Barreau.'

'How about Lagé?'

'Still walking up and down between Pissarro's place and the Hôtel Central with his camera. He's got quite a portrait gallery. Nobody we know, though. Or, rather, nobody we know who's mixed up in crime. Quite a lot of local business-men and representatives.'

'Nothing else? Did you get Robinson to check those workings Cormon did?'

'Robinson's in England,' Darcy said. 'I telephoned. Not due back until the weekend.'

Pel picked up the paper. Philippe le Bozec and his brothel adventure seemed finally to have sunk without trace. On the front was the Tour de France which was now down in the South and beginning to build up tension. One had it with breakfast, lunch and dinner. He noticed that Pissarro's man, Maryckx, was still well down the list.

'There was a telephone call for you, by the way,' Darcy said.

'Brisard, I suppose?'

'No. Not Brisard.'

Pel put the paper down. 'The Chief?'

'No. It came from Vitteaux.' Darcy grinned. 'Very come-to-bed voice, Patron.'

Pel glared. He was never one to enjoy his private life being bandied round the office.

'What did she want?'

'She asked me to apologise for not being in touch before but she said she was likely to be involved at Vitteaux for some time still. She said she'd written.'

Pel's heart leapt. He hadn't had a letter from a woman for years. It probably said nothing very important but he felt sure he could manage to read a lot into it if he tried.

Darcy's smile remained. 'You've been sending her roses, Patron.'

Pel stiffened. 'What's it to you?' he demanded.

'Nothing. Nothing at all. I'm all in favour. Only a French-man knows how to send roses – the exact colour and the exact number. I hope you got it right.'

'I took counsel,' Pel said with a sniff.

'Well done, Patron.'

'How about here? Nothing at all?'

'A quiet day, Patron. Made a nice change. I rang Robinson's place at Montbard and had a chat with that guy, Rivard, who runs the place.'

'And doubtless with Mademoiselle Guillemin also.'

'Oh, yes.' Darcy never hesitated to admit his peccadilloes. 'Her, too. I'm going over there tonight. Take her out to dinner.'

'What happens about all the others?' Pel asked in wonderment. 'Joséphine-Héloïse Aymé. And that one who worked at the University.'

Darcy smiled. 'Oh, I manage things,' he said.

'One of these days one of them will doubtless shoot you.'

Darcy grinned, clearly untroubled. 'How about you, Patron? You bring anything back?'

Pel fished out the drawing Jacqmin had done of Rambot. 'Only this,' he said, laying it in front of Darcy.

'It looks like me. Who is it?'

'Very probably the type who killed Cormon.' Pel smiled sourly. 'It *isn't* you, is it?'

When Pel reached home Madame Routy was watching the latest on the Tour de France. From the noise, it sounded as if the participants were fighting, not racing.

'Letter for you,' she shouted above the din.

As Pel picked up the letter, she hung around, dearly itching to know what was in it. Anyone, Pel thought, would imagine he never received letters.

As a matter of fact, he didn't. One occasionally from the sister who was married to a draper in Chatillon and one from the sister who had married a British soldier after the war and lived in the north of England. The rest all seemed to be bills.

Out of the letter came a formal death notice, a folder on fine paper, printed in grey and black. 'Monsieur et Madame Jacques Clarot; ses enfants, Monsieur Jean-Jacques Clarot, Monsieur et Madame Georges Matrel; ses petits-enfants... He glanced down the list of names of the family announcing the death of one Madame Michel Olivier – née Louise Picard

– and the obsequies in the Church of Notre Dame du Val at Vitteaux, until he found that of Madame Geneviève Faivre-Perret tucked away among the nieces and nephews. She was worried, he decided, that he might not have believed she'd gone to bury her aunt. After all, going to a funeral was an office boy's excuse when he wanted the afternoon off. It indicated, he decided, that she was concerned for his regard.

It pleased him. Then he noticed there was a note to go with it, which pleased him even more and he turned and gestured at the television. The Tour de France when he was about to read the only letter he'd received from a woman in years was like sacrilege.

Madame Routy sullenly turned down the volume but she didn't turn it off.

The note was disappointing. Hardly worth the effort of moving the switch. 'I have heard about the roses. Though I fear I shall not manage to return in time to see them, I am very touched. I'm afraid I shall be here for some time yet, but when I do return I hope you'll call round and take tea with me. Geneviève Faivre-Perret.' It could hardly be called a love-letter and there wasn't a lot that was heart-stirring. Try as he might, Pel found it hard to read much into it. It *might,* by a wide stretch of the imagination, hint that she was dying to reappear in Pel's sphere of influence and was longing to see him again, but in his heart of hearts he couldn't really feel that it did. At least, the roses had touched her, though people could be touched by being helped across the road.

Pel sighed. And she'd be in Vitteaux for some time yet. If Evariste Clovis Désiré Pel had been Menelaus and Madame Faivre-Perret had been Helen of Troy and he'd led the Greek fleet to rescue her, he'd probably arrive to find she'd gone off to the country for the day to visit her aunt, or that somebody had done for Castor and Pollux and there was a message for him to return home at once to lead the enquiry. Romance didn't seem to intrude very far into Pel's life.

'Anything important?' Madame Routy asked.

'No,' Pel said, determined that she at least shouldn't bandy his affairs around. She already suspected him of having a mistress somewhere and considered he was off to an illicit love affair every time he put on his best suit. He looked at the letter again. Sadly, he decided there *wasn't* anything in it. He almost began to wish Didier Darras would turn up. Between them, they could always reduce Madame Routy to a state of explosive fury by disappearing just when she'd cooked a meal. At the very least, they could have played scrabble in the kitchen, which was always better than trying to read through the clamour of the television. Even when Madame Routy watched a programme on the Churches of France, she made it sound like the attack on the Malakoff.

As he'd expected, it was a wearing night. It wasn't the Churches of France that Madame Routy was watching. It was a quiz competition and the sheer fatuousness of it drove Pel early to bed. The following morning, in a foul temper, he arrived at the office to find the telephone already ringing.

It was Madame de Saint-Bruie again and the shock was as powerful as last time, while the screech down the telephone like an eagle stooping to its prey – almost shattered his eardrum.

'My dear Mijo tells me you were in this area yesterday,' she yelled. 'Your young man came to see her. Why didn't you come to see me?'

Pel hummed and hahed over an excuse. It sounded shamelessly made-up, but she seemed not to notice. 'I had to know, – Evariste,' she shouted. 'I had to know. Have you unearthed any clues yet?'

It left Pel feeling faintly dazed. To have one woman requesting his presence was extraordinary, to have two was unbelievable.

Madame de Saint-Bruie was a new experience for Pel. Unusual, daring, slightly weird. But obviously wealthy. To a policeman as poor as Pel considered himself to be, wealth was important. She'd talked of a houseful of treasures. What was more, she'd kissed him. It was a long time since Pel had been kissed and it was an explosive experience. And there was no getting away from the fact – she appeared to be interested in him. She telephoned. She wanted to know how he was, what he was doing. For all her quiet elegance, Madame Faivre-Perret seemed to show a curious indifference. Bachelordom had long since palled for Pel; he needed to be needed, and Madame de Saint-Bruie seemed to be indicating the way.

He was still sitting at his desk, his eyes blank, when Nosjean put his head round the door. He held a newspaper.

'Patron,' he said, 'have you seen this?'

Pel lifted his head. 'What is it? Jacqmin turns out to be a member of the Ecole du Louvre in disguise?'

Nosjean gave a twisted smile. 'Not quite, Patron. But you'd better look at it.'

The newspaper was the one Darcy had been reading, the front plastered with the details of the shooting in Paris.

'This is of interest to *us?*' Pel said. 'Like insurrections, assassinations in Paris are nothing new. They've happened too often before.'

'All the same,' Nosjean said, 'just take it into your office, Patron, and read it through. I'll wait outside.'

Pel read the story carefully, wondering what Nosjean had found. It didn't seem to have much connection with the châteaux robberies, the loss of the panel at St Sauvigny or Cormon's death on the hill down to Destres. It seemed to be connected with an unannounced visit of the Prime Minister of Great Britain to the President of the Republic. The visit seemed to concern some projected getting-together over arms, which in itself was quite an occasion, considering De Gaulle had taken France out of Nato some years before. The meeting, it seemed, was to duplicate weapons as a means of standardising training and generally to pull up a few socks in the West in face of the danger from the East. Pel read on, puzzled.

The dead man, it seemed, was a British official by the name of John Ford, and he had been shot while the Prime Minister and the President had been dining together. With his chief safely surrounded by the security forces of the Republic, he had stepped out of the Elysée Palace into the Faubourg St Honoré; to be met with a fusillade of bullets which had killed him at once.

It was the next paragraph that made Pel sit up. Men had been seen running away and shots had been exchanged. As was usual in such cases, a civilian or two had been hit and slightly wounded but, with the security men shooting better than normally, one of the assailants had been killed. He had not yet been identified but in his possession had been found drawings of the dead British official, obviously provided as an identification.

Pel folded the paper carefully and called for Nosjean and Darcy. All the warmth he'd been feeling was dispersed and he was coldly efficient again.

'Sit down,' he said.

He looked at them as cigarettes were passed round.

'I begin to think we might have put our foot into something we didn't expect,' he said slowly. 'This looks a bit bigger than industrial espionage, bigger even than robbing châteaux.' He looked at Nosjean. 'This clearly struck a chord, *mon brave*. You were thinking of the quick sketch that was done yesterday by our friend, Jacqmin, and were wondering if this sketch they found in Paris was done by the same man.'

Nosjean nodded. 'That's right, Patron.'

Pel looked at Darcy. 'These gadgets Cormon was involved in making,' he said. 'Could they be explosive devices? For assassinations? There was some talk, wasn't there, of one of them looking like a switch. Could it be a trigger device?'

Darcy shrugged. 'I wouldn't know, Patron, but it's my guess it could.'

Pel stared at his blotter for a moment then he lifted his head, brisk and on the ball, the efficient half of his dual personality well to the fore. 'Better get a message off to Paris,' he said. 'Tell them what we've stumbled on. Make it tentative for the moment, because so far we have no proof. In the meantime, Nosjean, get in touch with the police at Châlon-sur-Saône. Tell them to pick up Jacqmin.'

There was a tenseness about the office as the morning wore on. It involved talking to Brisard, which was unfortunate, but Polverari had returned and Pel asked him with his experience and influence to sit in on the conference, too, and to bring the Chief.

'Why wasn't I told of this?' Brisard tried at once to be difficult, but Polverari shut him up immediately.

'Because it was only in the papers this morning,' he said. Though Polverari was small and fat and smiled more than most, he was shrewd and could be as sharp as anyone when he wished.

'I should have been given an opportunity to talk to this man, Jacqmin.'

'Doubtless, in good time, you will,' Polverari said. 'How much do you think this Jacqmin was involved in the business in Paris, Inspector?'

'So far,' Pel said, 'I haven't the slightest idea. It might be nothing more than a coincidence. But it seems worth investigating, because whatever this thing's about in Paris, it's bigger than what we've been involved in so far in this area. This Englishman seems to be some sort of secret military adviser to the British Prime Minister and that takes us out of the realms of industrial espionage into international terrorism, which is a different thing altogether.'

As they talked, there was a knock on the door and Nosjean appeared, pink and flushed as if he'd been hurrying.

'Châlon rang up, Patron,' he said. 'Jacqmin's disappeared. His girlfriend Léonie Sars, by name – doesn't know where he is. He went out last night, soon after they'd been watching the news on television – that's when the first report of the incident in Paris was given, it seems – and he didn't come back. She said he seemed upset.'

'He can't be far away,' the Chief said, brisk and commanding at once. 'He's got to be found. Put out a general request to all forces and all sub-stations, Nosjean. In the meantime, Pel, under the circumstances, I think we'd better let Paris know that your suspicions appear to have been confirmed.'

The atmosphere in the office was electric and when Lagé appeared to ask how much longer he had to parade up and down between the Hôtel Central and the works of Louis-Napoléon Pissarro, he was told to get on with it and not argue. When Misset appeared, mistaking the silence in Pel's office for calm, to demand the night off, he received the mother and father of a dressing down.

'If you find plain clothes work so wearing,' Pel snapped, 'I can always arrange for you to go back to the uniformed branch and have you put on traffic control at the Porte Guillaume.'

Misset vanished at full speed.

Everything seemed to have come to a stop. Nosjean and Darcy were still pursuing their enquiries but they were avoiding getting in too deeply, in case their presence was demanded elsewhere in a hurry, and they sat at their desks with their ears cocked for the first cries of alarm. It was noticeable that neither of them got involved with telephone calls to girls. For a change Odile Chenandier, Charlotte Rampling and Mijo Lehmann were not in Nosjean's mind and when the girl from the university rang up asking for Darcy, he told the man on the switchboard to tell her he was out on an enquiry.

None of them knew quite what direction the reaction from Paris would take and when it finally manifested itself, it surprised them all. The roof fell in. Pel was summoned to report at once to New Scotland Yard in London.

fourteen

'London?'

Pel was shocked. London was at the other end of the earth. The fact that he could fly direct from the city to Gatwick in a matter of two or three hours and be in London an hour later was immaterial. London was in England and England was not only outside Burgundy, it was outside France and, like a delicate wine, Pel considered that he didn't travel well.

Shaken, he went home, put on the suit he kept for the day when he met the President of the Republic – just in case he had occasion to greet the Queen of England – and packed a small suitcase.

'You going away?' Madame Routy asked.

'Yes.' Pel said.

'Holiday?'

'No. Business. London.'

'You'll be away a day or two then?'

Gloomily, Pel admitted that this was more than likely and Madame Routy smiled. With Pel away that long, she could really enjoy herself with the television, merely doing a quick skip round the house with a duster just before he returned.

'When are you due back?' she asked, making her preparations already.

'I don't know.' Pel wasn't too depressed not to respond at once to the challenge. 'It might be two days. Or three. Or a week. It might be tomorrow.' If she didn't know when he was due to return she'd have to remain on her toes – at least, as far as Madame Routy ever remained on her toes.

Returning to the office, he found Polverari waiting to greet him.

'They want you to go to Buckingham Palace,' the judge smiled. 'To receive the Order of the Garter.'

Pel wished he could.

As they talked, Brisard came in. 'You're going to London, I hear,' he said.

'Yes.'

'I'll go straight home and pack. You'll need me with you. Legal affairs need legal minds. I'm involved in the case. Deeply involved.' Brisard managed to make it sound as if he'd been doing all the leg work.

Pel glared bitterly at him. It would be nice, he thought, if it could be arranged for a steam roller to drive over him – slowly.

Polverari caught the expression on his face and turned to Brisard. 'You consider this your affair?' he asked.

'Of course.' Brisard had no doubt. 'It's far too important to leave to a mere policeman.

Polverari looked at Pel. *'Tiens,'* he said. *'Les clichés.'* He clicked his fingers. 'The instructions, Pel.'

Pel handed over the telex that had come from Paris. As Brisard turned to the door Polverari looked up. 'One moment, my friend,' he said. He held up the telex and read it out. ' "Inspector Pel to report at once to New Scotland Yard, London. To see Commander Fergusson." ' He looked up again at Brisard. 'Do I see any mention of Judge Aristide Brisard?' His eyebrows rose. 'No, I don't. This,' he said cheerfully, 'is nothing to do with you, my young friend.'

A plane was leaving the city late that afternoon and Pel was pushed aboard, faintly awed at the importance he seemed suddenly to have acquired. He arrived at Gatwick to find the red carpet laid out for him. New Scotland Yard weren't wasting time. A young man was standing by the steps as he emerged from the plane and whisked him through Customs before the other passengers had even started to head for the terminal building.

'I'm Inspector Goschen,' he introduced himself in passable French. 'Charles Goschen. I'm taking you home to my place for the night. My wife's expecting us. I hope you enjoy English food. I'm to wheel you in to see Fergusson first thing in the morning.'

Inspector Goschen lived in a large semi-detached house in a quiet side street. The houses around all looked much the same and the evening was full of golden-bronze light and the sound of birds. In France, Pel reflected, they would probably have been shot by some eager hunter determined to add them to his bag. French huntsmen shot at anything that moved, whatever its size, sometimes even at each other.

Goschen's wife was about the age of Madame Faivre-Perret and he was surprised to find she was quite neat and smart. The house was bright and colourful, and there were two young children who were vastly intrigued by Pel's accent. It made Pel wonder what qualities one had to have to acquire such a wealth of comfort and happiness.

The meal, better than he'd ever dreamed the British could manage, consisted of roast beef and something he'd never heard of before, called Yorkshire pudding, and it all appeared on the same plate, which hitherto he had considered a barbaric British habit but now, charmed by Goschen's wife, he felt was merely a delicate touch.

Goschen produced an unexpectedly good wine and afterwards, because it was still warm, they went outside to have coffee on the lawn. Pel studied the immaculate garden with its roses and flower beds and the grass that looked like green velvet. It made his own lawn look like the stubble of a cornfield.

'It is permitted to walk on it?' he asked.

The following morning, as Goschen had promised, he was wheeled in to Commander Fergusson, who was an older man with greying hair and a clipped moustache. Coffee was produced and they got down to business with Goschen standing with his back to the door so that no one came in.

'Do you know who this man is who was shot in Paris, Inspector?' Fergusson asked.

'I have his name,' Pel said. 'John Ford.'

Fergusson frowned. 'That's the name he goes under. His real name's something else entirely. But that doesn't matter. It wasn't an IRA shooting, of course. It's been made to look like one but it isn't. It's connected with arms and arms secrets, but I won't go into that too much. Just sufficiently to say that your country and ours are trying at last to come to terms with each other instead of competing. You have a few secrets and so do we. The meeting between our prime minister and your president was to conclude the arrangements. It was somewhat marred by the shooting of Ford. Fortunately for the relations between the two countries, an incident wasn't entirely unexpected, though it was thought the Prime Minister or the President rather than Ford would be the target.'

'Why was he shot?' Pel asked.

'Because clearly it's to the advantage of what I might call our enemies to prevent the exchange of secrets taking place. Ford was well aware of the people who were involved.'

'Do we know them?'

'Unfortunately, not for certain. Ford played his cards close to his chest.'

'Please?'

'I beg your pardon.' Fergusson gestured. 'I meant he was secretive about what he was doing, because he had to be. We thought he was quite unknown but someone clearly identified him and we think we know when. There was another unannounced meeting in Paris recently. Between the two Defence Ministers on the same subject. Ford was with our man. Because it was unannounced and because Ford wished as usual to remain anonymous, he was kept well away from the press and we know no one was able to photograph him because vehicles were placed so that no one could use a zoom lens. It's possible a secret camera picked him up, though, and that the drawings which identified him were made from that. Though we doubt that, because there would be no point in changing a photograph to the less certain medium of a drawing. I gather now you've turned up some dubious character who specialises in this sort of thing. Instant portraits.'

'That's so.'

'Will he be arrested?'

'Almost certainly. We were on to him within an hour or so of him disappearing.'

'Let's hope we catch him. What about these drawings I've heard about?'

Pel explained about Cormon's death and the scratchy drawings and workings that had been found among his papers.

Fergusson paused to light a pipe and blow out smoke. He did it with a casualness that Pel envied.

'Ever heard of a Capitaine de Corvette Edouard de Fransecky?' he asked.

'Yes.' Pel nodded. 'I wasn't involved, but he was the man who was accused of selling naval secrets.'

'Exactly. *British* naval secrets, which had been exchanged with your navy for secrets of your own. Simplified plans for a thing that was popularly known as the *Nebelwerfer,* and more exactly as the Double-Edged Sword. There were other more technical names in both countries. In fact, it was a device for launching from ships multiple homing missiles for destroying submarines. It was very important. We suspect now that the Russians have it. De Fransecky was involved in that, and we believe that somehow the plans were stolen and were copied – either by photographing or by an artist. Because of their size, we suspect the latter.'

Pel said nothing, his mind working furiously.

'There was also,' Fergusson went on slowly, 'the explosion of a high-speed launch – the Loupet type. What it carried is of no importance here, but let's just say it was built at the Werf Gusto yard in Schiedam for the Germans, the designs were passed to us and to you, and it was then fitted with prototype devices agreed on by all three navies. It was a good Nato project that also involved your country. It exploded off the coast near Sainte Marguerite as it was leaving the mouth of the Loire from St Nazaire. Divers were sent down to recover the gadgets with which it was filled, but the explosion had mostly destroyed them and the work had to be started all over again.'

The slow puffing of the pipe stopped and Fergusson looked up. 'We'd like to see the drawings and workings you found among this man Cormon's papers. Can you let us have copies?'

'At once,' Pel said briskly. 'If I may use a telephone.'

There was a lot more talk then Pel was led by Goschen to a room where books containing photographs were spread out on a table.

'Take a look at some of these,' Goschen said. 'They're our men. International men. Shadowy people – and God knows there are plenty about these days with terrorism on the increase. Any you're interested in, make a note of the numbers and we'll have them copied and sent on to you.'

Pel spent the rest of the day going through the pictures, looking for one who looked like Darcy. There were several and he marked them.

Goschen took him to dinner in Soho in the evening and the following day they were joined by a cold-eyed Frenchman called De Frobinius from the Sûreté who had flown over from Paris. He appeared to regard Pel as a mere country bumpkin, and seemed surprised when he was invited to sit in to hear what was going on.

They saw filmed shots of known terrorists and of the weapons they used, and were informed about the workings of early warning systems and new fail-safe apparatus that were coming into use. Pel found it all rather overwhelming and was awed by the magnitude of the information he was being given. Obviously someone somewhere – probably the Chief – had given a good report on him.

By the end of the day, even De Frobinius seemed to have accepted him and, drawing him aside as the others were sipping their apéritifs before dinner, he began to pump him a little about Jacqmin.

'You'll remember the murder of that bar owner who was killed near the naval base at St Nazaire,' he said. 'Or, to be more exact, who was found dead in a burned-out boat off Les Rochelets. Type called André Malat. Bit of a drunk. Had a bar at Pomichet, the back of which overlooked the river. He could see everything that went in and out of St Nazaire or Nantes.'

De Frobinius frowned. 'I expect they got rid of him because he was becoming dangerous and beginning to talk.' He paused, sipping at his pernod. 'There were drawings,' he went on. 'Technical drawings. And we found a telescope. He was reporting on the movement of naval vessels. They go in and out of there like buses past the Gare St Lazare. He was only the operative, however, There were others between him and what we can only assume was the Russian Embassy.'

Pel wondered how it affected him, but De Frobinius didn't enlighten him and he could only assume it was a quiet suggestion that he keep an open mind on anything he found.

Finishing work on Sunday, he decided to spend Monday looking round London. Watching the changing of the Guard, he was struck dumb as a large black limousine containing a figure in pale blue came through the gates of Buckingham Palace. It was only when he heard cheers and realised the flag on the bonnet of the car was the Royal Standard that it dawned on him that he was looking at a Queen, and he removed his hat and stiffened to attention. As a good Republican, he was a splendid Royalist.

In the evening, he took Goschen and his wife out to dinner – on expenses, of course. Setting off for home the following day, he was still faintly awed by what he'd learned and humbly pleased that he'd found some new friends.

'Come and see us if you're ever in London,' Goschen said.

Pel wished he could offer the same sort of invitation, but Madame Routy would have mutinied had guests turned up at the house in the Rue Martin-de-Noinville.

He flew back via Paris because De Frobinius wished him to meet his chief. By this time, Pel was beginning to feel important. They called at Interpol headquarters at 37, Rue Paul-Valéry where Pel studied more photographs, then he was fed at government expense in one of the best restaurants in Paris, before being put on the train south.

As soon as he had reached home and dumped his bag, he rang Darcy to find out what had happened in his absence.

'How was it, Patron?' Darcy asked. 'How did the Grand Quartier Général stuff go?'

'Everybody was helpful,' Pel said modestly. 'I'm a bit exhausted with talking rosbif, of course, but then, if one visits the land of Rosbifs, I suppose one has to accept that. What about Jacqmin? Have we picked him up yet?'

'Yes, Patron. Couple of hours ago, as a matter of fact. It's just come in. He's on his way here now. We picked up the knife he had, too. Nosjean's alerted the lab about it.'

'Where was he?'

'Lons-le-Saunier. He said he was going on holiday. But that doesn't seem to tie in with what this girl he lives with says. I think he was bolting to Switzerland to lie low for a bit.'

'We'll see him in the morning,' Pel said. 'Inform Nosjean. In the meantime get Châlon to enquire into his finances. The girl ought to know.'

fifteen

When Jacqmin appeared in Pel's office, Nosjean, Darcy and Pel were waiting for him like a tribunal. He looked nervous and a little dishevelled and tired.

Pel produced copies of the drawings of Ford which Fergusson had given him.

'Did you do these?' he asked.

Jacqmin looked at the drawing. 'They're my style,' he said.

'Did you do them?'

'How do I know? I do so much. I can't remember everything.'

'Why were you in Lons-le-Saunier?'

'I was taking a short holiday.'

'Without your girlfriend?'

'Occasionally I take off on my own.'

'That's not what *she* says,' Darcy pointed out.

'Well, she's new to the game, isn't she? She's only been with me a short time. I don't like getting too tied down.'

'Were you heading for Switzerland?'

'I like Switzerland. All those mountains.'

'You were bolting,' Pel accused. 'Where were you heading?'

Jacqmin looked lost. 'Switzerland. I haven't enough money to bolt any farther.'

'You've had money, though, haven't you?' Nosjean asked. 'Châlon police have discovered that at times you've been quite a big spender. And how did you manage to buy that house? Morlieu said you were on your beam-ends when you left Royan.'

Pel pushed forward the pictures of Ford again. Alongside them he placed the picture Jacqmin had drawn of Rambot, the one that looked like Darcy.

'We've had these studied,' he pointed out. 'They're by the same artist. The Director of the Galéries Richelieu swears to it. Do you still say you didn't draw these pictures of Ford?'

Jacqmin drew a deep breath and seemed to collapse like a punctured balloon. 'I drew them,' he said.

'Why?'

'Because I was asked to.'

'Who asked you?'

'Some guy Rambot brought along. He said he had a job for me. A well-paid one. I was to go to Orly with them and stand in a crowd of airport loaders. It was when the British Defence Minister came a month or two back. Whoever fixed it knew they weren't going anywhere near the VIP lounges and there were high vehicles all round where the aircraft stopped. Somebody must have paid the foreman of the loaders to have me included, because nothing was said.'

'Make a note of that, Darcy,' Pel interrupted. 'If nothing else, somebody's taking bribes. Pass it on to Paris. They'll find the time and date and pin him down.' He looked at Jacqmin. 'Go on.'

'I was given a clipboard with some loading lists on it. A large one. Underneath the top sheets was drawing paper. There was a man with me who pointed out the man I had to draw. *He* wasn't a loader either. At least I never saw him do anything that indicated he was. He just stood alongside me. We were searched for cameras but nobody questioned the loading lists. The people who got out of the aeroplane stood talking for a while. Only a few feet from me. The loaders were all round me. I did the sketches, making it look as if I were ticking off numbers and times – that sort of thing. It wasn't difficult. He had an easy face.'

'*Easy* face?'

'Well –' Jacqmin shrugged ' – round faces are hard to catch. No outlines. His was lean and thin. All angles. Very simple to get on paper.' He tried a weak smile. 'I think they were good likenesses.'

'Too damn good,' Darcy growled. 'What happened then?'

'After they'd all gone, we walked back to the loading area and the man who was with me pushed me into a car and we drove off. The drawings were taken from me. I was given a thousand francs and put on the train south with a ticket in my hand. I had no idea what it was all about.'

'Do you think we believe that?' Pel asked.

'You can do as you please.' Jacqmin shrugged again. 'It was an easy thousand to me. I didn't ask questions. I didn't know who the guy was I drew. I didn't know he'd get himself killed.'

'But he did, didn't he?'

'When I saw his photograph in the paper,' Jacqmin said, 'I knew at once who it was and I got scared. I bolted.'

'Was it Rambot who arranged it?'

'I don't know. *He* was just somebody I'd worked for. He brought the guy to see me. It wasn't Rambot who was with me at Orly.'

'Had Cormon anything to do with it?'

'I don't know. I shouldn't think so.'

Remembering what he'd been told, Pel leaned forward. 'These gadgets Rambot asked you to draw: Why weren't they simply photographed?'

'Mostly they were black plastic with bits of metal attached. It was clearer to draw them. They'd have photographed badly.'

'Describe one.'

'Well, one I did was black plastic – or bakelite – something like that – and it seemed to have a series of wires and a coil and a small magnet attached to it. At least it stuck to my penknife when I was turning it over.'

'Do you know what it was?'

'Some sort of switch, I think. I'm no expert.'

'Ever copy anything like plans?'

Jacqmin's face changed and he looked more wary than ever. 'I've often done that,' he said. 'There's more industrial spying goes on than people realise.'

'This wasn't industrial spying,' Pel said. 'It was more important than that. About eighteen months ago. Did you do anything of that kind about then?'

Jacqmin frowned. 'No.'

'It won't take us long to find out if you're lying.'

It was a bluff and Jacqmin fell for it. His face sagged and he nodded.

'All right then,' he admitted grudgingly. 'Yes, I did.'

'What was it?'

'I wouldn't know. It looked like radio. But I'm no expert. There was also a thing that looked like a set of organ pipes.'

The Nebelwerfer, Pel thought. The Double-Edged Sword.

'I had that for nine days,' Jacqmin said. 'I had to work all through every night to get it finished in time. And all the time this type kept telephoning to see if I was through.'

'Which type?'

'The type Rambot brought along. I slept for a week after it was over.'

'What was it, do you think?'

Jacqmin tried a grin, but it was uncertain. 'It could have been a new organ for the cathedral at Royan, for all I know,' he said.

Nobody smiled and his grin died.

'I don't argue,' he went on. 'I can't afford to. There'll be three of us soon and Léonie's – well, you know how women are. She wants the best for the baby. They paid me thirty thousand francs for it. You don't sneeze at that sort of money.

He was trying desperately to excuse himself, but his very protestations proclaimed his guilt. It was clear he'd been well aware that what he'd been working on was dangerous, even if he hadn't known what it was.

'Who brought the plans to you?'

'This type Rambot brought along.'

'Was Rambot there?'

'No. But I think he had something to do with it. There was another type, too. Looked like an officer. Cold, didn't say much. Kept in the background, but I noticed when this type Rambot sent was explaining what he wanted, he kept saying things that sounded pretty technical to me. Things like "We have to have the return springs clearly shown" and "The loading carriage hasn't been made clear." I don't know what he meant but he seemed to know all about the plans. I think he was an officer.'

'So do I,' Pel said. 'And that his name was De Fransecky. He's now doing time for selling naval secrets.'

Jacqmin pulled a face. 'He involved me in that?'

'Didn't you know?'

'No.'

Pel didn't believe him. Jacqmin's conscience was the sort that could always be swept aside when he was in need of money.

'Were any names mentioned?'

'No. Well – they were whispering as I started work. I heard them talking as if other people were involved.'

'But no names?'

'No. Perhaps Rambot's was one of them.'

As Jacqmin stopped there was a long silence, then Pel gestured. 'You'll be staying here for a while,' he said. 'Someone will doubtless come down from Paris to talk to you. I might even say "grill" you. So you'd better be prepared to tell the truth. And when he's finished there'll probably be someone else, well and truly backed by the Surete', who'll come from London. He'll want to talk to you, too.'

'What about?'

'For the love of God,' Darcy snapped. 'A man's been shot! A big boy, too. I think you got yourself into something bigger than you expected, my friend, and those drawings of yours make you an accessory after the fact. We'll need to find out a bit more about you.'

Jacqmin looked uneasy. 'I tell you I didn't know what it was for,' he insisted.

Pel frowned. 'It'll come out in the wash,' he said. 'If there's nothing known about you, you'll probably be allowed out and eventually get a suspended sentence. *Avec sursis.* Conditional on not appearing again. If it turns out differently, it could be a *"fermé"*, which means you'll end up at 72, Rue d'Auxonne, for a while.' He gestured to Darcy. 'Take him away,' he said. 'Identité Judiciaire would like to have him to *passer au piano.*'

Jacqmin looked scared. 'What's that?'

'Have your fingerprints taken.'

As Jacqmin vanished, Pel sat staring at his blotter. After a while, he took out a cigarette, lit it, decided he was being weak again, pinched it out and was about to put it away for later when he decided he was wasting good money and life was too short, anyway, to shorten it further by worrying.

Lighting up again, he sat drawing in the smoke, relaxed, his eyes bright, his mind racing.

Spying was something new for him. But was it *just* spying? That seemed to be over and done with, with the arrest of Capitaine de Corvette de Fransecky. The continued involvement of Jacqmin, however, the drawings he'd been doing, seemed to indicate the affair wasn't finished yet. At the same time, neither De Frobinius nor Fergusson in London had mentioned other secrets that had gone missing. Was it something else? Was he involved with terrorists? Were there to be more assassinations?

He sat frowning for a long time. Terrorism and assassinations weren't quite the normal run of the mill in his area, any more than involvement with spying was. There weren't even any important national figures around who could be hated enough for anyone to wish to kill them. Only income tax inspectors, he remembered, and *they* were liable to assassination any time and anywhere. Yet neither London nor Paris had been forthcoming about where the terror gangs they had referred to were coming from and he had to suppose there were many things for which they had to keep their lips buttoned up.

Yet terrorism couldn't be ruled out. Men like John Ford still occasionally got themselves killed and bombs still went off – the latest, he remembered, in Lyons, which wasn't all that far from his own backyard.

Finding links with terrorism on your own doorstep was always faintly disturbing. Like drugs, they normally belonged in capital cities, where there were ugly suburbs and emotions ran higher, where personalities tended to be more twisted, where psychoses were more involved, and above all where important people came and went. It left him with an uneasy feeling of groping into cotton wool, seeking something yet not quite sure what it was. There seemed little else to do but pursue the enquiries he was already engaged on and hope they produced something that might be of use not only to Fergusson and De Frobinius but also in discovering who had forced Cormon off the road at Destres and thrust the knife in his brain as he struggled to escape.

Frowning, he called for Darcy and gestured at the chair at the opposite side of his desk.

'We've heard a lot about little black boxes,' he said. 'About the size of tape cassettes.' He tapped the newspaper in front of him. 'Bombs,' he said. 'Letter bombs.' He paused and went on slowly. 'This reverser switch of Robinson's: Has someone got hold of it and are they using it to manufacture letter bombs? It would be about the right size, wouldn't it?'

Darcy frowned. 'Cormon, Patron?' he asked.

'It crossed my mind. Let's have another check on him. See what he did with his spare time in addition to losing his money on horses. He went to Paris occasionally. There've been bombs in Paris. Was he supplying the trigger mechanisms? Let's find out if he had any connections with any subversive organisation that might be responsible for this latest rash. After all, Lyons isn't at the other end of the world and they've had them there.'

As Darcy vanished, Misset put his head round the door. 'That Pissarro type, Patron,' he said. 'I've got the report from Durois of the Chamber of Commerce. It seems that he's not quite what he seems to be.'

'What *does* he seem to be?'

'Well, Durois did a quick sniff around and it seems Pissarro's not as wealthy as everybody thinks he is. He has debts.'

'Who doesn't?'

'His are substantial. He also has a woman in Annonay, near St Etienne. Name of Adrienne Morcat, 17, Rue Louis-Vinneroy. It seems also that he's been overspending – '

'Backing his fancy in the Tour de France, doubtless.'

'Not just that, Patron. It seems he likes girls. Any girls. That type has to wear monogrammed pyjamas, so his wife will know when he's in her bed. The general impression is that he's clever all right, but that he's a big talker and enjoys showing off.'

'I think,' Pel said, 'that we'd better go and have another talk with Louis-Napoléon Pissarro. Even his name sounds too good to be true.'

As Misset vanished, the telephone rang. It was the Chief.

'How did your trip to London go?' he asked.

'So-so,' Pel said. 'I'll be putting in a report.'

'I shall want to talk to you about it before then. In the meantime I've something to show you. Just come in here a moment, will you?'

The Chief was standing by his desk when Pel arrived, looking at a small black box from which wires protruded. With him was another man, small and stout and bald.

'This is François Coppet, Pel,' the Chief said. 'When you pay your electricity bill, he's the type who collars the money.' He gestured at the box on the table. 'He brought this in.'

The box meant nothing to Pel and he peered at it uncertainly as if it might leap off the desk and bite him in the leg.

'We were lunching together and got talking,' the Chief went on. 'And this thing cropped up.'

'What is it?'

'I don't know what you'd call it,' Coppet said. 'We haven't given it an official name yet. We call it "Mirror", for reasons I'll explain. We're trying to keep it as quiet as possible.'

'What does it do?'

Coppet smiled. 'It defrauds us. That's what it does.'

The Chief leaned across the desk. 'You'll have read in the paper of these meter frauds, I suppose?'

Pel nodded and Coppet gestured. 'They've been private prosecutions,' he said.

Pel poked at the black box, wondering what it had to do with him.

'We've been having a lot of meters tampered with by householders and apartment owners,' Coppet said. 'It's my job to check these things and track them down. Quite clearly, their meters were being interfered with and we brought them before the courts. Electricity meters, of course, as you'll imagine, are well sealed against people trying to tamper with them if only because of the danger – but we continued to get the frauds, though we never managed to find out how they were worked until recently. Nobody talked. Then two months ago we had a case out at St Antoine-du-Val – a farmer called Defournay. His current usage of electricity was half what it normally is and we investigated. He said it must be a faulty meter and offered to pay anything that was necessary. But his wife took our man on one side and produced this. She was suffering from a crisis of conscience and couldn't hold her tongue any longer. When we tackled her husband, he admitted it was a device for reversing the meter.'

Pel's head jerked up. '*Reversing* it?'

'Back to half of what he'd used. Since he normally had a heavy load, we were already suspicious.'

'You'd think he'd have a bit more sense,' the Chief said. 'A little less, and he could have argued they were economising.'

'Well – ' Coppet shrugged ' – the device seems to be not all that easy to control. It turns the meter back pretty fast, you know. In effect, with this thing they can actually put it into reverse. It's what I would call an extremely sophisticated device. And it's not the only one. We've discovered several others, all more or less based on the same principle. There'll be other prosecutions.'

'How does it work?'

Coppet smiled. 'That's something I'd rather not reveal. We're keeping it secret for obvious reasons and we decided to give it the code name, Mirror, so that nothing's given away. Enquiries are being made by our investigators all over the country. Somebody's been flooding the rural areas with these things and they're so simple we obviously can't reveal details.'

Pel poked at the black box. 'Much loss of revenue?' he asked.

'About twenty million francs,' Coppet said. 'Apart from that, the public should be warned about the extreme danger of electrocution that exists. You don't tamper with all that many volts without danger. In the north of France fifty-six thousand spot checks have been carried out in a twelve-month period and at least two thousand cases have been reported. In Defournay's case, the reading had been reversed by eleven kilowatts an hour. That means, if you ran twenty-two single-bar fires for an hour there would be a nil reading on the meter with one of these things attached.'

Pel was growing interested and his eyes were sharp and shrewd. 'This man you found with it – Defournay – where did he get it?'

'He said it was brought to him by a man who used to work for him. I don't believe him, of course. I think it was the man who's making them. He attached it to the meter on four or five days every month. The rest of the time he kept it hidden in the barn.'

Pel's nose was within inches of the black box now and Coppet laughed.

'Don't get too near it,' he said. 'If I attached it to your watch it would start it going backwards.'

'You've been worried by gadgets, haven't you, Pel?' the Chief asked. 'Are you interested?'

'Yes.' Pel nodded, his mind ticking away like a time bomb. 'In fact, I'd like to borrow that for a while, collect Darcy and go to see this farmer of yours to find out where he got it?'

'Can you?'

Pel sniffed. 'I ought to be able to,' he said.

sixteen

Defournay was a short, sturdy man whose farm was situated at the bottom of the slope at St Antoine. It didn't look a particularly efficient farm. The buildings were ramshackle, the fences were broken and the stone buildings in need of repair.

'You'd better come in,' he said heavily.

As they sat at the kitchen table, Madame Defournay produced a bottle of white wine and glasses, and they stared at the black box Pel had placed on the table.

'I told him not to touch it,' she said. 'But he wouldn't listen.'

'Be quiet, woman,' Defournay growled. 'I didn't realise it would work as it did. I didn't intend the damn clock to go racing backwards like that, I thought we could just say we'd been economising. Save a few francs.'

'It's still dishonest.'

'Yes – well –' Defournay scowled and started to light a pipe. 'Everybody tries to do the government down, don't they, Inspector?'

Pel lit a cigarette and sat back. 'Where did you get it?' he asked.

'This type came round with it.'

'Which type?'

Defournay shrugged. 'I don't know his name. He showed me how to attach it and switch it on. I didn't believe him. So he made it work and, sure enough, the meter went into reverse.' Defournay sighed. 'He must have been cleverer with it than I was, though, because when I did it, it raced back as if it had gone mad.'

'Have any of your friends got any of these things?'

Defournay was wary. 'I know of one or two.'

'Then,' Pel said, 'you'd better advise them to get rid of them quickly. The authorities are on to them and anybody who seems to be using less current than he was last year will be investigated pretty sharply.'

Madame Defournay nodded and Defournay gave her a sullen look.

'You could have gone to prison,' she said. 'Instead of just a fine.'

'Not if I'd learned to use it properly,' Defournay grumbled. 'They haven't found old –' he stopped dead and gave a sheepish grin ' – not yet, anyway. I'll go and tell him this evening.'

Pel didn't smile. 'I think you'd better,' he said.

Defournay leaned across the table, his lined face interested. 'It's clever, though, isn't it?' he said. 'How does it work?'

'I don't know,' Pel admitted. 'And if I did I wouldn't tell you. Neither would the electricity authorities. It obviously wouldn't be a good idea.'

'Have you come to arrest me?'

'I've come to find out where you got it.'

'This type came. I told you.'

'What did he tell you about it?'

'He called it a reverser. He said it would reverse the current or something so that it flowed the other way. Perhaps that's not what he meant but I'm no electrician. He told me to attach it at odd times and not to do it all at once.'

'How much did you pay him?'

'Five hundred francs. It seemed a lot but he said they weren't cheap to make, but that the price would be saved in two quarterly bills.' Defournay grinned. 'If I hadn't been caught, it would, too.'

'And he never mentioned his name?'

'Would *you*? I think he wanted to keep it dark.'

'Suppose it had gone wrong? How could you have got in touch with him?'

'That was a chance I had to take. He wasn't risking his neck, I suppose. At first I thought I'd been a fool and there'd been some sleight of hand or something, but when I attached it, it worked. I didn't argue. Not then, anyway.'

'Was his name Cormon?' Pel asked.

'He never mentioned his name.'

Pel gestured and Darcy fished in his briefcase to produce a copy of the picture he'd taken from Madame Clarétie's sideboard.

'That him?'

Defournay studied the picture. 'It might be. It's always difficult in black and white. He had a reddish face. It doesn't show here. And his hair was fair.'

'Fair hair often shows dark in a black and white picture,' Darcy pointed out.

'Then it could be him. Except that he looks younger in that.'

'He *was* younger in this,' Darcy said. 'It was taken ten years ago.'

As they headed back towards the car, Pel lit a cigarette, offered one to Darcy, and stopped to light them. Dragging the smoke down to the soles of his shoes, he let it leak slowly out, then, coughing like a tubercular in the last stages, he waved his hand as it hung about his head and gestured at Coppet's black box.

'Are you thinking what I'm thinking?' he wheezed.

'I think so, Patron,' Darcy said.

'Gadgets.' Pel's breath gradually returned. 'Robinson's reversals. It's quite a nice-looking little gadget, isn't it? A reversing gadget. Properly made. Neat plastic case. Dial. Everything. Not home-made.'

'Do you think Robinson was making them, Patron?'

'No.' Pel shook his head. 'But I think Pissarro might have been.'

When they returned to the Hôtel de Police, however, and Darcy made a discreet telephone enquiry for Pissarro at his works, he learned that he wasn't there.

'He left early.'

'Where for?'

'Home, I suppose.'

Trying Pissarro's home, they were answered by his wife. There was the sound of children's voices in the background and constant cries of '*Tais-toi!*' from her as she told them to be quiet.

'He's away on business,' she said.

'Where, Madame? Do you know? This is Produits Mercurie. We have a query.'

'I'll make a note and let him know you rang. I expect he'll be in touch. He'll be home before the weekend. He's gone to St Etienne. He has a customer there.'

Darcy put the telephone down and looked at Pel. 'He's gone to see his *poule*, Patron,' he said. 'That Madame Morcat.'

Pel smiled. 'He might get a surprise tomorrow when we turn up. In the meantime let's have a watch placed on his house in case he returns unexpectedly. Who've we got?'

'There's Lagé and Misset. Nosjean could help at a pinch.'

'Leave Nosjean,' Pel said. 'He's busy. Get Misset and Lagé on the job. Then see the Chief and tell him what we're up to and ask if we can borrow from Inspector Goriot's squad. You and I'll interrupt Pissarro's tête-à-tête with Madame Morcat in the morning.'

As they left the office, the telephone rang. His feet aching, Lagé had just entered with another batch of pictures. He had long since come to the conclusion that taking photographs in hot streets was a mug's game. In fact, he was beginning to wonder what he ever saw in photography. It was expensive, the equipment he carried was heavy, and at his age he'd have been much wiser going fishing.

He listened to the telephone ringing for a while, trying his best to ignore it, but he was too conscientious and in the end he picked it up.

The voice at the other end belonged to a police sous-brigadier called Quiriton who was ringing from St Denis-sur -Aube, and Lagé hadn't the slightest idea what he was talking about.

'I don't know anything about a yellow Passat estate,' he said. 'Whose is it? Has it been stolen?' The telephone clattered in his ear again and Lagé allowed his photographic equipment to slide from his shoulder to the table. 'Hang on, I'll make a note of it. What are you ringing about? We haven't lost a yellow – '

He felt the telephone gently removed from his hand and looked up to see Nosjean.

'It's mine,' Nosjean said.

As Lagé thankfully disappeared to the dark room, Nosjean listened quietly.

'Thank God there's somebody there who knows what I'm talking about,' Quiriton said. 'Was it you who was enquiring about a yellow Passat estate?'

'Yes, it was. You found it?'

'No.' The man at the other end of the wire laughed. 'But one of my men reported a car similar to the one you want round here.'

The arrest of Jacqmin and his own connection with it had involved Nosjean in a great deal of work, so that he'd almost forgotten the châteaux thieves. Now, however, he was on the alert at once. 'When?' he said.

'Two nights ago. I've just seen his report.'

'Get the number?'

'No.'

'Naturally.' Nosjean felt bitter.

'Hang on a minute,' Quiriton protested. 'He wasn't all that stupid. He'd been out on a break-in at the pharmacy at Liffol. Kids after drugs, I think. It's easier to pick them up at country pharmacies than in the town. He was there until late and was returning home at one in the morning when this Passat came out of a side turning, nearly hit him, and shot past. He cursed a bit but didn't intend to do anything about it – after all, there hadn't been an accident – then he remembered we'd been told to look out for a yellow Passat estate, and the lateness of the hour made him wonder. You don't get many cars at that hour round Liffol – there's nothing to take them there – so he decided to chase it. But by the time he'd turned, it was out of sight, and he never saw it again. It must have nipped down one of the side lanes.'

'No identifying marks?'

'He noticed it had some big dents in it. The front was bashed in and there was another mark on the side. Different ages, as if the owner was a bad driver and made a habit of running into things.'

'Well, that's a help. Did he see who was in it?'

'He thought a kid with long hair. Said it looked a bit like a mop.'

'That all?'

'That's all.'

The description didn't seem to fit Pierrot-le-Pourri, his friend, Poupon, or anybody else Nosjean had been investigating either.

'Have you got any *châeaux classés* round there?' he asked.

'We've got Lebouchon-Roy.'

'Big?'

'Yes.'

'Anything valuable in it?'

'I wouldn't know.' Quiriton chuckled. 'The only antique I know anything about is my grandmother's armchair which is in my parlour. It's not pretty but it's damn comfortable. I can find out.'

'Don't bother.' Nosjean was wondering whether he ought to go down to St Denis but he decided in the end that the fact that a yellow Passat was around didn't really mean a thing.

'Look,' he said. 'I have to slip to Paris. There are a couple of bright boys I'm watching there, I'll go and check on their alibis. It doesn't sound like them, but you never know. If you spot this car again or anything suspicious, let me know. In the meantime, keep your eye on the château.'

seventeen

Pissarro was in the garden of Number 17, Rue Louis-Vinneroy, at Annonay when Pel and Darcy arrived. He was
standing among the rose bushes with the heavy horn-handled
knife they'd seen him use for pruning at his home, cutting
blooms for the woman who stood alongside him. She was a
languid blonde past her prime and she held a shallow
gardener's trug in which she was laying the roses that Pissarro
cut. They assumed she was Madame Morcat and the scene
was one of rustic charm. It didn't impress Pel much.

As the car drew up, out of the comer of his eye, he saw
Pissarro spot him. Abruptly, his face changed and, turning,
his head down between his shoulders, he began to push
further into the rose bushes. Pel went after him like a dog
after a rabbit, the woman watching, startled, from the door
of the house. As he drew nearer, Pissarro, aware that he'd
been seen, put on an elaborate show of innocent affection,
plucking petals from a rose and beaming at the woman as he
dropped them to the ground.

'*Je t'aime.*' A petal fluttered from his hand. '*Beaucoup.*'
Another petal twisted down. '*Passionnement.*' A third left his
fingers. '*A la folie.*' The next petal was plucked with a
gesture. '*Pas du tout.*' He glanced at the woman, pulled a
face and went on faster. '*Je t'aime. Beaucoup. Passionnement.*' He stopped at last, dropped the ruined rose to the
ground and called out. 'I love you passionately, *chérie.*'

As Pel appeared alongside him, popping up from among the roses like the devil through a trapdoor in a ballet, he affected a start. His smile had enough gold in it to be dazzling.

'Inspector Pel!' Slowly the smile grew wider and more confident. 'Fancy seeing you here!'

Pel gave his imitation of a snake about to strike. 'Fancy seeing *you* here,' he replied. He glanced at the woman. 'A business associate?' he suggested.

Somewhat uneasily, Pissarro introduced her. 'Madame Adrienne Morcat,' he said. 'An old friend of mine.'

'So I've heard,' Pel smiled. 'And of Madame Pissarro's too?'

Pissarro's smile dried up. 'Well, ah – no,' he said. 'Not exactly. We're just old friends. Known each other for years. Long before I was married.' The walls were trembling with his efforts to convince.

As Pel watched him, unconvinced, Pissarro put on another big show of innocence. 'We were just discussing the chances of our team in the Tour de France, Inspector.

'*Our* team?'

'Madame Morcat is the widow of Martin Morcat, who owned Plastiques St Etienne. A small firm, which is included in the *"Touts Produits"* title, which covers all the other firms helping to finance our team. Pis-Hélio-Tout, you'll remember. "Pis" for Pissarro, "Helio" for Héliogravure Sud.' He was talking at full speed, as if he hoped that by doing so he could stop Pel asking questions. 'Everybody talks about the Tour de France, of course, at this time, don't they?'

'I don't,' Pel said, his voice as flat as a smack across the chops.

Pissarro tried to struggle on a little longer. He gestured at the paper lying on the terrasse. 'After all, it's an industry, isn't it?' he said. 'It requires seventeen hundred regular employees, a changing work force of eight hundred new personnel a day, four thousand police at bridges, roads and sprint areas, three hundred vehicles, seventy motor cycles, two helicopters, an entire fleet of radio planes to relay television and press reports, and media coverage greater than the Paris Peace Conference. The only comparable organisation was D-Day.'

'It also,' Pel said coldly, 'disrupts traffic, ruins the journeys of thousands of totally uninterested people and disorganises the forces of law and order which could be better used in stamping out crime.'

Pissarro made a last despairing effort. 'I hope you've got your money on our man, Maryckx,' he said. 'He's going to be the winner, you know.'

'He's not lying anywhere near the front, I notice,' Pel said.

Pissarro managed a weak smile. 'Well, he's hardly an "untouchable" but he's splendid in the mountains and he's got the deep chest of a sprinter. It's the purest sport in the world, cycle racing – a man on a shiny steed alone. It's like the old knights in armour again. He'll pull up, you see.'

'He's got a long way to go,' Pel pointed out.

Pissarro smiled and shrugged. 'Well, perhaps we're just deluding ourselves,' he admitted. 'Perhaps we shall lose a little money on the deal. But, let's face it, Van der Essen or Filou might well be using one of our sprockets. I shall be at the feeding point at Boine to cheer them past.'

He gestured towards a chair, his face a mask of affability, snapped the horn-handled knife shut and slipped it into his pocket before sitting down and giving up the struggle. 'Still, I don't suppose you've come here to talk about the Tour de France,' he said. 'What can I do for you?'

'Just a little talk, Monsieur,' Pel said patiently. 'Preferably in private. I'm sure it can be arranged.'

Pissarro turned to Madame Morcat who was watching from the door. '*Ma chérie,*' he said. 'Business.'

As she headed into the house, Pissarro gestured at the bottles on the terrasse. 'A drink, Inspector?'

'Not on duty, Monsieur.'

As they sat down, behind Pissarro's head Pel saw a line of ducks trudging across the wall. In the corner was a tiny butterfly with a broken wing.

'Nice picture,' he observed.

'Yes.' Pissarro smiled. 'I had it done as a birthday present.'

'By Maurice Jacqmin?'

'Who, Inspector?' Pissarro's face was blank.

'Maurice Jacqmin. Sometimes known as Jean Casse-le-Papillon.'

Pissarro gave a shrug. 'I don't know, Inspector. I don't know his name.'

'But you said you commissioned it. Surely you must have chosen the artist.'

'Well, no.' Pissarro looked uncomfortable. 'I had a Swiss friend, you see, whose work I admired, and thought he could do the job. But he insisted he never did that sort of thing and promised to find someone in his place. This fellow turned up. That's how it happened.'

'Did you never find out what his name was?'

'Er – no. Never.'

Pel studied the picture. 'How much did it cost? I'm a great admirer of art but I can never afford it.'

'Oh –' Pissarro gestured airily ' – two or three thousand francs. I'm not certain now. It's been there some time.'

'Expensive,' Pel observed. 'Pay cash?'

'No, the usual way –' Pissarro stopped dead and Pel smiled.

'Cheque?' he said. 'Then how did you make it out if you didn't know his name?'

Pissarro floundered and finally came up with the story that he'd paid his Swiss friend who had then paid the artist. Pel didn't believe that either.

'Name?' he asked.

'Of whom?'

'The Swiss friend.'

'I forget now.'

'But you commissioned the picture through him?'

Pissarro's mouth opened and shut. 'It's some time ago now, of course,' he managed. 'You can't expect me, with all the things I have to carry in my head about business, to remember things like that.'

There was a long silence in which Pissarro hurriedly rose and poured himself a drink. Pel watched him, his eyes icy. As Pissarro sat down again, he leaned forward.

'We're interested in some of the gadgets you've been making,' he went on. 'Ever make anything concerned with reversing electric current?'

Pissarro took a lot of pains to appear deep in thought. 'Not to my knowledge. Why?'

'I had occasion yesterday to inspect a device which seems to have been appearing in large numbers in the north of France.'

Darcy had quietly appeared and seated himself alongside Pel. Pissarro didn't seem to notice.

'It seems to have been used in the north rather than around here,' Pel went on. 'For purposes of security, I imagine. It's a device that's been troubling the electricity authorities for some time, a device for reversing electricity meters to produce a considerable reduction in the current used, a device to defraud that has caused the electricity authorities a great deal of concern. It interests me for a different reason.'

Pissarro frowned. 'And you wish to ask my advice about it?'

'More than that,' Pel said smoothly. 'The man who sold the one I saw yesterday seems to have been Claude-Achille Cormon, lately in your employ.'

Pissarro looked startled. 'Cormon? Good God! I knew he was a funny chap but I didn't think he was dishonest.'

'He'd been in prison,' Darcy said. 'He also only recently left your employ and found work with an Englishman who runs a small factory at Montbard. A man called Robinson, trading as Accessoires Montbard.'

'I've never heard of him.'

'He's not very important,' Pel admitted. 'Except to us. One of the things he's engaged in making is a gadget in use in electric lifts and single-handed sailing. A device that can reverse things electronically. So that a rising lift could be made to descend. So that a sailing vessel on a starboard tack could be brought on to the port tack. You understand me?'

'Of course, of course.' Pissarro was all ears. 'It sounds fascinating.'

'It does indeed. It occurs to me that your former employee, Cormon, saw possibilities in this device and managed to steal one. He then, I suspect, made a mock-up of the device I saw yesterday and tried it himself before eventually manufacturing a similar device in numbers. The authorities are worried. So are the police. Whoever made them is likely to be the subject of prosecution.'

Pissarro was looking nervous suddenly. 'It's a good job in a way that he's dead,' he said slowly. He paused. 'I don't mean that exactly, of course. What I meant was – well, the disgrace. That sort of thing. Making electrical devices at home to defraud the authorities.'

'He couldn't have made at home the device I saw yester-day,' Pel said quietly. 'It was a complicated affair inside a sophisticated black box.'

There was a long pause. Pel and Darcy were both closely watching Pissarro.

'*Could* Cormon have made these devices?' Darcy asked.

'Oh, most certainly. He was quite capable, I imagine.'

'Could he have made them at your place?'

Pissarro paused. 'It's possible, of course. People who have benches, drills, lathes, saws and soldering equipment will always use them for their own purposes. It's one of the perks of the trade. The number of cigarette lighters that are made must be enormous. When I did my military training, I was in the workshops and everybody was making them. The case of a cannon shell made a splendid desk lighter. A 303 cartridge case made an excellent pocket lighter. You must be aware of it.'

'I am,' Pel said quietly.

'Well –' Pissarro seemed to be talking for the sake of talking ' – as you can imagine, television switches are repaired when they go wrong. Radios are fixed. Bills are high and they're bound to take advantage of the situation. Chiefly in their lunch hour – ' he smiled ' – or when they're supposed to be doing overtime. I'm not always there, of course, and even if I were, I don't see everything, and they each have a drawer for their private equipment. Things can disappear pretty quickly into a drawer. They're all at it, I'm sure. Even the foreman – '

Pel held up a hand to stop the flood of information on the iniquities of the working population of the Republic. 'But Cormon was no longer in your employ,' he pointed out. 'He left you some months ago.'

Pissarro pulled a face. 'He must still have had friends at my place. He probably contacted one of them and got him to make these things for him.'

'I would suggest it's probably more sophisticated than that. That it would need careful work, not merely a little after hours or in the lunch break. It wasn't made with your approval, was it?'

Pissarro gestured feebly. 'Why do you ask?'

Pel nodded at the painting on the wall. 'The man who painted that – and I know exactly who it was, Monsieur – was approached by Cormon to draw a device that was brought to him. One of Accessoires Montbard's gadgets, I suspect. Doubtless Cormon "borrowed" it long enough to have it copied and then returned it. Then, with the drawing, the dimensions, et cetera, and with his own skill, he got his sophisticated device made to defraud the electricity authorities. Probably with the help of a man called Rambot.'

There was a pause and Pel looked hard at Pissarro, 'Ever met a man called Rambot?' he asked, 'He looks like Darcy here.'

Pissarro shook his head, 'Never. What is he? A manufacturer?'

'We don't know what he is. We'd like to know. He sounds interesting.'

'I've never heard of him. How does he come into it?'

'He also contacted your artist friend to have some drawings made. Perhaps for the same device. Perhaps something else. We'd like to know. It could have been the sort of thing that appears in a letter bomb.'

Pissarro shook his head, a pained expression on his face. 'What are you suggesting?'

'I was wondering if your association with Maurice Jacqmin went as far as Cormon's. And Rambot's.'

Pissarro looked indignant. 'In the name of God,' he said. 'I wouldn't do a thing like that! I'm a straightforward man.'

Looking at the painting on the wall and at Madame Morcat who was moving about inside the house, Pel felt he had good reason to doubt the statement.

eighteen

From Annonay they drove towards Rambillard to see Robinson. Though Pissarro wasn't aware of it, Madame Morcat's house was already being placed under surveillance. A short conference with the Commissaire at Annonay had made it possible.

'Leave it to me,' he said. 'We'll keep tabs on him.'

For a while in the car, Pel was silent. When he spoke, it was slowly, as if he were chasing ideas through the busy channels of his mind.

'Did you check on Cormon's background?' he asked.

'Yes, Patron.' Darcy kept his eyes on the road. 'We'd already done it once, of course, and found nothing. This time I concentrated on his political views. He seems to have been Leftish – but never enough to be Left. He wasn't a communist or anything like that. Just a sort of pink socialist. I've found provincials tend not to be too definite in their views.'

'Belong to any organisations?'

'Only a union. Nothing else. Doesn't seem to have been to any political meetings or anything of that nature. Of course – ' Darcy shrugged ' – he'd hardly let it be obvious if he belonged to something subversive, would he?'

At Rambillard, Doctor Robinson met them with what appeared to he genuine pleasure.

'Inspector Pel,' he yelled. 'Come in! Come in! And Sergeant Darcy, too! What joy! You're staying to lunch, of course! I'll

182

see my wife and arrange it all if you'll just hang on a moment!'

As they awaited Robinson's return, Pel decided that the British had let him down badly in recent weeks. He'd always thought them boorish and humourless, standing about in draughty country houses, wearing checked caps like plates, accompanied by dozens of dogs and possessing wives as flat as boards and about as interesting, to say nothing of eating food which wasn't fit to give to the pigs. He could see he would have to reconsider his position.

Sitting behind a pernod big enough to drown a cat in, he explained what they were after. He described the investigation into Cormon's death, and Jacqmin's connection, and voiced the suspicion without mentioning any names that the electrical reversing devices that had been found were being manufactured within a hundred kilometres of Montbard.

Robinson listened carefully, not attempting to interrupt until Pel finished.

'I would suggest, Inspector,' he said slowly as Pel sat back, 'that you make a few enquiries round the works of one Louis-Napoléon Pissarro.'

Pel sat bolt upright. 'You've had problems before with this Pissarro?' he asked.

'I know very well that one of my gadgets turned up in television sets manufactured in Lyons and when I enquired I traced it back to Pissarro.'

'Did you now?' Pel said thoughtfully. 'Was that after Cormon came to work for you?'

'No. Before. I wouldn't like to suggest that the thing was deliberately copied. But there *are* pirates who copy things – everything from films, books, tapes and gadgets of a minor nature. They're covered, of course, but it's very difficult to prove they've been copied because it's always possible for two people to have the same idea – or even for someone to have an idea put into his head by something he's read or seen

– without being aware it's already covered by a patent or a copyright.'

'Have you ever been contacted by this man called Rambot you saw with Cormon?'

'No. And the name means nothing.'

'He could have used an alias, I suppose. We've learned a bit about him.'

Robinson shook his head. 'Who is he?'

'We haven't got that far yet. Probably some sort of industrial spy. Perhaps more than that. Are you manufacturing anything at this moment that Cormon might have copied while in your employ? Something he might have been able to remove for a day or two, perhaps, without being noticed and then returned? An important part of one of your inventions?'

Robinson suddenly became blank-faced. 'I've turned out nothing new for a long time,' he said. 'Not since I made the reverser switch.'

Pel explained the electrical fraud device. 'Could that have been part of your device?' he asked. 'Could Cormon have stolen part of your reverser – the main part – and fitted it into this device he built to defraud the electricity authorities?'

Robinson frowned. He looked worried. 'It's possible,' he said.

'What about bombs?'

'Bombs?' Robinson looked startled.

'Letter bombs. There've been a few about lately. Could your switch device have been used in some way?'

Robinson looked even more startled, then he frowned and was silent for a while, considering the possibilities. 'It could have,' he admitted. 'It's got a tumbler device inside that wouldn't require much to be made into a trigger mechanism.'

'Is it something a good instrument maker could do?'

'Most certainly.'

'Cormon?'

'I should think so. On the other hand – '

'On the other hand, what, Monsieur?'

Robinson drew a deep breath. 'I'm rather concerned,' he said. 'I'd better explain.'

He poured more drinks. 'Lately I've only been doing private work in my workshop here. I told you about it. It's secret and I have only one helper, a man called Cortes who's been with me for thirty years. I've been working on something rather serious and even with him I permit him to see only part of it at a time. I have the only key to my workshop so no one can get in when I'm not here to supervise.'

'Do your people at Montbard know about this new thing you're working on?'

'No. Cortes does, of course. Or at least I'm sure he has an idea. He's not stupid. But only small parts of it were manufactured at Montbard, though I suppose it's possible to put two and two together and come up with some sort of answer. But I was always careful to give the prototypes to different people and at different times so they didn't have a clear picture. However, they might have talked. Rivard, for instance, is a sharp young man. Sometimes, I think a little *too* sharp. He may have come to some conclusion.'

'What is this thing you're working on, Doctor? May we know?'

Robinson hesitated then he shrugged. 'It's a government-backed idea,' he said. 'I should say a *British* government-backed idea, though the French government's involved, too. I do the work here because it's well away from prying eyes and, since all documents and letters are in English, it's kept more secret. When I was in London last year I saw possibilities for my reverser that had never occurred to me before and I took the idea along to the Government. The Ministry of Defence to be exact. There were talks. The last time in April. I was taken to see various scientists, manufacturers and government advisers and eventually I was told to go ahead.

Cash was provided. It's been going forward since then like a steam train.'

Pel paused. 'Have you ever met a man by the name of John Ford, Doctor?' he asked suddenly.

Robinson frowned. 'The man who was shot in Paris?' he said.

'Exactly.'

Robinson's frown grew deeper. 'I've met him,' he admitted. 'But I didn't know him by *that* name. He was one of the men in England I had talks with. About my idea.'

'What is it, Doctor? Some sort of secret weapon?'

'No.' Robinson seemed reluctant to answer. 'Do you have to know?'

'It would help,' Pel said. 'I think you can trust us. If you prefer, however, I could arrange for someone to come down from Paris. A man by the name of De Frobinius, with whom I've been working.'

Robinson frowned and thought for a moment. 'I know De Frobinius,' he said. 'He's Ford's opposite number in this country.' He drew a deep breath. 'I think I'd better tell you everything, Inspector, without, of course, giving you the details. You might say my idea is a counter to an already-established weapon, the guided missile.' He paused and lit a cigarette as they waited patiently. 'You might even say it's a device to effect the reversal of computors.'

There was a long silence. Pel was a little out of his depths but he was beginning to realise that whatever it was Robinson was engaged on was important.

'Perhaps you don't realise the implications of that,' Robinson went on. 'Most major weapons these days are worked by computors, which work out range, speed, et cetera. Torpedoes. Air-to-air, air-to-ground and ground-to-air missiles. Even artillery. Practically everything bigger than small arms. I was an artilleryman in the war and I learned a lot about it, particularly as, by then, artillery ranging was already being done mechanically. Do you see what I'm getting at?'

Pel was beginning to.

'My gadget,' Robinson went on, 'won't exactly reverse an artillery shell so that it'll turn round and head back to the gun which fired it. Any more than it will return a computor-directed enemy missile to its base.' He grinned suddenly. 'That would be quite a feat, I think. But an inter-continental ballistic missile hurtling through the stratosphere suddenly headed back to where it had been launched would have quite an effect on war, wouldn't it?'

Darcy whistled. *'Formidable,'* he said.

Robinson smiled. 'Exactly. *Formidable.* My device isn't as big as that yet. But I feel – and the British government feels – that even if we couldn't return a missile to its base, if it were computor-directed we could turn it back to the country of its origin. There are already counter-measures, naturally, but none of them as simple, small and lightweight as the one I'm working on. Of course, my device is only a small part of a much more sophisticated affair which is being developed by Sud Aviation in France and General Electric in England. It fits into a complicated switch system which is attached to a much larger protected-computor autopilot system. We think it will do exactly what we expect it to do.' Robinson gave a shy smile and rubbed his shapeless nose. 'I might add, Inspector, as you seem to know, that this was the reason for the recent meeting between the heads of state. You might say it's top-level material.'

As Robinson finished, Pel sat in silence for a moment. 'It occurs to me, Doctor,' he said eventually, 'that you ought to have some sort of guard here.'

Robinson smiled. 'That would be the one thing to draw attention to us,' he said. 'And that's the one thing I don't want. I feel very firm about it.'

'But if this thing, this valuable thing, disappeared, a great deal's lost. Has anyone heard of it?'

Robinson smiled. 'I suspect someone has. These things get around, you know. People in government are often indiscreet and a whisper spreads.'

'Has anyone ever tried to steal it?'

'Once. Someone got into my workshop here. It was quite obvious they'd been looking for it, from the way things had been scattered around and drawers opened.'

'You're certain it was this device of yours they were after?'

Robinson gave a neigh of laughter. 'There's nothing else,' he said. 'Nothing of any real value at all. It could only have been that.'

'How did they effect entry?'

'With a key, I imagine.'

'I thought you had the only one.'

'I have, and, of course, I immediately changed the lock and took extra precautions because there was no sign of forcible entry. The door was unlocked and wide open when Cortes arrived the next morning.'

'But they didn't get it?'

Robinson gave his neigh of a laugh again. 'It was in April and that was when I went to England. I took it with me, as well as all the papers.'

As they drove away, Pel was deep in thought.

The business was growing complicated. What had started with an art theft at St Sauvigny seemed to have turned into a murder enquiry, and from that into some sort of underhand espionage deal – international or at the very least industrial – with another murder in Paris.

Who was behind it? He dismissed Madame Clarétie at once despite the large knife Darcy had seen in her hand when he'd visited her. She somehow seemed unconnected with the affair save for her relationship to Cormon. Was it Pissarro? He seemed active enough, but there seemed an awful lot lacking in him, as if most of it was pure show, put on to please other people and boost his own ego. But under the bounce, was he really just a straw man? Jacqmin? His feet, legs and eyes seemed to preclude murder, but Pel had found, in fact, that physical disability was barely a draw-back if someone really wanted to kill. Rivard, Robinson's manager at Montbard? If nothing else, he had the drive to be dishonest and, Pel suspected, he was already cheating Robinson in a few small ways.

And how were all the enquiries connected? Because they seemed somehow – by some sort of tenuous thread held chiefly, it seemed, by Jacqmin – to *be* connected. Cormon's murder seemed somehow to be attached through Jacqmin to the murder in Paris. But Jacqmin's knife, according to the Lab, hadn't a trace of human blood on it, let alone blood of Cormon's group. Was it the knife that had been used? Was there another knife?

For a long time Pel said nothing, smoking one cigarette after another, his dark eyes sharp, his mind busy enough for him not to notice the speed at which Darcy drove. After a while, he sat up.

'We're on an international level now,' he said abruptly. 'It's clear Cormon stole the gadget that works Robinson's reverser switch to make the device for defrauding the electrical authorities. Then, at some point, perhaps with information fed to him by someone we don't know – this De Fransecky or Rambot, whoever he is – he tried to get hold of the new gadget Robinson's working on. It must have been Cormon. He'd got his baccalaureat in locksmithing. He could open any door. Then, either because he knew too much or because he was scared, they got rid of him. Somebody forced him off the road on the slope down to Destres.'

'And when they went down to make sure he was dead, they were horrified to see him crawl out of the wreckage.'

'Exactly.' Pel lit a cigarette and drew a deep breath. 'Our friend Robinson *needs* a guard, I think.'

'He said he didn't want one, Patron.'

'He's going to get one all the same. I'll get the Chief to see him. If necessary, the people in Paris. Somebody's already had a try for his gadget. We can't take a chance on them having another go.'

He was silent for a moment, studying his cigarette. 'It leaves you a little scared at the size of it, doesn't it?' he said.

He was beginning by this time to see the importance of the meeting he'd had in London. Someone at the other side of the Channel – even someone on his own side, if the speed with which he'd been sent to London were considered – had seen the connection between Robinson and the shooting of Ford in Paris, and was wondering how much the enemies of the West were involved.

'It seems to me,' Pel went on, 'that this mysterious Rambot who keeps popping up's the key figure.'

'Think he belongs to the other side?' Darcy asked.

Pel sniffed. 'I'm beginning to wonder,' he said.

At about the time Pel and Darcy were leaving Rambillard, Nosjean was hearing once more from Sous-Brigadier Quiriton at St Denis-sur-Aube.

'It's been seen again!' he yelled excitedly down the telephone. 'Just now!'

'What's been seen?'

'The yellow Passat! Here! In this village!'

'Get the number?'

'No! In God's name, this damned vehicle's more elusive than a spectre! I saw it shoot past the window, going out of the village towards the south. Same one. Dent on the side. Front bashed in. There was a dent at the back, too, just for your information. I rushed out to get the number but the bastard had just shot round the corner. I got my car out and shot off after it, but it had already gone. It disappears faster than a rat up a drain. Whoever's driving it *must* be up to something, to disappear that fast.'

'Same driver?'

'Same driver. Mop of hair. I didn't see his face, just this mop of hair. Looked like a kid. Tall but slim with a small head, shoulders and jaw.'

'What colour was his hair?'

'Could have been anything. Dark. Red. Mousy. Blond. I don't know. It moved too fast and the shadow inside the car made it just look dark. I got two of my boys out at once in their car but we didn't find it.'

Nosjean thumped the desk with his fist in his anger and frustration. 'They've got their eyes on Lebuchon-Roy,' he said. 'I'd bet my wages on it.'

'That's what it looks like.'

'But we can't watch the place everlastingly.'

'Hang on,' Quiriton said. 'I haven't finished yet. I think it's tonight. Or tomorrow. Or sometime soon, anyway.'

'Why?'

'*We've* done a bit of sniffing as well as you.' Quiriton sounded pleased with himself. 'I've just been to have a talk with the *gardien*. There was a party round here yesterday. Private party. Antique dealers, decorators and students. It seems some of the questions were about chairs. Boulard? – is that the name? – Boulard chairs?'

'Go on.' Nosjean was growing excited.

'The *gardien* was cagey and he didn't give anything away. He's not exactly bright but he was clever enough to remember that.'

'Did he describe the type who asked the questions?'

'Yes. Small. Bit effeminate. Smart-suited. Little beard and whiskers.'

'It sounds like Pierrot-le-Pourri,' Nosjean said. 'Can we raise a few men?'

Quiriton laughed, clearly delighted with himself. 'I'm sure we can and I'm sure we will. It's the most exciting thing that's happened in St Denis since the butcher's shop caught fire. I can raise five, but I can get one or two from Barrois and some from Fricourt-le-Duc. Are you expecting a break-in?'

'It begins to look like it,' Nosjean admitted. 'I'll come down. Perhaps they're getting greedy, because it isn't very long since the last one at the Manoire de Marennes. Perhaps they think they're cleverer than the poor old flatfoots.'

The sous-brigadier laughed again. 'A lot of people think that,' he said. 'They're not always right.'

'Let's see what we can do, shall we?' Nosjean said. 'I'll check up on my types in Paris and see if they have an alibi for when you saw the Passat, then I'll come down and join you.'

As Quinton rang off, Nosjean dialled Pierrot-le-Pourri's number in Paris.

The sound of the bell was answered immediately and to Nosjean's surprise it was Pierrot-le-Pourri himself who answered. Surprised, Nosjean talked for a while then suggested that he'd like to talk to Poupon, Pierrot's sidekick.

'Of course, *chéri*,' Pierrot gurgled. 'He's right here beside me.' The voice grew fainter. 'The sergeant wants to talk to you, darling. Hurry up, do.'

Poupon's voice came on the wire. There was no mistaking it, and Nosjean frowned.

'Do you mind hurrying, dear,' Poupon said. 'We're just on our way to the Bobino. We got a party up. All our friends. Dinner in Montparnasse and then the music hall. *French* theatre. Not that tourist rubbish you see at the Folies Bergère.'

Nosjean found a few trumped-up questions to ask and put the telephone down, frowning and angry. If Pierrot-le-Pourri and his pal, Poupon, were in Paris, they could hardly have been passing Ouiriton's sub-station in the yellow Passat Nosjean was seeking. And clearly, if they'd organised a party to go to the theatre, they clearly didn't intend to be in Quiriton's area that evening. Yet – Nosjean frowned – there was something a little too pat about this theatre party. It sounded like a carefully arranged alibi. Perhaps someone else was doing the job and Poupon and Pierrot-le-Pourri were just waiting for the stuff to arrive. Perhaps the thieves even looked a bit like them: Perhaps they'd even been deliberately chosen as a sick joke to make the police flounder. The thought confirmed Nosjean's belief that tonight was when the job was to be pulled. It *had* to be tonight. The party going to the Bobino seemed to confirm it. Both Pierrot and Poupon had sounded highly amused to hear Nosjean's voice and he suspected they were enjoying his discomfiture.

Ringing off, he contacted the Quai des Orfèvres and asked if the premises in the Rue Vanoy could be watched. Though Nosjean himself might be somewhere else, it wasn't hard to summon help.

He put the telephone down with a thoughtful frown on his face. Despite the precautions he was taking, he suspected it was probably all a waste of time because, if the job *was* pulled as he expected and the thieves got away with it, Pierrot and Poupon would hardly be stupid enough to allow the loot to arrive on their doorstep just when they would guess the police would be watching. They'd surely have arranged for it to turn up somewhere other than the Rue Vanoy. They probably even had a warehouse somewhere outside Paris – Rambouillet, Melun, Corbeille, Tournan, Chantilly, Pontoise or somewhere like that – where it could be left until the heat died down.

As he replaced the telephone, Nosjean looked at his watch. Chagnay was near St Denis-sur-Aube and, if he got off early, he might even manage to telephone Mijo Lehmann.

He went in search of Pel but Pel and Darcy had disappeared, so he took his problem to the Chief who listened carefully to his theories.

'You'd better get down there at once, my boy,' he advised. As Nosjean was stuffing notebooks and pens into his pocket the telephone rang. It was Odile Chenandier wondering where he'd been.

'I've been busy,' Nosjean said. 'It's been hell here.'

'Are you still busy?' She sounded lost and full of reproach.

'Yes.' Nosjean was quite unable to consider his private life when there was a job to be done. 'I'm just on my way to St Denis-sur-Aube. We've had a tip-off and I'm handling it because the Old Man's not around and we can't waste time.'

She tried to find out more but he rang off hurriedly before he had to indulge in explanations which, while they weren't lies, weren't the truth either. He hadn't seen Odile Chenandier for some time and he felt as guilty as hell.

nineteen

When Pel arrived back at the Hôtel de Police, Misset was in the sergeants' room with Lagé.

Unaware of Pel in the doorway, he was reading aloud from *L'Equipe*. His face looked as though he'd just learned he had a terminal disease and his voice was in mourning. The newspaper, apparently, carried an unexpected angle.

'Filou's dropped out,' he was saying in aggrieved tones. 'I had two hundred francs on him, too, and he'd just had a terrific ride on the Ballon d'Alsace and was lying seventh.'

'Never mind Filou,' Pel snapped from behind him. 'Who's minding the shop?'

Misset leapt to his feet in a panic. 'Pissarro's?' he yelped. 'One of Goriot's men's watching it at the moment, Patron! I relieve him.' He gestured at the paper. 'Just working out who'll win the Tour! It's a close one this year. It looks like Van der Essen now. He's red-hot in the mountains and that's what separates the men from the boys! Clam's nowhere!'

Pel glared at him. Misset was a fool, he decided, and as soon as he could he intended to shift him to someone else's team.

'Lagé,' he snapped. 'I want to see those photographs you took outside Pissarro's.'

'At once, Patron!' Lagé almost leapt to attention and saluted.

He had been busy and the pile of pictures he had taken was quite considerable.

'You said not to miss anyone, Patron,' he pointed out earnestly.

Pel shuffled the photographs like a dissatisfied child trying to play cards. 'And all these are suspicious types?' he asked.

'You never know, Patron,' Lagé said. 'They might be.'

'You've cost the department a fortune.' Pel jabbed a finger at one of the pictures. 'That one looks so old, he'd be too tired to be a crook. His feet look bad, too. Like mine.'

He thrust the photographs into a pile and drew forward the pictures which Goschen had sent from London. Several of them seemed to match.

Sweeping the matching prints together, he nodded to Darcy. 'Come on,' he said. 'Let's go and see that hotel-keeper at Voivres. For all we know Rambot's one of this lot. I'd like to know which he is.'

The bar at Voivres was full of customers. At one end, two routiers, their great lorries standing outside, were carving at slices of steak and stuffing the meat into their mouths with bread and wine. Inevitably the television was going. Inevitably it was showing the Tour de France.

'Filou,' the announcer was saying, 'has been taken to hospital. He was going well on the slopes of the Col d'Est when he fell three kilometres from the summit. He regained his machine but collapsed a second time further on, and this time he was unconscious and the kiss of life was tried. What heroism he showed! What courage!'

What with the customers and the new angle on the Tour de France, Vandelet, the hotel proprietor, was too busy to attend to them just then, but the day was warm and they felt they could wait. Taking their drinks outside, they sat in the sunshine until they saw the lorries move off, then, going inside, they found Vandelet, his wife and helpers all busy washing up.

As Pel explained what he was after, Vandelet came round the zinc counter. Spreading the photographs on a table, Pel gestured.

'The type who came in here with Cormon,' he said. 'The one he called Rambot? Remember?'

Interrupted from time to time by shrill cries from his wife who kept accusing him of dodging work, Vandelet bent over the photographs.

'It could be him,' he said, pointing. 'On the other hand – '

There was another accusing yell from the kitchen and he lifted his head and roared. *'Tais-toi,* woman! Can't you see I'm busy?' Still muttering angrily about his wife, he jabbed a finger at the photographs. 'That one,' he said. 'That's the one. I think it's him. No doubt. Yet – '

His conversation still punctuated by bitter accusations from the kitchen, he had narrowed his choice down to three when his wife appeared. She was narrow-faced with a sharp aggressive nose and a thin-lipped mouth as tight as a gin trap.

'It's the police,' Vandelet said, spreading his hands in a gesture that included the whole of the hotel.

'But, of course!' Her shoulders lifted and her hands flew. 'They have nothing better to do!'

'They have problems.'

'So have I!'

'Then attend to them, in the name of God!' Vandelet dismissed his wife with an upward sweep of the hand, as though he were tossing her accusations over his head and out of the window. 'That one,' he said at last. 'That's the one. I'm certain.'

Pel picked up the picture. The man in the picture was dark, and strong-looking. He compared it with Darcy.

'He's not a bit like you really,' he observed to the sergeant. 'He's good-looking.'

It seemed pretty obvious by this time that, despite Pissarro's protestations, he *had* been involved in whatever dirty business Cormon had dreamed up and Pel was beginning to wonder how much Robinson's anti-missile device was involved, too.

'Get the pictures to Paris,' he told Darcy. 'Then we'll try them on Robinson. He can confirm it or otherwise.'

While Darcy was having copies made, Pel bearded the Chief in his office. He listened quietly as Pel indicated the need for a watch to be placed on Robinson's place.

'Is it necessary?' he asked.

'I think it's very necessary,' Pel insisted.

'Will he accept it?'

'No. But it's still necessary.'

'We can't intrude.'

'I think we should try. If necessary, we should bring Paris into this. It's big and I think he needs protection. If not him, then at least what he's doing.'

By the time Darcy appeared with the pictures, the Chief had contacted Robinson and had his request that a watch should be placed on him turned down flat. He was busy now trying to contact De Frobinius in Paris.

'Don't worry,' he said to Pel as he headed for the door. 'I'll bring pressure to bear. We can get the Ministry of Defence in on it if necessary.'

As Pel and Darcy headed for Robinson's home again, Pel suggested they tried his works first.

'It's Wednesday,' he said. 'And Wednesday's the day he's supposed to go there. If he isn't there, it'll delay the meeting a little and give him time to get over the Chief's call. He doesn't strike me as the sort of man to bear malice but you never know and it's always easier to talk to someone who's calmed down. If he is there, it'll save us a journey. Besides – ' his eyes glinted ' – that young gasbag, Rivard, might have something to add. He seems to know more than is good for him. He might even know Rambot.'

Robinson was not at the works. Elodie Guillemin, who was eating a sandwich at her desk, suggested he might have been too busy.

'He doesn't always come,' she said. 'Only usually.'

'What about Rivard?' Darcy asked.

'Oh, *he's* here.' She produced a big smile and indicated the works. 'They're at lunch now, though, but I expect it's all right to go through.'

When they reached the workshop, however, they found the place empty except for one angry-looking middle-aged woman.

'Where is everybody?' Pel asked.

She indicated the photographic processing department. 'They're all in there,' she said.

'Eating their lunch?'

'That's what they say.'

Darcy glanced at his watch. 'They take a long time, Patron,' he observed. 'And they choose a funny place to eat. What the hell are they up to?' He looked at the woman. 'Are there women in there, too?'

'They call themselves women,' she snapped. 'They try to get me to go in, but I won't.'

'Why? What are they up to? Sex orgies?'

As Darcy spoke, there was a burst of laughter from the closed door of the processing laboratory. It was followed almost immediately by a shout of glee.

Darcy looked at Pel. 'This,' he said, 'I find intriguing. Think it's a new kind of union meeting?'

The laughter came again and Pel looked at the woman sitting alone at her bench, eating a sandwich.

'Do they do this every lunch break?'

'No,' she said. 'Once a week.'

'What have they got in there? A strip tease show?'

She flushed. 'You'd better ask them.'

Darcy and Pel studied each other, then quietly walked to the bench alongside the door of the processing room and sat down to wait. After another ten minutes, there was a great yell of laughter and a burst of clapping. Then, where there had been silence, they heard the noise of chattering voices and shouts of *'Bis'* and 'Bravo.' A moment later the door opened and two flushed-faced girls appeared. A man followed, grinning, and pinched one of the girls' behind. As she shrieked, Pel and Darcy watched with interest. As the man saw them sitting on the bench, he turned quickly.

'Jean-Pierre!' he shouted. 'The flics!'

There was immediate silence. The chattering and giggling died at once and half a dozen girls and several men filed out silently, all looking sheepish, and headed for their benches. Putting his head round the door, Pel saw Jean-Pierre Rivard standing by a projector. Opposite there was a white-painted wall devoid of shelves.

'Having a show?' Darcy asked.

'Yes.' Rivard indicated the wall. 'On there. They enjoy them. Makes the dinner hour pass more quickly.'

'They *want* lunch time to pass quickly?' Darcy asked in surprise. 'What were you showing them?'

Rivard was fiddling with his lunch box on a table alongside the projector. He turned abruptly, reached out, picked up a spool of film, glanced at it and held it out.

'This.'

Darcy studied it. ' "Horses in the Camargue," ' he said. 'They found that funny?'

'No. Just interesting.'

'They did a lot of laughing.'

'They get a lot of fun.'

'They must do.' Darcy pushed into the room and, as he did so, contrived to let his arm catch against Rivard's lunch box. As it fell to the floor, it burst open. A half-eaten sandwich, an apple, an empty beer bottle and a circular black container rolled out. Rivard made a dive for the container but Darcy got there first. As he picked it up, Rivard tried to snatch it back, blushing furiously. Darcy held him off, studied the container then passed it to Pel.

' "Kleinekino," ' Pel read. ' "8mm movies in standard-8 and super-8 colour. *The Black Stockings.*" ' He looked at

Rivard and continued to read from the end of the box. ' "Dirte is bought a set of black underwear by her boyfriend, Karl. But Karl insists on putting them on for her – and then emotion takes a hand." ' He turned the box over. ' "A light-hearted look at sex." Well, well.' He studied the back of the box. ' "Cartoons. Comedies. Titillation." German, too.' He looked up at Rivard. 'They're great ones in Germany for this sort of thing.' He turned to Darcy. 'You can get space films, science-fiction, and a large selection of explicit amorous adventures,' he explained. He looked again at Rivard, then out into the workshop. 'No wonder Doctor Robinson considered he had a happy work force here,' he said. 'How long has this been going on?'

Rivard gave him a sullen look. 'A while,' he growled.

Pel's manner grew more harsh. 'How long?' he snapped.

'About a year.'

Darcy smiled. 'Smuggled in, in lunch boxes, with the apples and ham sandwiches, eh? Where do you get them?'

'Denmark. Sweden. Germany. I get them through a cata-logue. They don't come here direct.'

'Where do they come to?'

'Charles Rudeau's. He's one of the packers. We use his place as an accommodation address. We've had one or two packages seized.'

'I'll bet you have. Doctor Robinson didn't approve, of course.'

'He didn't know.'

'I imagine not.' Pel looked at Rivard. 'I came here today thinking you might be able to help me. But I don't think you're the man, after all. Perhaps we'd better see Robinson himself.' He studied the box in his hand again, then looked up at Rivard once more. 'While this sort of thing was going on, who looked after the shop?'

Rivard frowned. 'No one.'

'*You* were supposed to, weren't you? Suppose someone had walked in and helped himself to something?'

'We had nothing worth stealing.'

'You had gadgets.'

'Nobody knew what they were.'

'Cormon did. Did he go in there with you?'

Rivard flushed. 'Since you mention it, no.'

Pel did his snake-about-to-strike act. 'Cormon, my friend, is under suspicion of, at the very least, industrial espionage, probably a great deal more. And what he stole probably came from here.' He tossed the container to Darcy who slipped it into his pocket.

Rivard's eyes followed it. 'You going to keep it?' he asked.

'I think we'd better, *mon brave,*' Darcy said. 'I've no doubt it came through Customs described as something else entirely. It might be a good idea to pass the information on.'

Rivard flushed. 'It was only a girlie show,' he said. 'Everybody enjoyed it. Even the women. It was a bit of fun, that's all. Nobody worries about a little bit of pornography these days.'

'No, my friend,' Darcy smiled. 'But for public shows you still need a licence.'

'You going to do anything about it, Patron?' Darcy asked as they drove away.

'Shouldn't think so,' Pel said. 'It's none of our business, unless it led to a lack of security. If Cormon did use lunch-hour breaks of that sort to lift things, then it'll all come out in the wash. Let's go and see Robinson. We've got to face him some time and if he's not here, he'll probably be at Rambillard.'

As they talked, they had the car radio on because it was giving warnings of where the Tour de France was expected at certain times of the day – something of importance to any traveller – and suddenly the announcements were interrupted by a flash message.

'Doctors,' the commentator said, 'have pronounced Aurélien Filou dead and have refused permission for interment.'

Darcy glanced at Pel who reached forward to turn up the volume control.

'They considered it abnormal,' the announcer went on in awed tones, 'that a young and physically well-prepared athlete should die in the course of a competition for which he had trained.'

Half an hour later there was another flash. The pockets of Filou's racing jersey had been found to contain two medical containers, one empty and labelled tonedrin, the other half-full of anonymous tablets about the size of aspirin, and among his baggage a box had been found which contained various tablets and medicines, among them tubes of tonedrin and stenamina, both drugs in the methyl-amphetamine group.

The awed tones of the commentator were understandable. Cycling under the influence wasn't something to be encouraged, not even if the rider won, because the sponsors liked to be able to say that success came from the use of their cycles rather than the use of drugs.

'It's not unknown, though,' Darcy said. 'There was that case a year or two ago of someone trying to cheat the urine test they have to take by giving a sample from a rubber bulb in his racing shorts. Even doctors and race officials have been implicated.' He smiled. 'If *I* were trying to pedal up the Col d'Est, I'd need everything I could get.'

Pel considered that *he* wouldn't even get beyond the nursery slopes, not even with jet aid. An idea occurred to him.

'Think Pissarro's involved?' he asked. 'He's a damned sight too interested in the result.'

Darcy shrugged. 'If everybody interested in the result of the Tour were involved in things like this, Patron, then half the manufacturers in Europe would be in gaol: Raleigh.

Gitane. Coca-Cola. Peugeot. Besides, it's not heroin. It's only amphetamine-based drugs.'

Pel frowned. 'Well, Robinson's already had trouble with Pissarro,' he said. 'He might have something to say. At the very least, he'll be interested.'

But when they reached Rambillard, they found Robinson wasn't interested in anything any more. There were police cars outside the house and a doctor just emerging.

'What in the name of God's happening?' Pel asked.

The doctor shrugged. 'You might well ask,' he said.

twenty

With the aid of Sous-Brigadier Quiriton, Nosjean felt he had every road in the district covered. All round the Château de Lebuchon-Roy police cars waited out of sight behind high hedges, deep in woods, and tucked into the yards of friendly farmers. Nosjean had scouted the area thoroughly and, because he was anxious that his suspects shouldn't be aware of his presence, he had taken care not to have the cars placed anywhere on a direct route to the château. If anybody was coming, he didn't want them put off. He wanted them to arrive, collect their spoils, then catch them red-handed.

It was hardly what could be called prevention of crime, which was what the police were supposed to exist for, but sometimes cure was better than prevention. A man put away for a year or two was often more effectively stopped for the future than a man who was merely frightened off. The do-gooders might have had it other ways, but Nosjean was a policeman and didn't believe in feather-bedding criminals. Sous-Brigadier Quiriton's men had been warned not to stop a yellow Passat estate if it appeared, merely to watch where it went and report by radio to Nosjean, who had taken station with Quiriton in a yard belonging to a farmer friend of Quiriton's, with Quiriton's car tucked away out of sight behind a haystack.

It was Bastille Night and Quiriton's men were a little sullen that they were missing it. Bastille Night didn't normally have a great deal of effect on St Denis beyond a few drunks and a few flung fireworks, but this year the village was en fête. A platform had been set up for a disco where music was already thumping out, a bar had been erected, and on the slope above the village a snake of coloured lights was beginning to appear as schoolchildren carrying lanterns prepared to head for the square. Quite apart from the fact that the older of Quiriton's men had been hoping to see their children in fancy dress, they had also been hoping – in addition to preserving the face of republican dignity among the misrule – for a few free beers behind the canvas at the back of the bar. Instead of which, they were sitting in their cars among the shadowed lanes waiting for a gang of thieves they firmly believed would not appear.

As the summer evening changed to dusk and the trees in the distance changed from blue to purple, Nosjean sat quietly on the shafts of an old cart, trying to work out the relative qualities of all the girls he knew. He wasn't thinking too much about the job in hand as he waited, but policemen are much the same as other men and have the same distractions. Charlotte Rampling at the library had disappeared into the limbo of lost loves and it was now a toss-up between Odile Chenandier and Mijo Lehmann. At that moment Mijo Lehmann was leading the field. She was better-looking and more chic, but he had a feeling that Odile Chenandier might well prove the more faithful. Unfortunately, however, faithfulness could sometimes turn into possessiveness and Nosjean was nervous about that.

There were few cars about as dusk came: A green Peugeot brake with two young men in it, both wearing red and white scarves and hats, as if they were returning from a sports event, a big Merc with a fat man in it with a young girl, who looked as if they might be heading for a big seduction scene, a few battered cars that belonged to farmers. As darkness came, the cars seemed to consist entirely of young men and girls out courting.

Still they watched. There was no sign of a yellow Passat. Later in the evening, the farmer's wife appeared with coffee and brandy because, despite the warmth of the day, under the shadow of the hills it was surprisingly chilly. Still no Passat. Pork sandwiches appeared, brought out by the farmer's daughter. She was about twenty and attractive, and Nosjean looked at her with interest before thrusting her out of his mind – he seemed too occupied with girls already – and instead sat in Quiriton's car listening to a portable radio which he kept turned down as low as possible so that he would miss nothing that came over Quiriton's police band. The news seemed to consist entirely of the unexpected death of Aurélien Filou and the courage of his team in deciding to continue.

At midnight, Nosjean decided he'd made a bad guess and that Sous-Brigadier Quiriton's report of a yellow Passat had concerned merely a couple of tourists. Whose it was, he didn't know, because, as he'd long since discovered, neither Pierrot-le-Pourri nor his friend, Poupon, possessed anything other than expensive Citroëns.

'Let's have a prowl round,' he suggested to Quiriton. 'Warn your men we're coming.

There was a brief talk on the radio before they set off.

'They've not been seen round the château,' Quiriton said.

'All the same – ' Nosjean shrugged ' – let's go. But no lights. Let's not warn them if they're around. Besides, we'll see better in the dark.'

For some time, they drove around. Against the pale summer sky they could see the heavy bulk of the château, its square shape, its turrets and chimneys. There was no sound. All the cars they'd seen earlier seemed to have vanished. Once they heard the shrill yelp of a fox and a hullabaloo from a hen-house as though it had got in there. Dogs started barking, one after the other, picking up the signal as it was passed from farm to farm. But no cars.

They were moving slowly, the engine almost silent, and Nosjean sighed.

'I think we've missed them,' he said. 'Or else they haven't come.'

'We saw the Passat,' Quiriton insisted. 'Just as we'd been told to look for.'

'Let's prowl round the back of the château,' Nosjean suggested.

Quiriton started the engine and, lights out, engine very quiet, they got into motion again. Passing another of Quiriton's cars, they were informed that no one had seen any yellow Passat.

'They haven't come,' Nosjean said bitterly.

'Perhaps they caught on or got a tip-off we were waiting.'

Nosjean frowned. 'Well,' he said, 'if they haven't come, at least nothing's been stolen.'

They were just moving slowly under a belt of trees, both of them yawning, when they heard a motor car engine start. Immediately they sat up, alert at once, to see a green Peugeot brake shoot out from a ride in the woods. It swung on to the road, rocking wildly, its lights out, and came towards them, its engine racing. Quiriton swung the wheel furiously, cursing at the top of his voice.

'*Les bougres! Ils ont foutré la bazar,*' he yelled as the other car caught their front wing, bounced off, swung across the road and disappeared into a ditch. Cursing, Quiriton fought with the steering, dropped a wheel into the ditch at the other side of the road and disappeared beneath Nosjean as the car flipped over on to its side.

Without waiting to find out whether Quiriton was alive or not, Nosjean thrust open the door of the car with an effort, scrambled out, his feet all over Quiriton, and started to run. A man wearing a red and white woollen hat was scrambling from the green brake but, hearing Nosjean, he dived into the trees. As he crashed off into the distance, a second man, also wearing a red and white hat, scrambled clear and had just started to run when Nosjean took a flying dive at him, grabbed him round the legs and disappeared with him into a ditch smelling of wet earth and leaf mould. For a moment, there was a frantic scrambling to get on top, then Nosjean wrenched himself free, grabbed the man's wrist and wrenched it up behind his back. The man yelped with pain and, flinging him on to his face, Nosjean slipped the handcuffs on his wrists. Only then did he think about Quiriton.

Dragging the man with him, he found Quiriton, a cut on his forehead dripping blood into his eye, climbing out of his car.

'We've got one,' Nosjean said. 'You hurt?'

'Not enough to worry,' Quiriton said. 'Let's have a look at him.'

He switched on a torch and in the beam they saw a young man little more than twenty with a beard and a pale frightened face.

'He's not from round here,' Quiriton said. 'Is he one of yours?'

Summoned by Quiriton's radio, the other cars came into action at once and the second man was caught with the first light of the following day at the other side of the woods.

In the meantime, Nosjean had taken a look at the green Peugeot brake lying with its nose in the ditch. Its rear seat was down and into the space it made were jammed two chairs. It didn't take Nosjean long, with the knowledge he'd acquired, to identify them as Boulards.

'Well,' he said triumphantly, 'we've got two of them.'

'Complete with loot.' Quiriton grinned. 'What's more, there's a crowbar in the car, to say nothing of a complete housebreaker's kit, which includes a screwdriver and a 30-millimetre drill.'

'Which was doubtless used to bore holes at Boncey-Morin, Marennes, and a few other places.'

Two hours later, sitting in Quiriton's office, with the two young men securely under lock and key, Nosjean swallowed a mug of coffee and a celebratory brandy which Quiriton produced.

'You deserve a commendation for this,' Nosjean grinned. 'The guy in the yellow Passat must have been the one who cased the joint and these two turned up later to collect the goods.'

'Name of Jean-Jacques Raméai and Henri Prez. From the Belleville district of Paris. Are they connected with your pal, Pierrot-le-Pourri?'

Nosjean had already been on the telephone and it was a point he had been careful to question.

'They swear they don't know them,' he said. 'But I'm not sure I believe them. It's my view these two were on the way to get rid of the goods in the Rue Vanoy. Two days from now you'd never have recognised those chairs.'

He borrowed the telephone again to ring Auxerre and inform Sergeant de Troquereau, whose chief emotion seemed to be one of sadness at missing the pick-up.

'Pity the top boy wasn't with them,' he said. 'The one who supplied them with information.'

Nevertheless, Nosjean was more than satisfied with the night's work. The two chairs, magnificent to Nosjean, stood in the sub-station at St Denis, their backs medallion-shaped, their arms rose-decorated, their seats tapestry-covered. For the benefit of Quiriton he turned one of them over and indicated the estampille of the craftsman.

'Boulard,' he said. 'That's his signature.'

Quiriton lit a cigarette and pulled a face. 'Can't see what they see in them,' he observed.

'Kings of France probably sat on those chairs at one time or other,' Nosjean pointed out indignantly.

Quiriton ran a hand over the tapestry that covered the hard wide seats. 'Must have had good sitting bones,' he said.

Breakfasting at Quiriton's house, Nosjean decided it might be a good idea to inform the owners of the château of their good fortune. They might be pleased enough, he thought cheerfully, to offer him anything he wanted – their lands, their castle, the hand in marriage of their favourite daughter.

They were breakfasting when he arrived, having risen somewhat later than he had. The owner turned out to be the fat man they had seen in the Merc the night before and the girl turned out to be his wife. Somehow, they both failed to bear the look of the old nobility.

'I didn't know they'd gone,' the man said.

'It wouldn't have mattered, anyway,' the girl commented casually. 'We could easily have afforded some more.'

Disgusted and annoyed, Nosjean headed back to Quiriton's sub-station. Perhaps what Madame de Saint-Bruie had said was right. The owners of some of this beautiful furniture he'd been expending so much energy on defending didn't deserve to have it.

It might be a good idea to go and tell her so, he decided. She'd be pleased to know she was right. Besides, he might make his number with Mijo Lehmann, too, which would be even pleasanter. In the meantime, he'd better let Pel know what he'd been up to.

As he waited for his call to come through, Quiriton appeared. 'Something's come up,' he said. 'It might be interesting. On the other hand, it might not. I had my men go over the ground where the Peugeot had been parked. In case of footprints.' He held out a piece of stained paper. 'They found this. It obviously doesn't come from round here and I wondered if the address rang a bell.'

Nosjean took the paper. It was the sort of paper that was wrapped round food and was delivered in vast rolls that were attached to the side of a shop counter. It was greaseproof, and printed across it every few inches, so there'd be no mistaking where it came from, was the address – Charcuterie Espinasse, Rue Vanoy, Paris, 7ème.

'Charcuterie Espinasse,' Nosjean said slowly. 'I remember buying a sandwich there once. It's just down the road from Pierrot-le-Pourri's.'

His heart thumping, he rang the Quai des Orfèvres in Paris at once and arranged for them to pick up Poupon and Pierrot-le-Pourri, who were going to have some explaining to do, then set about ringing Pel. He could just imagine the delight, could just imagine himself being welcomed back, the hero of the hour.

There seemed a great deal of difficulty getting through to the Hôtel de Police, however, and when he finally did so the man on the exchange sounded flustered.

'What the hell's going on?' Nosjean asked.

'Something's come up,' he was told. 'Hang on, I'll put you through.'

Getting through to Pel's office, Nosjean was thankful at last to hear Darcy's voice. It didn't offer any congratulations, however. It didn't even stop to find out.

'Where in the name of God have you been?' Darcy demanded furiously.

'I've been down here in St Denis. I've been – '

Darcy wasn't interested in what Nosjean had been up to. 'For the love of God,' he said. 'Get back here! Fast! You're needed. Doctor Robinson's been murdered.'

twenty-one

Robinson had been found bludgeoned to death in his workshop.

His wife was in Paris at the time and it had been his elderly helper, Cortes, who had found him on arrival at work. The door of his little workshop had been forced and the material on the benches had been scattered everywhere.

There were smudges all over an iron bar which had been found outside and it had been sent to Judiciaire d'Identité to get them matched up. Since they were well and truly daubed everywhere, Pel had a suspicion that whoever had left them had worn gloves and wouldn't be identified.

'Anything missing?' he demanded.

'His work's missing,' Cortes said.

'What work?'

'He was engaged on some gadget.'

'What was it?'

'A switch.'

'Come on,' Pel said sharply, pulling the old man aside. 'He told us a bit about it. He was working on a computor reverser. A device that could throw computors into error. Was that it?'

Cortes looked worried. 'Not all of it,' he said. 'What he was working on was just the core of the thing.'

'And that's what's been stolen?'

'Well, it isn't here and there was nothing else of any value.'

'What's it like?'

'Flat. About eleven centimetres by five. A box made of plastic.' The old man dived into a drawer and produced a small black plastic container. 'Like that. One of those fitted into the lift mechanism he devised enables a lift to return to the basement without anybody pressing switches. It's used chiefly in warehouses. Loick Fougeron was interested in it for his yachts. It shifted his sails without any effort from him.'

'And that's all that's needed to throw computors haywire?'

The old man shook his head. '*Nom de Dieu,* no! That's only *part* of it. The device it fitted into was – ' he gestured with his hands ' – about twice the size of a shoe box. What he was working on was only the trigger mechanism.'

When Pel returned to the Hôtel de Police, his expression was bleak and angry. After their early success, things seemed to have gone badly wrong. Darcy met him with a worried look on his face.

'Pissarro's disappeared, Patron,' he said.

'What!' Pel's face went red. 'How in God's name did he manage that? We were watching him here and at Annonay. Who's responsible?'

'Misset, Patron.'

'I'll have him back on Traffic for this!' Pel stormed. 'What happened?'

'He was watching the house and Pissarro was safely there when he took over. He'd been followed all the way there in that old Bentley of his by a police car from Annonay. Goriot sent a man out at once. He was relieved by Lagé, who was relieved later by Misset. The Bentley was still there. Misset was short of cigarettes so he went down to the bar to get some. The Tour was on television and he dawdled to listen to the guff about Filou. While he was in there, he heard the

Bentley start up – you can imagine what a roar it makes – but when he ran out he was too late. Pissarro had vanished.'

Pel was pale with fury but there were other things to occupy his mind beyond Misset's stupidity.

'What about Rambot?' he asked. 'What have we learned about him?'

'I sent Nosjean up the motorway to Paris with more photographs,' Darcy said. 'He's just telephoned. He saw De Frobinius. Rambot turns out to be a man by the name of Adrien Ladour. Only he's not as French as he sounds.'

'Commissar of all the Russias, I suppose?' Pel said grimly.

'He might well be,' Darcy said. 'De Frobinius identified him at once. Name of Haroun Dagieff. Arrived in France some time ago claiming to be a Russian dissident and demanding asylum. There was a bit of to-ing and fro-ing, but the Quai d'Orsay finally agreed to back his request and he was allowed in. He changed his name to Ladour, he said, because he was afraid of retribution. Interior kept their eye on him, because planting an agent in the shape of a refugee's an old dodge, it seems. They had him watched and they recently discovered he's been depositing large sums of money with Credit Lyonnais. They did a bit of digging and found the account was in the name of Sardier, but it was our friend, Rambot – Ladour – Dagieff – take your pick – who was depositing the cash. He was interested in aeroplanes, they've discovered, about the time that double-agent, Le Mai, disappeared. *He* was one of the contacts of that English guy, Philby, if you remember. They were never able to pin anything on Le Mai and he was around for years before they decided to pick him up. He went out just in time. Dagieff, it seems, had set up the plane business as a feint, and while they were watching Dagieff and the airport, La Mai went down the Loire by boat from Nantes or St Nazaire to a ship, and went to Turkey and then across Iran.'

'It makes sense,' Pel growled. 'In fact, a lot of things begin to make sense. Rambot's obviously after this thing of Robinson's.'

'There's more to come, Patron,' Darcy said bleakly. 'Our friend, Rambot – Ladour – Dagieff, was also in that brothel in Paris when they raided it and found the Russian attaché and Philippe le Bozec from the Ministry of Defence.'

'Who *was* passing secrets, after all?'

'Seems so. He's been arrested on our say-so.'

Darcy tossed across a folder giving the details. A great many policemen who had expected to be drinking bocks of beer at their local bars or even romping in bed with wives or girl friends, had found themselves unexpectedly on duty, and all over France premises had been raided and arrests made. A few people with well-known names had been found where they shouldn't have been – one member of the House of Representatives in the bed of the wife of another – and among those arrested had been two policemen, an army officer and a naval lieutenant.

'They recovered a few things from La Bozec's apartment,' Darcy said. 'Designs. That sort of thing. You ever heard of the Breux-Magnus machine gun?'

'New one, isn't it?'

'Revolutionary, they tell me at the Ministry. Developed with the Americans and the British. There were also plans for a new injector or something for jet engines that's used at the airport here.'

'While doubtless at the barracks here, in the Rue du Drapeau, they have the Breux-Magnus?'

Darcy managed a twisted smile. 'No, Patron. That's not ours. That comes from Clermont-Ferrand. But there's also some sort of nuclear trigger which has been lifted from the establishment near Aignay. A few minor bodies have also been pulled in on the strength of what we've discovered. A storeman. An NCO at the airport. A sous-lieutenant of the

Chasseurs Parachutistes. It seems they've been bringing them in in dozens all day.'

'What about Dagieff or whatever his name is?'

'Paris is watching him.'

'Is that all?'

'That's what the Chief says. They've got a line on his movements. They know he wasn't in his apartment the night Cormon was killed.'

'I expect he was here removing Cormon from the scene.'

Pel was angry enough to bite the heads off nails. 'Send Misset in! He should be cut into strips and fed to the pigs.'

Judging by the look in Pel's eye, Darcy decided he probably would be.

By the time Misset left Pel's office he was pale, shaken and wishing he'd joined the Sanitary Department instead of the police.

'In the name of God,' Pel snarled, glaring at the door, remembering Robinson's kindness and determined to work out his anger on someone, 'I'd get rid of him if we had anyone to replace him. But we haven't. We've been functioning one short ever since Krauss was killed. Tell the Chief I'm coming to see him.'

The Chief listened to Pel's tirade calmly but he wasn't the slightest bit put out.

'Krauss' replacement is being selected at this moment,' he said. 'We're taking care. He's got to be good. The fault, in any case, didn't lay with Krauss' absence. Inspector Goriot filled the gap very adequately. The fault lay entirely with this man, Misset, from your team.'

In which, of course, he was dead right. It was hardly Pel's fault that Misset was stupid and careless, because he'd not chosen Misset himself, but there was no answer and the ultimate responsibility rested on the shoulders of the head of the section – Pel.

'Has it raised problems of security?' the Chief asked coldly.

'God forbid,' Pel said. But he wasn't so sure, all the same.

'I think you'd better find Pissarro,' the Chief said.

'What about Rambot – or Dagieff or whatever his name is? We ought to be picking him up too.'

'Leave him alone,' the Chief advised. 'He's obviously in close touch with the Russian attaché and if they're together the Russian will immediately claim diplomatic immunity and that'll throw a spanner in the works straight away. Leave it to Paris.'

'A man's been killed! Two! Three, if you include the man in Paris.'

The Chief shrugged. 'You'll not get far if the Soviet Embassy's involved. We need to catch them red-handed. Then, at least, the Government can raise a storm about what they're up to and demand that a few of them be sent home. The Press has been howling for weeks that there are too many, anyway. Just don't stick your neck out without orders. Let the Ministry handle it. That's what they're there for. Paris has him under a twenty-four surveillance. Just pick up Pissarro.'

Back in his office, Pel sat staring furiously at his blotter. France was a thousand kilometres long and roughly the same distance wide and – thanks to Misset's carelessness – somewhere inside its frontiers at a spot unknown to Pel was Pissarro, who now seemed to hold the key to all their questions.

'Suppose,' Darcy suggested, 'that this time it wasn't Rambot.'

'What do you mean?' Pel growled.

'Well, Cormon's murder sounds like the work of Rambot. Somebody cold-blooded with a lot to lose. But Robinson was killed by somebody else – somebody different – somebody with a lot to lose but more likely to be ham-handed enough to use an iron bar.'

'Pissarro?'

'Why not, Patron? He was in debt. And he was keeping two households going and needed money.'

'Yes, he was.' Pel frowned, deep in thought. 'That house of his at Daix,' he said slowly. 'What was it called? *Ker Boukan,* wasn't it? That's a Breton name. His wife's a Breton from La Roche Bernard, and he said they still have a house belonging to her mother at Penestin that he visits.' He stood stock still, staring at his feet, his mind racing. 'And Brittany borders on the Loire near Las Rochelets where Malat, that bar owner who reported the naval vessels in and out of the Loire, was found murdered. His place was at Le Pornichet just to the west.' He snapped his fingers, suddenly excited.

'In the name of God,' he said, 'Le Bozec represents Muzillac just to the east of there and Pissarro's father-in-law sat in the House of Representatives until two years ago for Villaine next door! Don't tell me Pissarro didn't know Le Bozec!' He looked at Darcy, his eyes bright. 'Even De Fransecky was stationed only a few kilometres away at St Nazaire. All within a stone's throw of each other! All on the same doorstep!' He slapped the desk. 'They knew each other! They must have done! I'd bet my salary on it. They probably even met in Malat's bar. If it wasn't Rambot who got rid of Malat, it must have been one of *them.* It's Pissarro who's got Robinson's gadget!'

Obtaining a warrant from Judge Polverari, they tore Pissarro's house apart. His wife was in tears and it jabbed at Pel's liver to see the fear in the eyes of his children. But it had to be done. It wasn't the job of the police to be sentimental. Pissarro had been playing a dangerous game and, unfortunately, not only Pissarro but his family, too, had to suffer for it.

They lifted the carpets, removed the floorboards, and went through every drawer, every bookshelf, every tin and packet in the kitchen. They found nothing. Back at the Hôtel de Police, tired, exhausted and angry, they rang the police at Châlon-sur-Saône. On Pel's instructions, they had been taking Jacqmin's house apart, too, and they had also found nothing, any more than the police at Annonay, who had been stripping the home of Pissarro's lady friend, Madame Morcat.

'Any sign of Pissarro yet?' Pel asked.

But Pissarro hadn't been seen in Annonay and they could only leave instructions that he was to be arrested if he did turn up. Frustrated and angry, Pel had just slammed down the telephone when he remembered something Pissarro had said. Jumping to his feet, he stuffed cigarettes into his pocket and started yelling for Darcy to get the car.

'Boine,' he said. 'Head for Boine!'

'Boine, Patron?' Darcy looked worried. 'It's bang on the route of the Tour de France. It's even a feeding point. We won't want to get snarled up in that lot!'

'We'd better not,' Pel grated.

'But why Boine, Patron?' Darcy swung the wheel and changed gear to head out of the parking area. 'That's nowhere we're interested in.'

'Yes, it is. It's where Pissarro is.'

At Euchatel, policemen were standing in a line across the road. As the car approached, one of them stepped forward and held up his hand.

'You can't come this way, my friend,' he said.

'I think I can,' Pel snapped. 'I'm Pel, Police Judiciaire.'

The policeman looked through the window. Pel was far from an impressive figure and the policeman thought he was someone trying it on to get a good view of the Tour.

'And I'm the President of the Republic,' he jeered. 'Turn round.'

Darcy produced his badge and the policeman flushed, leapt to attention and waved them past.

'Go by Blitterans, sir,' he said. 'That way you'll miss the barriers. Straight on, down the hill to the right, on to the main road, fork right to Jean-de-Bresse, then right, then left, and up the hill to Verne. After that the signs are clear to Boine.'

'Got that?' Pel said as Darcy drove on.

'No,' Darcy said. 'Have you?'

'No.'

They took the turn on to the main road as instructed, forked right, right again, then left – and found themselves in a farmyard. Darcy swore. Pel waved a hand. 'Take your time,' he said. 'No need to get in a temper.'

Backing out, they wandered down a lane or two and turned up outside Jean-de-Bresse, hard up against a barrier placed there by the police: '*Route barré. Tour de France.*'

Darcy glared at it through the windscreen. 'Shall I shift it, Patron?' he asked.

'No.' Pel's teeth were clenched but he was hanging on to his temper. 'We're well ahead of them. Just keep calm. If we disrupt the Tour we shall have the whole of the French press down on our necks and our image is bad enough without being accused of spoiling the great sporting public's interest in the all-important question of who's the fastest cyclist in France.'

As they headed down the hill and turned right, a farmer was just driving out of his gate in a battered Renault.

'Which is the way to Boine?' Darcy yelled.

'Follow me,' the farmer yelled back. 'I'm going there myself.'

He let in the clutch and jammed his foot on the accelerator so that the Renault shot away with spinning wheels, a shriek of tyres and a cloud of dust. Darcy hurriedly reversed and set off after it but it had already disappeared.

Pel was scowling as they asked the way again. 'You're better going over the top,' they were told.

But 'over the top' was blocked by an enormous road-roller.

'You can't come this way,' the driver announced.

Darcy climbed out of the car. 'Police Judiciaire,' he said furiously. 'We've got to get to Boine. We need to pass.'

'Well,' the driver of the roller said. 'It's no business of mine and I can reverse down there to let you go, but you'll probably disappear from sight in a hole that's been dug for a new water main. It goes right across the road. It's closed for the rest of the morning.'

Beginning now to grow worried, they sped back the way they had come and found themselves once more at the barrier outside Jean-de-Bresse.

This time all Pel's frustration burst out of him in an explosion of rage. It contained all he felt about Misset and his everlasting newspaper reading, everything he felt about Pissarro and his self-important gestures, everything he felt about Madame Routy and her interest in the television, even everything he felt about the Tour de France and the national obsession with sport. As the valve went, the rage came out like steam.

'God damn and confound it to everlasting hell,' he raged. 'Get it out of the way!'

Under a sky that was showing an ominous purple darkness, the whole hillside at Boine was covered with vehicles as locals and tourists climbed banks and walls to get a good view. There were adverts for *Le Vélo, Le Monde Sportif* and *La Vie Au Grand Air,* but the village carried no mention of Clam or Van der Essen. Instead the walls were plastered with the name of one of the more obscure members of Clam's team, who came from the neighbourhood and was firmly expected to lead the column up the main street of his own village.

They had arrived only just in time and the first publicity cars were already flinging out free gifts of cigarettes and ball point pens to the spectators, who were waiting four deep, carrying flags and wearing coloured caps. Following them came the mattress cars, the rice-package cars, the chocolate and drink cars, then six jeeps, two sexy white cars with half a dozen sexy white model girls, insecticide cars with giant flies on their roofs, a car decked with ribbons like a wedding limousine, a car like a buffalo, a car like a zebra, a fire engine, an old car dispensing balloons, and a bus in which a bank was operating for the benefit of the Tour employees and followers. Everybody in the vehicles seemed to be dressed in bright-coloured overalls, and they were tossing out caps, posters, car stickers and lollipops. Loudspeakers by the dozen were filling the air with their harsh-tongued spiel, each drowning the one next door. Even the Post and Telephone van driver was crooning a jingle in an iron voice until the radio car of ITT-Océanic began to announce that Van der Essen had a four-minute lead. To the dazed locals it was like an invasion from outer space.

As the circus vanished, there was a lull and business at an ice cream van among the crowd began to pick up, then, as motor cycle outriders began to appear the ice cream ceased to be a matter of interest and everyone began to crane their heads again.

A wedding procession walking back from church pushed in alongside a flock of nuns beneath a banner announcing 'Jo Clam, you are the strongest,' and three generations of one family waited outside their door on kitchen chairs, a fourth, a woman at least eighty years old, hanging out of an upstairs window with a pair of field glasses.

An excited '*Les voilà!*' set everybody staring down the valley then the motor cycle police appeared, and finally at the bottom of the hill as they turned from a down-gradient to an up-gradient, the cyclists came in a tyre-squealing nightmare – grey and rainbow-striped jerseys, orange and carmine jerseys, blue and gold, chequered, diamond-patterned – and began to agonise uphill. As they turned, pedals touched and two riders came down, bringing with them a whole group of cursing, sweating men.

The feeding point was on the brow of the hill, a banner announcing '*Contrôle de Revitaillement*' snapping in the breeze. Here, for a kilometre, team officials waited with musettes, small bags of food, ready to hand them to their riders to be slung over sweating shoulders for distribution into the pockets of racing jerseys. In a bar an Italian reporter was shouting into a telephone at the speed of a race commentator, only to go purple and throw up his hands in fury as he discovered he'd been disconnected.

As the riders laboured upwards, standing on their pedals, their faces tortured, one of the spectators, excited to the point of hysteria, tried to give his favourite an illegal push up the hill, and for his trouble was hit smartly over the head with the plastic water bottle normally attached to the bicycle frame so that he fell back in the arms of laughing friends. Another man, trying to throw water on his favourite, let go the bucket by accident and instead of helping, brought his man down and limped away with a black eye from the resultant scuffle with his supporters in the crowd. The Tour, Pel felt, was well up to form.

As the riders swished by in the growing purple light of the approaching storm, they were greeted with christian names. Their teams and the firms they represented were announced on the backs and fronts of their jerseys, Italians advertising French products, Dutchmen advertising British cycles. Patriotism always ran a little thin in professional cycling.

Empty water bottles and musettes were exchanged for full ones as the flood of riders swung by, taut-bodied men wearing black shorts, golfers' gloves and huge wrist-watches. Jerseys caught the light as they whipped past in a dazzle of colour, followed by the television and radio vehicles beaming reports to the national press, support cars with rear doors cut away for a mechanic to lean out with a screwdriver to a cycle even as its rider bowled along, ambulances, medical wagons, repair wagons, team cars carrying spare frames and wheels, first aid kits, water bottles, Dutch cigars, burgundy, armagnac.

A desperate rider with a bursting bladder flung his machine down, disappeared into the hedge to pee, then scurried back clutching a fresh water bottle thrust at him by one of his team.

The police were holding back the usual lost and baffled motorists who were trying to reach a destination on the other side of the route and keeping the excited crowd out of the way. As Pel pushed forward, Pissarro's bulk was clear but to Pel's surprise he was already heading back towards his car.

As Darcy took his arm, he looked at Pel, his gold teeth showing in a wide smile. 'Come to watch the race, Inspector?' he asked.

'I'm arresting you,' Pel said.

'What for?'

'Suspicion of being involved in robbery, for a start, and very likely of being involved in murder, conspiracy and one or two other things.

Pissarro's face went blank. 'You're out of your mind,' he said. 'Who've I murdered?'

'I suspect Doctor Robinson, and very probably Cormon. Because of a small gadget they'd both been working on.'

Pissarro smiled. 'I've got nothing of Robinson's.'

The last exhausted cyclists arrived, eyes dull, heads nodding, legs rubbery, the very last – called the Red Lamp because he was the warning to following cars – driven onwards by the car balai, a vehicle with a broom attached to its cabin because it was supposed to sweep up those riders who were forced to abandon. As it passed, the sky, which had turned now to a smoky grey, seemed to part and large drops of water began to spatter down.

It was pouring as they took Pissarro to one of the police vans and made him undress. What he said was right enough. He had nothing on him that bore the slightest resemblance to a tape cassette such as they were looking for.

Pissarro looked amused. 'Wrong, Inspector?' he asked. Pel frowned.

'I was only watching the race, you know,' Pissarro went on. 'My man, Maryckx, has just passed. He's not as far up as I thought he'd be and I don't think he's going to pull it off now. Not unless he becomes jet-propelled. He'll finish up in the thirties and that won't win him any prizes.' He sighed. 'However, that's the way it goes, isn't it? Can I go now?'

'No.' Pel gestured to Darcy. 'Warn Judge Brisard and get someone to lock him up. And tell them not to make any mistakes. We don't want another stunt like Misset pulled.'

Darcy frowned. 'What do we charge him with, Patron?'

'Brisard'll find something.'

'He's supposed to be innocent until he's proved guilty.'

'Not in my book,' Pel snarled. 'I'm a policeman. With me he's guilty until he's proved innocent.'

twenty-two

'What did Brisard say?' Pel asked.

Darcy sat down at the other side of Pel's desk. 'He asked what we were going to charge him with? What proof had we?' Darcy looked worried. 'Patron, we *have* no proof. His fingerprints weren't on the iron bar or anywhere in Robinson's workshops.'

'He was wearing gloves,' Pel said. 'Everybody reads enough about crime these days to know that.'

'We've found nothing incriminating. He had nothing on him. He said he was watching the race and that's what he seemed to be doing. Just handing out musettes to his team. He'd certainly not got Robinson's gadget.'

Pel scowled. Surely, he thought, the Lord God of Hosts wasn't going to do it across him at this stage of the proceedings. 'Somebody's got the damned thing!' he said. 'Have you tried Paris? What's our friend Rambot up to?'

'They're still watching him. They've intercepted his post and tapped his telephone. His conversations were all unsuspicious and there was nothing in his mail resembling Robinson's black box.'

Pel stared at his blotter. Across it lay the newspaper, the front page announcing in advance the result of the Tour de France. Van der Essen, as had been predicted, was leading, and there was a picture of him, thigh muscles like steel bands, head down, heading for the last stage, his sponsor's name across his shirt, his cotton peaked cap over his eyes, his white musette on his back.

'The damn gadget must be somewhere,' Darcy said. 'He couldn't have got rid of it. Rambot can't have got it or he'd surely have bolted. But he seems to be quite unconcerned. They know every move he's made for the last few days. To the minute.'

'Has Pissarro said anything?'

'Patron, we've both had a go at him and so has Judge Brisard.'

Pel frowned. They were both worn out with working over Pissarro.

'Perhaps he's not involved after all, Patron.'

Pel scowled. 'I'm damned sure he is,' he growled.

'Well, all he's done is return from visiting his *poule* in Annonay and then dodge Misset and go to Boine. Perhaps he didn't even *dodge* Misset. Perhaps he didn't even know he was being watched and just got in his car and drove north to watch his man, Maryckx, go past.'

Pel lifted his head. 'Maryckx,' he said slowly. 'Maryckx!'

His voice rose. 'Maryckx,' he said again and suddenly he jumped to his feet and started stuffing pencils and notebooks and spare packets of cigarettes into his pockets.

'Paris,' he said. 'That's where Maryckx is going!'

'Of course, Patron. They're all going to Paris.'

'It's where *we're* going, too.'

Darcy looked puzzled. 'Won't the Quai des Orfèvres be watching that end?'

'Shut up and get the car,' Pel snarled. 'And, for the love of God, go by the motorway! This time I want to be in front of those damned cyclists and all the idiots who're watching them!'

'It's pretty obvious what's happened,' Pel said as they hurtled up the motorway, the windscreen slashed by an unexpected drizzling rain. 'Our friend, Rambot-Ladour-Dagieff-whatever-he's-called was the link to the Russian Embassy. Sometimes things were drawn – by our friendly neighbourhood artist, Jacqmin, who'd put anything on paper for anyone without asking questions. Doubtless he'd been doing it for some time for industrial snoopers and it got around where it mattered. He drew the fuel injector and the breech block for the Breux -Magnus. Probably even quite innocently, but he described something square and shiny that had a hook-shaped thing that moved backwards and forwards. It's a long time since I did my military service but to me that sounds like the breech block for a machine gun.'

Pel finished his cigarette and blew out smoke as if his life depended on it. 'When the drawings were done,' he went on, 'they were spirited away through agents found by Rambot or Philippe le Bozec from the Ministry.' Pel looked indignant. 'Where it started is anybody's guess but I dare bet Pissarro was in it all the way. Who better to put to good use the things they lifted? His whole firm was geared to copy things. He even *admitted* copying things. He'd probably been Le Bozec's man and Rambot's man for years. It was Pissarro who planted Cormon in Robinson's works and it was Pissarro who saw further possibilities in the gadget Cormon stole. Or found out what Robinson was up to – through Le Bozec, who more than likely got the information through his own sources at the Ministry.'

Pel was shocked. Despite 1940 and the Occupation, he'd believed in patriotism and the thought Frenchmen could sell their country's secrets left him shattered.

'It's quite clear Pissarro wanted Cormon to get hold of Robinson's latest and best,' he went on. 'What easier? Cormon didn't even need a jemmy. He knew all there was to know about locks. But it happened to be the time when Robinson went to England and he'd taken everything with him. It must have been about then that Cormon got the wind up and guessed that Pissarro was more than just a copier of industrial secrets. He was no hero but he was French and was worried about what was happening and decided to tell the police.'

Pel paused, lit two fresh cigarettes and handed one to Darcy. 'But he was also worried about what would happen to him for his part in it,' he continued, 'and thought he'd better contact Brigadier Foulot, that cousin of his. Perhaps he thought he might work a deal. He arranged to see Foulot, but Pissarro was suspicious after what had been said and went after him. He went to see him and learned from Cormon's sister that Cormon was on his way to see Foulot and knew that if he didn't act fast the game was up. He had to stop him or the lot of them were finished. Probably he picked up Rambot and, fortunately for them, Cormon dawdled, stopping for a brandy or two to give him courage and they caught him up near the hill down to Destres. That's where Cormon realised he was being followed and they started driving faster and faster, with Pissarro trying to nudge him off the road. It wouldn't have been hard. Cormon had a small Peugeot. Pissarro drives an old Bentley that's as heavy as a tank. In the end, either because Pissarro pushed him over or because he lost control, Cormon went over the edge and landed in the fields.'

'Where the car burst into flames.'

Pel nodded. 'Pissarro thought that was the end of it, but when they went down to have a look, they were horrified to see Cormon crawl out. Pissarro killed him.'

Darcy frowned. 'It's pure speculation, Patron,' he warned. 'We need proof that'll stand up in court.'

'We'll get it,' Pel said grimly. 'It *had* to be Pissarro. We'll find he knows how to administer Doc Minet's "hunter's thrust," I think. He's gone in for every other kind of sport you can mention – even big game fishing. His office was filled with pictures of him at it – holding everything but a gun. But that doesn't mean to say he'd never held a gun. And he had that knife of his that he used for pruning roses. He kept it in his pocket.'

'But, Patron,' Darcy protested again. '*We've no proof.* When we picked him up at Boine, he didn't have the gadget. We didn't find it anywhere and there was nothing on him even remotely resembling it.'

'No,' Pel agreed. 'But he'd had it nevertheless.'

Despite the weather, Paris was en fête for the arrival of the Tour. Tricolours hung in the rain like wet washing and half the buildings seemed to be plastered with signs. As they turned into the shining periphery road, the crowds were already gathering.

De Frobinius was waiting at the Quai des Orfèvres looking puzzled.

'Rambot's watching the finish of the Tour,' he announced.

'I thought he might be,' Pel said.

De Frobinius didn't argue and they climbed into Darcy's car and headed for the Champs Elysées, collecting policemen as they went. When they arrived, there was an atmosphere of tremendous excitement and a loud hailer was blatting at the air with instructions to spectators and officials and the placings of the leaders. Publicity vehicles were parked everywhere and there were police at every corner. The spectacle was in full swing. The road had been hosed down and brushed, and the two preliminary local races to work up the crowd's interest had just finished. The news was coming in from St Germaine-en-Laye, Côte de Masnuls, Côte de la Madeleine and other places.

'Van der Essen leads! Then it's Ruyère and Cecano! Then O'Reilly and Joop Martin! Clam's nowhere!'

Heads craned where the crowds huddled for shelter on café terrasses, stumbling over tables which the rain had transformed from something that supported after-lunch drinks to bird baths spotted by water dripping from canvas awnings. As Darcy edged the car forward barriers slowed them down and in the end they left it, shouted to a policeman to keep an eye on it and began to hurry. Pel was ahead of the others and beginning to run. A policeman shouted at him to keep back but he didn't hear and De Frobinius showed his pass and waved the policeman aside. Snatching people from his path, Pel plunged on, his feet splashing in the gutters. There were a few protests but he heard none of them.

'Here they come!' The yell went up and, as the pack flashed past, the first cyclist home could be seen above the heads of the yelling crowd, coasting past with his hands in the air in a boxer's handclasp of self-congratulation.

'It's Van der Essen,' Darcy said.

'To hell with Van der Essen,' Pel snapped.

Forcing himself through the crowd, the rain in his eyes, he saw the press and television reporters flood round the winner. Panting still with his effort, the man in second place was also disappearing under a crowd of friends, only slightly less hysterical than the winner's party. The rest of the pack was coming now and Pel was trying to identify them. Alongside him, a man staring at a rain-wet list of the riders, ticking them off as they passed, was startled as the sheet was snatched from his hand.

'Hé!' he yelled. He was just about to reach out for it when Darcy grabbed him.

'A minute, my friend,' he said.

'Who're you?'

'Police Judiciare.'

'Then arrest that type there! He's got my programme!'

'Sorry, *mon brave*. He's Police Judiciare too!'

The rain dripping off his hat, Pel was going down the sodden list with his finger.

'Lyeaux, Macorde, Maëlle, Mahon, Martin, Maryckx. Number 197.' He thrust the programme back at the startled owner and pushed nearer.

'There's Rambot,' De Frobinius said, gesturing across the crowd. 'He's here!'

'Of course,' Pel said. 'He would be.'

He was reading aloud the numbers of the riders as they swept past. '176...18...44...83

'Pissarro's man seems to be well back,' Darcy said. 'If that's the type you're looking for.'

'That *is* the type I'm looking for.'

'Do we arrest Rambot?' De Frobinius asked.

'Not until I say.'

'...79...62...85...for God's sake, don't say the damned man's fallen!'

'There, Patron!' Darcy said. 'One-nine-seven! That's him. Coming up now. He doesn't look much like the winner Pissarro thought he was.'

'He doesn't have to,' Pel said. 'All he had to do was finish.'

Maryckx, his rain-soaked diamond-patterned green vest bearing the words, *Pis-Hélio-Tout,* the peak of his cap turned up, was slowing down as he passed between the yelling crowd. He appeared to be looking for someone.

'Rambot seems to be one of his supporters,' Darcy said.

'I'm not surprised,' Pel said. 'Stand by.'

They saw Rambot, covered from head to foot in a grey plastic mackintosh, approach Maryckx as he stopped and began to wipe his brow with a red handkerchief. Rambot shook hands, smiled, slapped Maryckx's back and began to talk earnestly to him, pointing to the bicycle. As they talked, Maryckx began to fish in one of the pockets of his racing jersey where he stored the food he picked up in musettes at feeding points. As he withdrew his hand, Rambot moved forward.

'Now!' Pel said, and De Frobinius lunged with Darcy. As they grabbed Rambot, there was an immediate yell from the crowd.

'Get the cyclist!' Pel said, and policemen moved forward in a wave.

Resenting the interference with the sacred Tour, the crowd began to push and shout. In the scuffle, Pel was swept off his feet and found himself on the asphalt with his fingers trodden on. As he rose, cursing all athletes and everybody who was interested in athletics, he heard a shot. Immediately, there was a yell of terror from the crowd and, despite the crush, it managed to sweep back like a flood-tide. People fell and were trampled on. Several more shots rang out and a woman alongside Pel, on her knees, her head down between her hands, lifted her face to yell. *'Assassins! Anarchistes!'* she screamed and tucked her head down out of sight again.

As Pel scrambled to his feet, he saw that De Frobinius had Rambot, his mackintosh torn, surrounded by policemen and Darcy had Maryckx safely guarded. A wounded gendarme was being helped away.

'In his pocket,' Pel said. 'It's in his pocket!'

Thrusting his hand into Rambot's pocket, De Frobinius produced a small black plastic box, roughly eleven centimetres long and five centimetres wide.

'This it?' he asked.

'That's it.'

Maryckx was staring at it. 'He told me it was a film of the leaders,' he said. 'He said it was urgent and had to be handed over to Agence Presse Duval. This type – ' he gestured at Rambot ' – said *he* was Agence Presse Duval. It's nothing to do with me. I was just earning a few extra francs.'

'That's something we can check on,' Pel said. 'Bring him in.'

Darcy was staring at Pel. 'Patron,' he asked. 'How did you know he had it?'

'He was Pissarro's man,' Pel said as the pressmen crowded round. The photo flashes began to dazzle them and a television reporter shoved a microphone in Pel's face and started yelling questions. 'Pissarro said he was going to watch him at Boine. But why? If he was as interested in the race as he said he was, why wasn't he following it by car like everybody else with an interest in it? Why wasn't he an official, detecting and punishing misdemeanours? Because he had Robinson's gadget and he handed it over at Boine. In the food satchel. Maryckx dropped the empty one and Pissarro handed him the full one – and that contained the black box. It changed hands just before we arrived. It was the only way to get rid of it when he realised he was being watched. But what a way! He was one of the sponsors of the team and had every right to be at Boine. Nobody would interfere. Nobody's *allowed* to interfere. And it was almost as quick as by car. It had to be connected with the Tour. We couldn't get away from the damned thing. We were tripping over it everywhere we went.'

twenty-three

It was over.

The congratulations had come in thick and fast. Even from Paris and London. One from De Frobinius and one from Fergusson, both very official, and a third one, much more informal from Inspector Goschen – 'Well played.' It puzzled Pel because he'd been playing no game. He'd been in deadly earnest. Indeed, most of life was deadly earnest for Evariste Clovis Désiré Pel and, a modest man, he'd been surprised at the enormous success they'd had. What had started as a mere enquiry by Traffic had blown up to a size that involved the whole nation. It was perhaps not surprising, Pel thought modestly, that the Chief had talked of rewards and promotion. He might, after all, find occasion to put on that suit he kept for meeting the President of the Republic.

All he really needed to make it complete was someone to share it with.

There was even a short note from Madame Faivre-Perret but, Pel noticed bitterly, no Madame Faivre-Perret. She hadn't dropped everything and rushed back full of admiration. She was still in Vitteaux burying her aunt. Surely to God, Pel thought, she ought to have got the old biddy under the sod by this time.

He drank a little too much brandy in the Chief's office then went round to the Bar Transvaal with the members of his staff – noticeably leaving out Misset, who still hadn't managed to claw his way back into favour. Since his way home coincided with Nosjean's, they ended up together in the Bar du Destin, Pel a little heavy-headed but pleased with himself. In the mood he was in, he felt he could conquer the world.

'Your châteaux robbers, I'm glad to say,' he said to Nosjean, 'are also behind bars.'

Nosjean shrugged. His triumph had gone almost unnoticed in the greater glory of the department and of Evariste Clovis Désiré Pel.

'Not quite,' he said. 'All we've got are two unknown burglars who were employed to lift the stuff. And they're not talking.'

'You have the two in Paris.'

'We can't hold them, Patron.'

'You can always re-arrest them when they're released. Eventually they'll be nervous wrecks. *Prêt à grimper au mur.* Ready to climb up the wall. They'll talk in the end.'

Nosjean frowned. 'The one I wanted was the one who's behind it all. The brains. The expert. Madame de Saint-Bruie insisted there *was* an expert. Until he's found, we've not finished, and it'll all start again in a year's time when everything's quietened down.'

Pel paused. 'Perhaps,' he said slowly, 'I ought to go down and see Madame. Convey our thanks. Do you think a lunch ought to do the trick, Nosjean?'

Nosjean glanced at him, his eyes amused. 'Perhaps that would be a good idea, Patron,' he said.

Pel nodded. A campaign in the direction of Madame de Saint-Bruie, he thought, might stir Madame Faivre-Perret to action. He felt certain she'd get to hear of it. If she didn't, he could probably drop a few hints. And, if nothing came of that, well, there was always Madame de Saint-Bruie herself. She had shown a considerable interest in him. Not exactly a Madame Faivre-Perret, of course – but she was a woman. Pel felt sure something could be made of her. She also appeared to be wealthy, as Pel was not. Certainly, one thing Pel did not possess was the houseful of priceless treasures of which she liked to boast. All Pel had was an overworked television and the *comfort anglais* – the deep armchair which was more often than not occupied by Madame Routy. It might be nice, he felt, to live in a house surrounded by priceless treasures.

'I'll make a point of it at the weekend,' he said.

Nosjean smiled. 'I have to go down there tomorrow,' he said. 'You know what it's like. It takes ten minutes to arrest someone and two hours to fill in all the papers. I didn't get the chance before, because I was hauled back when Robinson was murdered.' He thought warmly of Marie-Joséphine Lehmann. 'It's my day off and I think I ought to manage one this week. I'll slip down, take out the girl from the shop for lunch as a reward for her help and inform Madame that you'll be along at the weekend to see her. Shall I arrange a meal, Patron?'

'You know a good place, *mon brave?*'

'The Hostellerie D'Artagnan at Coublon-le-Grand's first rate, Patron. Not expensive either,' Nosjean added, feeling sure that this would add to its appeal.

'Please do that,' Pel said.

As he shook hands with Nosjean and left, Nosjean stared after him. He was a funny old bugger, he thought to himself, but, at least, unlike some funny old buggers, he knew his job, and did it well.

Suddenly Nosjean realised he was surprisingly fond of Pel, especially when his frailties began to show. There had been a time when Nosjean, then a young sergeant who blushed whenever he was addressed, had been terrified of him, but over the months he had come to realise that, despite his sharp tongue, Pel was scrupulously fair. He came down like a ton of bricks on mistakes such as Misset made but he was never short on praise when someone pulled off something worthwhile. What was more, unlike some, he didn't claim the praise himself. A lot of praise had gone Darcy's way and a lot had come to Nosjean. Despite his uncertain temper, Pel was a good man to work for, a man who overcame his own uncertainties to behave with utter confidence when he was doing his job. Why shouldn't he go home feeling like the next President of the Republic? Why shouldn't he take Madame de Saint-Bruie out to lunch? Why shouldn't he take her to bed, for that matter? He'd got a gleam in his eye and, judging by what Nosjean knew of Madame de Saint-Bruie, she probably had one, too. It would, he decided, probably do the poor old bastard good.

The following day, Nosjean drove down to Chagnay. Mijo Lehmann greeted him with a wide smile. Madame de Saint-Bruie wasn't in the shop.

'She's been off colour for the last day or two,' the girl explained.

'Sick?'

'Oh, no. Moping chiefly. Between you and me I think some man's let her down. She likes men, you know. She liked your inspector.'

'I think he likes her,' Nosjean grinned. 'He's hoping to come down at the weekend and take her out to lunch. Think she'd go?'

'She'd probably jump at the chance. I think she's had a big disappointment. He's probably just what she needs.'

He persuaded her to shut the shop for half an hour and took her to a bar round the corner for a coffee and to arrange for dinner that evening. Everything was going very smoothly, he felt.

The man on the next table, who was reading *France Soir,* was looking oddly at Nosjean, and Mijo pointed out that he was looking at the picture of Nosjean which accompanied the story of the triumph in Paris.

'I think he's seen your picture,' she whispered. 'I have a copy myself. I bought it to show my friends.'

Nosjean borrowed the newspaper and they opened it at the picture, Nosjean talking loudly enough to confirm for the man on the next table that he was indeed one of the heroes of the episode. Eventually the man put down his paper and leaned over to touch Nosjean's shoulder.

'You this type in the paper?' he asked.

Nosjean blushed and modestly admitted that he was. 'Good for you, *mon brave,*' the man said. 'We need more like that.'

Pink with pleasure, Nosjean finished his drink and escorted Mijo back to the shop, even managing to snatch a kiss behind one of the tapestries that separated the office from the front.

'I'm terribly proud of you, you know,' Mijo said warmly. She opened the paper and spread it on a battered-looking escritoire. 'Everybody's talking about it.'

Nosjean studied the paper proudly. He was there with Pel and Darcy in the main story and even a second time with Quiriton in the smaller story on page 2 about the châteaux robberies. Everybody seemed to be in the paper, in fact – Phillippe le Bozec who'd started it all; De Franzecky; Malat; Lambov, the Russian attaché; the man they'd known as Rambot; Pissarro; Cormon. All lined up in a veritable rogues' gallery. Even Jacqmin, the artist, was there for his part in the affair. It didn't matter much now whether he'd done the drawings for the châteaux robbers or not. They'd got him in jail, anyway, and if he *had* been involved, at least he wouldn't be around to trouble art connoisseurs for a long time.

All the same –

Nosjean was just wishing they could have nabbed the expert whose advice had encouraged the robbers when Mijo spoke.

'I've met that one,' she said, pointing.

Nosjean came to earth. 'Which one?'

'That one. Jacqmin. He came in here.'

Nosjean sat up. 'In where?'

'In here. In this shop.'

'He did? When?'

'Oh, more than once. Not lately though.'

Nosjean was beginning to grow excited. 'When was the last time?' he asked.

'About a fortnight ago.'

'What did he talk about?'

'Furniture.'

'What sort of furniture?'

'Old furniture.'

Nosjean had almost forgotten his picture in the paper and Marie-Joséphine Lehmann's admiration, even the kiss she'd given him. Everybody's friendly neighbourhood artist, Pel had called Jacqmin. Into anything and everything – honest and dishonest. They'd suspected all along there'd been an artist involved in the robberies. Of course there had! It had been Jacqmin! As Pel had said, the news got around. Cormon had put Rambot on to him, and probably Rambot had put who ever was running the châteaux jobs on to him. Or the other way round.

'Did he meet anyone here?' he asked. 'I mean had he come by some sort of arrangement? He must have had an accomplice, an expert to guide him. Was there anyone else in the shop when he arrived? – someone he could talk to?'

'Only me and Madame de Saint-Bruie.'

Nosjean frowned. 'Only you and – ' he stopped dead, a sudden uneasy feeling gripping him ' – and Madame de Saint-Bruie?'

Mijo smiled. 'I think he was a friend of hers,' she said. 'He seemed to be trying to learn about furniture. He didn't know much about it but he liked it and she liked to take him off with her when she visited the *châteaux classés*. She was trying to teach him about it, I think.'

Nosjean drew a deep deep breath. It was painful enough to hurt his chest. 'They don't deserve to own such beauty,' she had said.

'This Jacqmin,' he said slowly, remembering the slim young man with the mop of wild hair Quiriton had seen as he had driven past his sub-station, the wild hair that could in the shadows have been dark, blond, mousy – or red. 'Did they go in her car?'

'Yes, of course.' Marie-Joséphine was looking at Nosjean in alarm. 'Are you all right?'

'Yes, I'm all right.' Nosjean spoke with difficulty. 'What is it? A yellow Passat Estate?'

'Yes.'

'With dents in it? At the front and rear and along the side?'

'Yes. She's a dreadful driver and sometimes when she's had a brandy too many at lunch time she runs into –' the girl looked at Nosjean, puzzled. 'How did you know?'

Nosjean hardly heard her. He was thinking sadly of Evariste Clovis Désiré Pel. It was all too clear, all the affected help that would put them off the scent, the constant references to the expert they sought as 'he', as if he were male, all the apparent interest in Pel that would deflect suspicion.

'Oh, no,' he said softly to himself. 'Oh, dear God, no!'

MARK HEBDEN

DEATH SET TO MUSIC

The severely battered body of a murder victim turns up in provincial France and the sharp-tongued Chief Inspector Pel must use all his Gallic guile to understand the pile of clues building up around him, until a further murder and one small boy make the elusive truth all too apparent.

THE ERRANT KNIGHTS

Hector and Hetty Bartlelott go to Spain for a holiday, along with their nephew Alec and his wife Sibley. All is well under a Spanish sun until Hetty befriends a Spanish boy on the run from the police and passionate Spanish Anarchists. What follows is a hard-and-fast race across Spain, hot-tailed by the police and the anarchists, some light indulging in the Semana Santa festivities of Seville to throw off the pursuers, and a near miss in Toledo where the young Spanish fugitive is almost caught.

MARK HEBDEN

PEL AND THE BOMBERS

When five murders disturb his sleepy Burgundian city on Bastille night, Chief Inspector Evariste Clovis Désiré Pel has his work cut out for him. A terrorist group is at work and the President is due shortly on a State visit. Pel's problems with his tyrannical landlady must be put aside while he catches the criminals.

"…downbeat humour and some delightful dialogue."
Financial Times

PEL AND THE PARIS MOB

In his beloved Burgundy, Chief Inspector Pel finds himself incensed by interference from Paris, but it isn't the flocking descent of rival policemen that makes Pel's blood boil – crimes are being committed by violent gangs from Paris and Marseilles. Pel unravels the riddle of the robbery on the road to Dijon airport as well as the mysterious shootings in an iron foundry. If that weren't enough, the Chief Inspector must deal with the misadventures of the delightfully handsome Sergeant Misset and his red-haired lover.

"…written with downbeat humour and some delightful dialogue which leaven the violence." *Financial Times*

MARK HEBDEN

PEL AND THE PREDATORS

There has been a spate of sudden murders around Burgundy where Pel has just been promoted to Chief Inspector. The irascible policeman receives a letter bomb, and these combined events threaten to overturn Pel's plans to marry Mme Faivre-Perret. Can Pel keep his life, his love and his career by solving the murder mysteries? Can Pel stave off the predators?

'…impeccable French provincial ambience.' *The Times*

PEL UNDER PRESSURE

The irascible Chief Inspector Pel is hot on the trail of a crime syndicate in this fast-paced, gritty crime novel, following leads on the mysterious death of a student and the discovery of a corpse in the boot of a car. Pel uncovers a drug-smuggling ring within the walls of Burgundy's university, and more murders guide the Chief Inspector to Innsbruck where the mistress of a professor awaits him.